Who Has Your Back?

Also By Beverly Hurwitz MD

WAR in the OR - A Novel
Is the Cat Lady Crazy? - A Novel
Nobody Else's Business - A Novel
Park City Hiking Guide
A Walker's Guide to Park City

Who Has Your Back?

Beverly Hurwitz MD

Surrogate Press®

Published in the United States by
Surrogate Press®
an imprint of Faceted Press®
Surrogate Press, LLC
Park City, Utah

SurrogatePress.com

ISBN: 978-1-947459-78-6

Library of Congress Control Number: 2023905591

Book Cover and Interior design by: Katie Mullaly, Surrogate Press®

This book is dedicated to all of the patients
who have suffered neglect and have been harmed
by a for-profit health care system.

Prologue

Back pain strikes four out of five people at some time in their lives. Healthy young adults are most likely to experience an acute episode, but the backs of children, teens, and seniors are also vulnerable.

The human spine supports the head and the entire body with a stack of thirty-three odd-shaped vertebrae aligned in a wavy column. Unfortunately, the four built-in curves of the human spine render it architecturally flawed and highly susceptible to trauma, overexertion, repetitive use, ordinary wear and tear, aging, and gravity.

Acute back pain often occurs when a mostly sedentary person shovels snow, moves a dresser or attempts some other physical feat they are not conditioned for. Without strong truncal and abdominal muscles for support, the precariously stacked backbones and their numerous tiny joints are easily overloaded.

Typically, an acute back pain episode lasts a few days, weeks, or months, but most sufferers make a full recovery. Unfortunately, back pain can also become recurring or chronic. Occasionally, scoliosis, cancer, arthritis, infection, or any number of other diseases underly back pain. Often, the cause cannot be precisely identified.

Surgical treatment of back pain has been prevalent for decades, but the long-term outcomes of some common surgeries have not proven favorable, while the long-term results of some newer procedures are not yet known. Resultingly, researchers have been developing drugs, devices, and non-surgical procedures to try to help back pain sufferers, but there's little agreement amongst "experts" as to the value of medication, massage, manipulation, exercise, braces, mattresses, behavioral training, acupuncture, regenerative medicine, anesthetic injections, nerve ablations, spinal cord stimulators, or various surgical approaches. One person's panacea can be another person's poison.

Billions of dollars are thrown at back pain every year, but the condition continues to plague humanity. Like the characters in this novel, we are all just the guinea pigs of modern medicine, its wonders, and its foibles.

The people and companies in this story are fictitious. Any resemblance to actual people or entities is coincidental.

Chapter One

At first, Sean Garmen didn't understand where he was. He must have been knocked unconscious. He felt his head for lumps and found a walnut-sized one in the middle of his forehead. Touching it left blood on his hand. When he was finally able to focus on his surroundings, he realized he was at the bottom of the stairs.

Then he remembered that Frieda had started to cry, and he'd tripped on something on the way up. He never saw what it was, but his right leg went right out from under him. He remembered twisting around and grabbing for the banister. After that, there was no memory.

The thought of Frieda crying jolted him. She was quiet now, but he had to check on her. What if she'd fallen? She'd been trying to climb over the rail of her crib for the past week, even more of a gymnast than her brother. What if she'd succeeded? She could crawl anywhere.

Sean couldn't bear the thought of his baby girl tumbling down a flight of steps, especially since he'd apparently just done that. He attempted to get up. Before he could lift his shoulders from the floor, he felt a strange click clack in his low back. A sharp pain shot across his butt and pierced his thigh. His stomach did a cartwheel. He immediately lowered his head and closed his eyes, nauseous, dizzy, and hurting.

It took a minute to catch his breath and then, he tried to roll to his side. He stopped when a hot poker stabbed him in the groin. He rolled back onto his back and tried to draw his knees up. His back muscles contracted like a rubber band as soon as he flexed his thighs.

Pain like this was out of his realm of experience. "Something must be broken," he heard himself say out aloud. He pressed on what he could reach, but nothing was particularly tender except the goose egg on his forehead. He tried to sense his feet; he could wiggle his toes. That made him think he was okay, so he sucked in a big breath and quickly sat up. A spinning room and intense pain overwhelmed him. He lied back down, confused and scared.

How could he be this injured? He was only twenty-eight years old, physically fit, and in good health. Always athletic, he'd just played a great game of golf on this beautiful September morning, walking and carrying his clubs with no pain at all.

He had no history of back problems; maybe a twinge now and then when his tall frame was bent over the engine of a low sports car, but nothing ever like this. All he had to do on the rare occasion when his back felt sore, was take some ibuprofen and a hot bath. But he'd never experienced anything like this. This was excruciating.

It must have just happened, he tried to convince himself. He hoped it would calm down in a few minutes if he just stayed still and focused on relaxing his muscles. He figured he'd be sore for a few days at worst. He listened for Frieda for a few more seconds until his eyelids drifted downward.

When Sean reopened his eyes, he saw flickering light. Had he passed out again? He didn't know. It could have been seconds or hours since he'd first found himself on the floor. When he was able to focus, he realized the changes in light came from the shadows of breeze-blown leaves, dancing on the wall alongside the staircase. Still midafternoon, he concluded. How long ago had Frieda started to cry? He had no idea. Now, there was no sound coming from her room. The image of her motionless and blue in her crib tore at his conscience.

"I have to get up," he told the shadows. "I have to check my baby girl."

Sean reassessed himself. Maybe the headache wasn't so brutal now, but the slightest movement of his torso caused a sharp pain to shoot across his buttocks. Even if not for Frieda's sake, he had to get to the phone and call Darcy.

He wondered where he'd left his cell phone. Had he taken it out of his golf bag? Left it in the car? He concluded it didn't matter because he probably couldn't even crawl to get to it.

Darcy might not be home for a few hours. It had become her Sunday tradition to go to lunch and a matinee with Sean's mother Rosemary. Today, they'd taken three-year-old Quinn with them, although they often left Sean to baby-sit both kids while they did their girl thing.

As long as he got to play golf Sunday mornings, he didn't mind baby-sitting in the afternoon. He was delighted that his son was already showing exceptional interest in cars, so he could work on his Mustang and simultaneously entertain his little boy.

Darcy and Rosemary's relationship had become a bonanza for all of them. Darcy had lost her own mother to breast cancer when she was five, and she'd had little mothering after that. Now, her father, step-mother and sister all lived far away.

Having grown-up himself without a father, Sean took pride in being able to provide her with a family. It was even more satisfying that his mother loved Darcy like a daughter. They'd become exceptionally close, and his children were enveloped in love.

But where were his wife and mother now that he needed them? Enjoying themselves at some kiddy movie. He was unable to even move, let alone take care of his infant daughter. He became determined to get to his feet.

He rolled onto his side and ignored the pain as he flipped onto his stomach. From there he pushed up to his knees. When he tried to bring one foot forward, a white-light pain bludgeoned his senses. He fell on his face and blacked out again.

When he awoke, the shadows on the wall had moved. Sound was coming from Frieda's room, and he held his breath to hear. She had just started saying 'mama' amidst a symphony of babble and squeals. She usually wanted a bottle shortly after waking and would cry to let them know. Her babbles turned to cries.

Sean took a deep breath, squeezed his eyes shut and pushed up from his stomach. Pain, dizziness, and nausea pummeled him. Perspiration diluted the blood that was trickling down his forehead and the mixture frothed into his eyes. Suddenly he was gripped with fear. What if he was paralyzed? What if he had broken his back and by trying to move, he had just injured his spinal cord?

His thoughts got louder then Frieda's crying. Paralyzed? How could he possibly work? How would he support his family? Would he even want to live? A feeling of terror set in, more unbearable than the physical pain. He shuddered and realized that tears were adding to the wetness of his face.

Then, Frieda's cries got louder.

His brain seemed to be in low gear. He had to think hard before deciding that he wasn't paralyzed because he had been able to move his legs and roll over. He could feel his thighs touching the floor. That had to mean that the spinal cord was intact. As relieved as was, he was less certain as to whether he should continue to try to get up.

Then, Frieda's cries became frantic.

He wished he knew what time it was. He wished he knew if it would be better to just lay still and wait, or risk injuring his spinal cord by trying to get to his feet. He wished Frieda would just go back to sleep. Then, when her cries became shriller, he imagined her with her limbs stuck in the crib side rail. As his headache hammered him, he envisioned himself in a wheelchair.

Chapter Two

Eva Rodeki had a sickening feeling as she took her seat at the corporate conference table. The gleam in Doctor Winslow's eye suggested she'd been summoned to play the ringer. She wondered which poor physician would be their next target.

It hadn't always been this way. When she was first promoted to the position of "Director of Provider Partnerships," the doctors she was launched to destroy usually didn't deserve reimbursement. She'd feel gratified to catch a cheater ripping off the insurance company or deceiving his patients. Now, those were the easy cases that others could handle. Her role had been developed to perform special services for Doctor Henry Winslow, the newest medical director of the WhiteGuard Insurance Company.

Under the previous medical director, WhiteGuard only went after physicians who they judged to be incompetent or dishonest. The old medical director was a highly respected, well-connected internist who also served as the governor's health advisor. Policy had been his to make, and he personally believed that the purpose of health insurance was to share the burden of the cost of human afflictions, instead of piling it all on the backs of the sick and injured.

However, the WhiteGuard Board of Directors had come to believe that the role of a health insurer was to guard against unnecessary expenditure in order to optimize returns to investors. The board execs decided that the politically smart way to develop the company's new direction was to hire a new CEO with the specific task of replacing the medical director They bought off the old CEO and recruited finance wizard C.L. Udall to become the new chief.

Clarence Lowell Udall Junior, or CLUJ, as he was called behind his back, rose to fame in the 1990s, when he mopped up some damages caused by the collapse of one-third of the U. S. savings and loan institutions. The WhiteGuard board was confident that if anyone could increase shareholder profits, it was a big bad banker.

There was no way CLUJ was going to work with a medical director who put ethics before profits. A handsome severance package kept the old medical director from fighting for his professional life. Two more medical directors came and went, until CLUJ found one that he could totally dominate.

Eva wondered how desperate Doctor Henry Winslow had become. Although his credentials were impressive on paper, his training in the most prestigious institutions had turned him into a run-of-the-mill orthopedist. Still, even a subpar surgeon could earn lofty community status and a fabulous income. Doctor Henry Winslow had all of that until the day his wife and three children paid him a surprise lunchtime visit, and found his receptionist having him for lunch.

After his wife Gloria divorced him, and after he married the receptionist, his children refused to have anything to do with him. It also turned out that the new wife was intolerant of alimony and child support, so she left Henry with more financial obligations and went off in search of greater riches.

When his OR colleagues started to smell alcohol on his breath, empathy was abundant in the small Southern city where he practiced. The surgery department chairman agreed to not turn him in for operating under the influence if Henry would just quietly go away.

Eva Rodeki knew all of this about Doctor Henry Winslow because she'd been a surgical scrub nurse in the hospital where he was practicing at the time of his indiscretions. The handsome orthopedist had also been a favorite topic of gossip.

Winslow however, had no recollection of ever having worked with Eva. She was just one of numerous face-masked subordinates who slapped instruments into his hands when he barked orders in the OR. When he arrived at WhiteGuard as the new medical director, Eva was as astounded to see him there, as she was careful to keep her knowledge about his past to herself.

Eva didn't know that Henry Winslow had recovered from his drinking problem, reconciled with his son Adam and daughter Jill, joined a large orthopedic practice in a Midwest city, and started operating again. Soon thereafter, Doctor Winslow had the misfortune to develop hand tremors.

His father and grandfather also had this genetic curse. Henry had learned early on that drinking alcohol made his hands steadier, but he was determined not to relapse. He tried some medications, but the tremors persisted. He believed he could still competently operate scalpels, saws, drills, hammers, and the other tools of orthopedics. Unfortunately, his tremulous hands unnerved patients, and none of his fellow orthopedists were supportive of a partner who made the practice look shaky. His contract wasn't renewed.

To keep up with alimony payments and child support, Doctor Winslow settled for shifts in urgent care clinics. Managing snotty nosed babies, urinary tract infections, high blood pressure, and the like was boring and paid poorly compared to a surgeon's income. His son Adam's medical school costs ate most of his salary.

Then, Doctor Winslow heard that the CEO of WhiteGuard Insurance Company was seeking a new medical director with a strong interest in healthcare economics. Hoping he could triple his income, Henry applied.

After interviewing with WhiteGuard's CEO, other candidates declined the job offer; but Henry held his nose and jumped right into the iron-fisted clasp of Clarence Lowell Udall Junior. With Udall and Winslow at the helm, the health insurance division of WhiteGuard was transformed in less than two years. Delivering maximal profit to stockholders became the company's top priority.

One of the first tactics CLUJ ordered Doctor Winslow to employ was "rescission," the practice of finding a technical reason to cancel the policy of someone with an expensive disease. By colluding with other insurers' data banks, WhiteGuard might tell a client that their policy was cancelled because they lied on their application about a history of headaches. "We found records of a doctor's visit for headaches when you were fourteen."

Another favorite tactic was to impose colossal premium increases for small businesses if one of their employees was stricken with a costly illness. This often caused the employer to drop the insurance policy and saved WhiteGuard from covering the costs of cancer or multiple sclerosis or some other horrible disease.

CLUJ's master plan also included getting rid of high-cost drugs and physicians whose services the insurer could consider ineligible for coverage. That's when Doctor Winslow would be put to the task of digging up data that the insurance company could use to justify WhiteGuard's denial of reimbursement.

If Henry couldn't find research or other doctors to support WhiteGuard's position that a particular physician was doing inappropriate treatment, then Eva Rodeki might be assigned to try to trick a physician into doing something that the insurer could label as a policy violation.

Eva dreaded whatever assignment she'd been called in on.

Chapter Three

Somehow, Sean Garmen managed to get to his feet. He'd limped to where he could see the clock and was relieved to realize that what he thought might have been hours of lying on the floor, was probably only about ten to fifteen minutes. Thankfully, Frieda was quiet again.

The thought of trying to get up the stairs was daunting. He plotted instead to find his cell phone and call Darcy. Then it dawned on him that she was probably in the theater with her phone turned off. Or would she keep it on vibrate? He didn't know. They hadn't gone to the movies as a couple since they'd become parents.

Every step was a tremendous effort. His head was pounding, and he wasn't sure if the returning nausea was from the pain in his back or from head injury. Finding his phone on the kitchen table took some of his anxiety away, but Darcy didn't answer when he called. Neither did his mother or his brother Michael. Michael sold heavy equipment to factories, and he was always traveling.

Sean pulled a frozen hamburger patty from the freezer and held it to his forehead. After a minute, the cold made him feel more alert. He went to sit down to alleviate his dizziness and think about what to do next; but trying to sit made his back hurt so badly that he opted instead to lean against a wall.

So, if he couldn't sit, how on earth could he get to the ER? Darcy still wasn't answering her phone, and he didn't want to leave a frightening message on her voicemail. Even if he could reach Darcy or Michael, how could they help him? What if his back was broken? The fear of being disabled grabbed hold of him again. After deliberating for a few seconds, he narrowed his options down and called 911.

Awaiting the ambulance, he managed to unlock the front door, gather up his wallet and insurance card, vomit in the sink, and prop himself against the refrigerator. Frieda was now crying, his head was throbbing, and he still worried that any motion could paralyze him.

"I hurt my head and my back, and I can't move," he told the ambulance attendants, "and I have an eleven-month-old baby upstairs who I haven't been able to get to."

The next thing Sean knew a voice was saying, "Can you open your eyes, Mr. Garmen? Do you know what happened to you?"

He thought he was dreaming until he felt something cold on his chest. Something, no someone, was pulling his socks off. He could smell vomit and a chemical odor. He presumed he was in the ambulance. He tried to open his eyes, but the light was too bright. Another wave of nausea overcame him. He was sweating and shivering simultaneously.

"Can you hear me, Mr. Garmen? Do you know what happened to you? I'm Doctor James. If you can hear me, squeeze my hand."

Sean realized there was a hand holding his and he gripped it.

"Good, Mr. Garmen. You're in the emergency room."

He saw the stethoscope on his chest and suddenly understood his situation. "My baby. Is my baby okay?"

"Your baby's fine, Mr. Garmen. She's over there with one of our nurses. The ambulance people tried to call your wife on your cell phone but couldn't reach her. Is there anyone else we can call? Follow the light with your eyes, Mr. Garmen."

Sean realized a man was attaching wires to his chest and a middle-aged woman with big eyeglasses was waving a penlight in his face. The light was too bright and there seemed to be noise coming from everywhere. Before he could even say he was nauseous, a hand stuck a pink basin under his chin. He wretched dramatically but just a little foam dribbled down his chin. As his nausea lightened, he became reacquainted with his aching head and the boring pain in his back. There was a stiff collar around his neck. A blood pressure cuff was tightening around his arm.

"My mother. No, she's with my wife. They're at the movies. My brother Michael. What hospital am I in? My brother lives near Community General."

"This is Mercy Hospital, Mr. Garmen. Community was backed up and your ambulance was diverted here. Do you know Michael's number?"

"I don't know anyone's number anymore. It's in my phone. Where's my phone? Where's Frieda?"

"Frieda?"

"My baby girl. Geez, I'm supposed to be babysitting."

"Your baby's okay. The ambulance folks brought her here with you. She's right over there." Doctor James pointed. "What happened to you, Mr. Garmen? Can you tell me what hurts?"

The neck collar wouldn't allow Sean to turn his head to see where the doctor had pointed. "My back, my right leg, and my head. I was going up the stairs and I tripped on something. I think I hit my head on the banister. Then I found myself on the floor. I lost time and I couldn't move. Am I paralyzed?"

"I don't think so, but we don't want you to move until we get some x-rays. We'll see if someone around here has your phone. Can you feel anything here on your foot?"

Sean felt a prickling sensation on his right foot, then his left. "Yes. Does that mean I'm not paralyzed? Can I see my baby? She needs a bottle. She's got to be hungry."

"Please try to keep still. Mr. Garmen. It's very important that you don't turn your head. You're a good parent, aren't you? I'll have them bring the baby over here so you can see her, but please try not to move. Do you know how long you were unconscious?"

"Just a few minutes I think, but I don't really know. I don't even remember the ambulance ride, so I'm not sure of anything. What time is it now?"

A nurse with a five o'clock shadow and onion breath said, "five-thirty." Sean started to feel queasy again. His headache was worsening, his neck and face were hurting, and he felt confused. He also felt thirsty.

"Can you give me something to drink?" he asked.

The physician shook her head no.

"How about something for the pain?'

"I'm afraid we can't do that until we get some x-rays and find out what you did to your head and spine. The plastic surgeon should be here by the time you get back from x-ray to repair that nasty laceration on your forehead. Wouldn't want to see an ugly scar on that handsome face of yours," Doctor James said.

As she finished the sentence, she moved on to the next patient on the other side of the curtain. The way the ER was backed up this summery Sunday afternoon, it would probably be another hour before radiology would get around to Sean Garmen. In the meantime, Doctor James wrote orders for a blood draw, an intravenous line, fluid monitoring, CT scan of the skull and brain, and x-rays of the neck and back. Then, she got interrupted and forgot about the missing cell phone and Baby Frieda.

Onion breath wasn't very talkative, thankfully. Sean estimated the pale-complexioned nurse to be about his own age, but it was hard to tell because the man looked exhausted. His conversation was limited to: "Please make a fist. You're going to feel a stick. Now a stick in your other arm so we can give you IV fluids. You're attached to this pole now. Don't try to go anywhere. Here's a urinal. We need to measure your pee." And then, he too was gone.

Sean could hear people bustling all around him, the din of multiple conversations, someone crying hysterically, a PA system crackling and paging Doctor James, monitors beeping, a telephone ringing, and somewhere in the distance, the wail of a siren. He tried to shout, "Where's my baby?" but no one came to answer.

Chapter Four

With the WhiteGuard quarterly report showing another drop in the profit margin, CLUJ became enraged about costs arising from the treatment of chronic pain. Baby boomers were living longer and seemingly less tolerant of pain than previous generations. Ever since the turn of the millennium, when federal law mandated that hospitalized patients be assessed and treated for pain, "the fifth vital sign," WhiteGuard's outlay for pain management had been steadily climbing.

The cost of some pain medicines was exorbitant, and more were being prescribed. Many of their insured were being referred to pain clinics, where more physicians were providing additional treatments that were more expensive.

Doctor Henry Winslow supported CLUJ's profit driven policies, especially when it came to pain management. Back in his operating days, whenever patients returned after surgery claiming their back pain was worse, he perceived them to be lazy people, trying to get out of work so they could sit around all day and get high on narcotics. He'd tell them to "just buck up" and send them on their way. Besides, CLUJ had made it known that Henry's job depended on getting rid of these mushrooming pain doctors.

Without even a hello, Henry's Winslow's trembly hands pushed a file across the table to Eva Rodeki. "We need you to scope out this Doctor Stefan Donilski. He came on to our panel as a neurologist four years ago, but now he's promoting himself as a pain specialist. He does numerous procedures and he hired two other doctors who are also doing the procedures. One of them is a psychiatrist and the other's a pediatrician. I don't know where a psychiatrist gets off doing procedures."

Henry Winslow rolled his eyes with arrogance. "Donilski's from Eastern Europe somewhere. He has an accent and a kind of smart-ass way of talking around whatever you confront him with, like he's some poor ignorant immigrant. He has all the right credentials; but he does a lot of alternative stuff, like acupuncture and prolotherapy. Now he's doing platelet-rich plasma and stem cell injections and his practice is growing like wildfire.

"Donilski and his partners also write a lot of narcotic prescriptions. We think he gets patients hooked on the drugs so they're willing to do his other voodoo. We've got two other pain doctors who say his treatments are a lot of bunk, but Donilski's got an army of patients who sing his praises."

"So, what's my cover?" Eva asked.

CLUJ's master of phony documents, pushed a file across the table. "You'll be Lisa Banks." In the folder was Eva's picture on a driver's license and a WhiteGuard insurance card and credit card, all in Lisa's name. A letter of referral from another physician said that Lisa had been complaining of severe back pain for five months, that various medicines hadn't helped, and that physical therapy had made her worse. There was also a disk with her phony MRI and x-rays.

According to Doctor Winslow, Lisa Banks's imaging studies didn't show anything that wouldn't be seen in any other fifty-year-old woman. "We want to see if Donilski recommends treatment for someone who has nothing really wrong with them."

Henry paused for a second. "There isn't anything wrong with your back is there? We want you to go in there with a perfectly normal exam and see if this guy puts you on narcotics just to keep us paying the bills."

Eva wasn't about to tell her boss that her back had been hurting for decades. Years as an OR nurse moving patients from the gurney to the operating table had taken its toll. Then, after her husband's untimely death, with three young children to care for, she'd learned that admitting to a bad back made her ineligible for clinical nursing positions, which also made it hard to get good health insurance.

Eva ultimately learned to keep her back pain a secret, and she wound up working more backbreaking jobs just to support her family. In fact, it was her bad back that made her leave clinical nursing and go into administration. Especially because she knew how Doctor Henry Winslow viewed people with chronic pain, she certainly wasn't going to divulge any of that now.

"Well, I'm insulted that at forty-eight you think I can pass for fifty," she quipped with her lilting Southern drawl, "but my back's an old workhorse that just keeps carrying the load."

Chapter Five

Rosemary didn't feel like coming in when she dropped Darcy off at her townhouse. As much as she loved her grandson, Quinn had become restless during the movie and whiney on the way home. She was perfectly happy to kiss the child goodbye and let Darcy deal with him. By the time Darcy had carried an uncooperative Quinn up to the front door, Rosemary had driven out of sight.

With Quinn in her arms, Darcy rang the bell for Sean to open the door. When he didn't, she figured he was probably in the shower. Feeding Frieda often meant getting splattered and Sean had no tolerance for baby burps. She put Quinn down and fished in her purse for her keys.

Once inside, she became alarmed when she couldn't hear water running, the TV playing, and there was no response to calling his name. Quinn stopped to play with a toy car at the bottom of the stairs, while Darcy galloped up the stairs to check on Frieda. When that proved fruitless, she assumed Sean was working in the garage and had taken Frieda with him. She only found his cars in the garage.

Even though he worked on cars all week, Sean still took joy in rebuilding cars on the weekend. His latest project was a sixty-five Mustang and there was an old Pontiac he planned to restore when and if the Mustang ever got finished

When she found the cars present but no Sean or Frieda, she ran to the kitchen to look for a note. It was a beautiful afternoon and perhaps he had opted to take a walk. It was totally unlike Sean to go out for a walk though, and he would have left her a note if he did something out of the ordinary. He was always considerate that way.

Darcy knew there must be a problem. Her anxiety doubled when she saw vomit in the sink and a raw hamburger patty on the floor. Something was very wrong.

She tried to imagine a better scenario. Maybe Corey had come by to pick Sean up for a car he was working on. Sometimes, an important customer would get emergency service on Sunday. It was a nice idea, but it didn't explain the vomit in the sink and the absence of a note.

Darcy ran to the foyer to find her purse and grab her phone. Damn it, she thought, she turned it off in the movie and forgot to turn it back on. Sean must have gotten sick and couldn't reach her. She dumped the purse, looked in every pocket of her clothes, and then in Quinn's clothes, but the phone wasn't anywhere.

Then it dawned on her that it must be in Rosemary's car. When Quinn started to get restless in the back seat, she gave him her purse to play with. He loved to open and close the Velcro flap of the compartment where she kept the phone. Now it was probably sitting under the car seat, turned off, so even if she or Sean tried to call it, Rosemary would never know. She cursed their decision to get rid of the landline.

She grabbed Quinn and ran next door to her neighbors, but they weren't home. Nor were the people in the next unit. Three doorbells later, an older couple invited her in, and she found herself standing in their kitchen on a corded wall phone. Sean's number only allowed her to leave a voice mail, and then she remembered he hadn't plugged it in last night. When he left for golf, he mentioned his battery might be low. Her next realization was that she didn't know anyone's phone number anymore, except for Rosemary's, but there was no answer there. Rosemary probably wasn't home yet.

Her kindly neighbor brought her an old phone directory while his wife tried to amuse the increasingly irritable Quinn. Darcy couldn't have been more flustered. Anyone she could think to call wasn't in the directory. As she pondered her dilemma, her neighbor said, "you know, Dear, I did see an ambulance go by a little while ago."

Darcy couldn't figure how that could be relevant. If Frieda was sick, Sean would have driven her to the hospital himself. So, it had to be Sean who was sick, but then where was Frieda? Her heart sped up as her imagination ran wild. Someone whose car repair went badly had kidnapped Sean and Frieda. Who else would want to hurt sweet Sean Garmen? She couldn't decide if she should call the police, the hospitals, or the ambulance companies?

Her neighbor, Stan Keegan, sensed her panic and stepped in. "You go comfort your little boy and let me see what I can do here."

Almost an hour later, they had learned that a 911 operator had sent an ambulance to the Garmens' address. It took more calls, prompts, and time on hold to learn that Sean had been transported to Mercy Hospital, a thirty-minute drive from the Garmens' end of town. The most frustrating call was the one Darcy made to Mercy hospital. She was able to learn that Sean was there, but privacy laws prohibited the clerk from giving her any information about his condition over the phone. And no, they didn't have any information about a baby named Frieda.

Darcy was too shaken to drive but was finally able to reach Rosemary. Of course, she would come and get her. Yes, Darcy's cell phone was found in the back seat of her car, still on vibrate from the movies. No, there weren't any messages.

Stan and Emily Keegan offered to baby-sit Quinn, but Darcy was bothered about leaving him in a strange environment with people he didn't know. She was confident they were lovely people, but she felt frantic about her missing baby, and she didn't think she could deal with worrying about Quinn too.

By the time they got to Mercy Hospital, it was almost seven. Initially, the ER front desk clerk gave them a hard time because when Darcy had dumped her purse to look for her phone, she apparently hadn't stuffed her wallet back in. The clerk wasn't any friendlier to Rosemary since the name on her identification was changed when she remarried. She was no longer Garmen but Cauthers.

"We have to be able to identify to whom we're giving information," the clerk repeated like a robot without ever making eye contact. Fortunately, the ER physician overheard Darcy begging to see her husband Sean and baby Frieda, and she intervened.

Sean had been sent to x-ray and Doctor James said that they really didn't know how badly he was hurt until they could see the films. "He shows symptoms of a concussion and he's hurt his back. He also needs a laceration repair."

Doctor James sent a volunteer to collect Frieda from the pediatric unit where she'd been parked in a playpen. She squealed with delight when she saw her mother. Rosemary, Darcy, and the children were directed to a COVID sanitized waiting room. The baseball game on a TV was hardly a distraction.

The kids became frightened when a young woman became hysterical. While she was whisked away by a nurse, her companion informed the rest of the waiting crowd that she'd just been told that her mother died. A strained silence replaced her cries, until Quinn started to cry that he wanted his daddy.

It was quarter to eight and they still knew nothing about Sean.

Chapter Six

A cancellation afforded Eva Rodeki an appointment with Doctor Stefan Donilski the next day. The receptionist advised her to come early "because, Ms. Banks, Doctor Stef wants you to complete a boatload of paperwork. Normally we'd send this to you ahead of time but for tomorrow, we'll need you to fill it all out when you get here."

Eva arrived an hour ahead of schedule. She was grateful for the extra time to just observe. If Donilski was making oodles of money, it would never be known from the appearance of his waiting room. It wasn't shabby, just small, plain, and dull. A young receptionist named Tonya, who had a slight accent, made Eva wonder if she might be the foreign doctor's daughter.

Tonya copied the fictitious insurance card and handed Eva a thick stack of papers: informed consent, privacy policy, insurance assignment forms, and an arbitration agreement. There were forms that asked her about her medical and surgical history, drug use, diet, job, hobbies, travel, and family. Another form asked her to mark her pain on anatomical drawings. One form asked how pain affected her ability to sit, stand, walk, sleep, drive, shop, eat, work, and have sex. Another asked about depression, anxiety, and mood changes. It was an overwhelming amount of paperwork.

Finally, there was a packet of information about Doctor Donilski, acupuncture, prolotherapy, platelet-rich plasma, and stem cell therapy. What little Eva knew about these treatments was that WhiteGuard wouldn't pay for them.

As she fabricated a history for Lisa Banks, Eva observed a pregnant woman walk out of the clinic with a man holding her arm. She looked like she might be giving birth before she got to the door. The couple stopped at the desk and the man told Tonya that the woman felt much better. "After all these miserable weeks, her sciatic pain is finally gone; just amazing." He paid cash.

As her attention wandered from the annoying stack of papers, Eva observed another waiting patient. He looked to be about seventy years old and even in a chair, he seemed stooped. When he was brought back to the inner office, he arose slowly and stiffly. He walked with short, shuffling steps. Thirty minutes later, he reappeared, standing almost upright. His gait was livelier, and his expression seemed relaxed. He told the receptionist that he couldn't believe what the doctor had done. He smiled as he handed her a credit card.

Eva got curious. She wondered if maybe she couldn't find relief for her own back pain with this very doctor her employer had sent her to destroy. She told Tonya she goofed up the form about her pain and needed to redo it. This time, she recorded her real symptoms instead of those she had created for the ratfink Lisa Banks. Just as she finished the last form, another patient emerged from the clinic. She was a delicate young woman, maybe in her early twenties.

"How'd you do today, Janelle?" Tonya asked.

"Great! Every time I come; the pain gets a little better. Right now, I can't feel the phantom limb pain at all, just a little of the stump pain. I wish I'd tried acupuncture ten years ago when they first amputated my leg."

Tonya looked at her paperwork. "No charge today, Janelle. Doctor Stef says if your insurance won't cover this, he'll treat you anyway."

Janelle looked dumbfounded. "Really? That's amazing."

"Well," Tonya said, "he has a soft spot for people who've had childhood cancer. When he was a kid, he lost his sister to leukemia."

Janelle said a tearful thanks and limped out the door.

Tonya took Eva's papers and about ten minutes later, Doctor Donilski came to the waiting room to greet her. He was a large, robust-looking man with a ruddy complexion and bushy gray hair and eyebrows. His age was hard to guess. He smiled broadly, but Eva sensed smugness in his demeanor.

"Just call me Doctor Stef," he said, "you Americans butcher Donilski." He didn't offer a hand to shake or gesture for her to go first. He turned abruptly, leaving her to follow him into an exam room.

Chapter Seven

Though exhausted, Darcy Garmen couldn't sleep. By the time she got home from Mercy Hospital it was ten-thirty and it took an hour to settle the kids.

Doctor James had assured them that Sean hadn't broken his back and wouldn't be paralyzed. However, he did have a skull fracture and a significant concussion. She wanted to monitor him overnight, keep him hydrated with an IV, and make sure there was no brain bleeding. If his vomiting improved and his blood count didn't drop, he could probably be discharged in the morning.

It was the first night in the six years they'd been married that Darcy had tried to sleep alone and sleep just wouldn't come. Finally, somewhere around four, she fell asleep, only to be awakened by a frightening dream. She was in bed with Sean, only somehow, Sean turned into her mother. There were big clumps of hair on the pillow and her mother just kept vomiting.

Darcy became a terrified child again, staring at her mother's yellow skin and balding head, knowing that something very bad was happening. The nightmare woke her, and she decided to get out of bed, rather than try to go back to sleep and have the dream return. She used to have nightmares like that for much of her childhood. Falling in love with Sean Garmen had mostly put the dreams to rest.

By six, she had showered and checked the children who were sleeping peacefully. She went to the kitchen to make coffee and was confronted by Sean's vomit still coating the sink. It rekindled thoughts of the dream and triggered memories she hated to dwell on, childhood memories of her parents, Ann and Rob Healy.

Darcy's mother Ann was an only child whose own mother had died of breast cancer before Darcy was born. Darcy's father Rob was also an only child. He worked as an accountant and did income taxes on the side. Darcy was five and Ann was seven months pregnant with Darcy's sister, when Ann was diagnosed with breast cancer.

After giving birth, Ann had mastectomies and was started on chemotherapy, but by then, the cancer had spread to her bones. She broke her spine when she fell on slippery pavement. Afterwards, Ann was essentially bedridden. A nurse would come to help her bathe and try to get her to eat, and Rob's mother came to take care of Darcy and her newborn sister. Darcy's most vivid memory of her mother was that of a yellow, skeleton-thin, balding woman who was always vomiting.

After Ann's death, Rob found it too difficult to work, date, and be a parent, so he sent his daughters to live with his parents who owned a farm in Indiana. Rob was a "menopause baby" and his parents were in their sixties when they assumed care of their granddaughters. Although the girls were materially well provided for, their grandparents weren't affectionate, and Darcy's teachers worried that she suffered from depression.

Rob remarried and when his daughters were nine and four, they returned to the home of Rob and his second wife, Noreen. Although Noreen tried to make a comfortable home for the girls, deep down she resented having to share Rob with them, and the sisters never felt entirely welcome.

Darcy moved into an apartment with a friend as soon as she finished high school. She worked as a waitress, and while she provided exceptionally polite and competent service, her generous tips were more a result of having a gorgeous figure and saucer-sized, violet eyes. Her eyes were so extraordinary that most people couldn't help but gawk at them.

When the antiquated Chevy that Darcy bought promptly broke down and got towed to Art Tobler Auto Tech, she met handsome, romantic Sean Garmen, the mechanic who loved old cars. Sean also had magnetic eyes. They were ocean green with flecks of copper and gold. Darcy envied his luxuriant auburn hair. Within a year of their first date, they married. Darcy finally felt loved, plus, she'd gained a devoted mother.

Darcy's little sister was also eager to leave home. After Darcy moved out, her sister found her pathway when a proselytizing Mormon missionary came to the door. She joined the church, and went on a mission to Argentina, where she met her prince charming and stayed. Although she and Darcy kept in touch by email, neither could be of much help to the other in times of need.

Darcy's family became more fragmented shortly after Quinn was born, when Rob was offered an accounting job in a Colorado mining firm managed by Noreen's brother. After they moved west, they came back to visit for grandson Quinn's first and second Christmases, but they had never even met their granddaughter Frieda. Their phone calls had become infrequent, and Darcy guessed they were pretty much caught up in new lives with Noreen's relatives. It wasn't like they had ever been a close family and she really didn't miss them.

Besides, Rosemary had become the mother Darcy had never had. She was warm, wise, caring, and fiercely loyal to her sons. Darcy so wanted to be the good parent to her kids that she didn't have in her own life, and she hoped she could be as good a mother as Rosemary.

By the time Darcy had cleaned up the kitchen, drank some coffee, fed, bathed, and dressed the children, emailed her sister, and reviewed their health insurance policy, it was quarter to eight; time to let Sean's boss know he wouldn't be going to work.

"Art Tobler Auto Tech." It was Arthur who answered the phone. Darcy explained to Sean's boss what had happened.

Arthur almost dropped the phone. "Please, no! We've got a dozen appointments for Sean this week. The boys are going to be in deep doo-doo. Look, you tell Sean he needs to get better fast; but not to come in until he's okay. You need my help with anything, just call. I don't care if it's day or night. Please tell Sean we're rooting for him and not to worry. We'll take care of things here."

The truth of the matter was that Arthur was very worried. It had come to the point that he felt he could not run his business without Sean. The guy was a genius mechanic, especially with high performance cars. People came from a five-hundred-mile radius for problems other mechanics couldn't solve. Sean could typically diagnose and fix any problem if they could just get the parts. If there was anything Arthur was still very good at, it was finding the parts.

Like his father before him, Arthur Tobler had once been a cracker-jack mechanic himself. But as cars became more electronic, he found his knowledge inadequate. He tried to take courses, but the technology was changing faster than he could keep up. He had become totally dependent on "his boys," his two sons, Ryan and Corey, and his employee Sean.

Ryan, the oldest, was a good kid; a reliable worker who genuinely liked to please his father and the customers. He had grown up in the business and learned everything his father could teach him, plus the electronics taught in tech school.

Corey was the really smart one. He could master anything he was interested in. The trouble was, he was mostly interested in getting high, driving fast cars, and getting it on with every good-looking female he encountered. Arthur had bailed him out of trouble more times than he could count. He'd also fired him several times. But then, Corey would promise to reform himself and Arthur would bring him back into the business because he was family, and because most of the other mechanics he had tried to hire weren't half as talented. Either they didn't know their stuff, or like Corey, they were unreliable.

For years, it seemed that most of the kids Arthur had hired out of the technical school just wanted to be entertained and collect a paycheck. Sean was the supreme exception, and for the better part of the eight years since he'd been hired, he'd been the main brain of Art Tobler Auto Tech.

Sean possessed some uncanny ability to diagnose car problems by sound and touch. He sensed things from the feel of driving a car and by listening to the engine that most people would never notice or understand. He was diligent, reliable, and he kept the garage scrupulously clean and organized. It was important to Arthur that his business appear first-class.

Sean also had a way of explaining mechanical problems to owners and other mechanics that was understandable, but would never leave them feeling embarrassed for not knowing what Sean knew. One referral to Sean always led to more.

The guy was also a good soul. When Arthur and his sons were dealing with his wife's deadly dance with COVID, Sean worked double time for more than a month and refused to take one extra penny for his efforts. He was also a positive influence on Corey.

So, when Arthur heard that Sean was seriously injured, it occurred to him that not only did he need Sean, but he also loved him like he was his own kid. When Darcy called back to report that Sean was being discharged from the hospital but needed a van or station wagon to pick him up because he couldn't sit, Arthur was as happy to help as he was upset that his ace mechanic was so badly injured.

Chapter Eight

Doctor Stef's exam room, like the waiting room, was surprisingly simple. There was no high-tech equipment, just an exam table, a sink, and a shelf with supplies. The nurse in Eva recognized the labels of Novocain and other anesthetics.

Doctor Stef looked at her paperwork. He asked some questions and then watched her do all kinds of position changes. He checked her strength, sensation, reflexes, and the range of motion in all her joints. Then he had her lie on her stomach on the exam table and did a kind of exam she'd never had before, carefully feeling each of her backbones and the muscles from her skull to her buttocks.

Finally, he moved her into a tiny little office where he sat behind a cluttered desk. While he studied the imaging she had brought, Eva tried to decipher the foreign language titles on his bookshelf. She couldn't even tell what language it was.

"Ms. Banks" he said "you have basic problem. MRI of back look okay, but only show you lying down. Physical exam show when you sit, left side of pelvis two inches shorter than right side. If back muscles not compensating for this, head and spine would be tilted left. Head not tilted because humans have strong reflex to hold head in middle; so muscles on right side of spine always pulling right to keep head from hanging to left. Since as secretary, you spend much time sitting, muscles on right side of back always contracted, overworked. On left side, muscles stretched out, weak. Imbalance has caused some spinal curvature. This hard to fix in person your age."

"So, what do I do?" Eva asked. "And how come the physical therapist didn't see this problem?" Eva was actually wondering why all of the doctors and chiropractors she had seen in her twenties, when her back first became painful, had never mentioned this. She remembered one doctor telling her that her left leg seemed short. A lift in her shoe was costly. It didn't help her back pain and it made her arch hurt.

"First thing we try is raise up short side of pelvis in chair with wedge cushion. Put under left butt cheek. At first, make you uncomfortable, but if use faithfully for few months, muscles adapt to new position, not pulling and stretching all day long."

"A few months? I've already been in pain enough months."

Doctor Stef pointed to an area on the MRI. "Surgeons probably tell you this disc need fixing, but disc not causing pain. Or they give steroid shots, but steroids not give equal size pelvic bones. You feel better after using cushion few months."

Eva needed to see if she could get Donilski to start her on narcotics, though she had no intention of taking them. She'd tried narcotics when her pain became chronic, but she couldn't tolerate them. They made her feel more tired, nauseous, constipated, and itchy than they were worth.

"Is that all you can do for me? And what if this cushion doesn't work? Can't you give me something to kill the pain while I'm getting more uncomfortable on the cushion? I've taken Tylenol and Motrin for months and they haven't helped. Now, you want to make me more uncomfortable? I'm the only source of income for my family. I have to go to work and sit all day long. Then I go home to take care of three children. I really think I've suffered enough, and I was hoping you could help me."

"Look, Ms. Banks, I want to help. Dozens of patients come here already on narcotics and even if I mechanically fix them, not always can they get off drugs. You try cushion first. If no help you, we try acupuncture."

"Will my insurance pay for acupuncture?" Eva knew perfectly well that WhiteGuard was still denying coverage for acupuncture, even though there was some limited coverage of acupuncture by some other insurance companies.

"Insurance pay for nerve blocks. Once you numb, acupuncture painless and for free. But try first cushion; safer, simpler, cheaper. Insurance not have problem with more basic treatment. You give these papers to Tonya. Come back in six weeks," Donilski said as he left the room.

It was going to take much more sophisticated tactics to entrap this doctor. Eva figured she'd probably even have to submit to acupuncture and other far-out stuff to gain his confidence. She wondered if maybe he could actually help her. Perhaps, she theorized, if she couldn't succeed at her job, maybe she could at least get some relief for her chronically aching back.

But, she worried, even the cushion had side effects.

Chapter Nine

The Toblers had a van that they used to transport parts. They worked feverishly to clean out the back and stock it with a cot, pillow, and blanket from the big box store. They bolted the cot to the floor.

Darcy returned to the townhouse of her newly befriended neighbors to thank them and give them an update. She was thrilled when they offered to baby-sit and again, they seemed happy to help. She was so thankful to have met these gracious people, strangers until yesterday. She was also relieved that she wouldn't have to again subject the kids to the hospital environment. It had been scary for them.

Had her neighbors not been available, Rosemary would have taken the kids, but Rosemary managed a huge dental practice and this week, she was struggling with three missing hygienists: one out on maternity, one on vacation, and a third with illness.

Lunchtime traffic was beastly all the way and Darcy worried that Sean had been tossed out of the hospital without help. She was both relieved and surprised to find him still lying on a stretcher in the hallway when she finally got past another privacy-obsessed clerk. The hallway was uncomfortably chilly.

Sean looked slightly better than when she'd seen him Sunday night, though he was now wearing a raccoon mask. His forehead was bandaged, but bruising had spread to the bridge of his nose and around his eyes. At least he no longer had that ghastly look of someone who was nauseous, a look that reminded Darcy of her mother coping with cancer. His IVs and monitors had been disconnected.

"They didn't have any beds in the neuro-intensive care unit," he explained, "so they kept me in the ER. With the loud noise and bright lights, and my head just pounding, I don't think I slept at all. There was this onion breath nurse that came around occasionally to check my IV and his breath made me even more nauseous. The one time I was almost asleep, he checked my eyes with a bright light."

Sean was never a complainer, so Darcy was persuaded he'd had a horrific experience. "Doctor James seemed very caring. Did she check on you again? "

"No. After she told us about the imaging results, I never saw her again."

"Why didn't they give you something for sleep?" Darcy asked.

"You know, I asked onion breath if I could have something for pain a half-dozen times, but he just kept saying that pain medicine could interfere with my neurological status, so I should just try to get some sleep. So then, I asked if I could have something to help me sleep, but he said that could also interfere with my neurological status. I got the same answer when I asked if they could give me something for nausea. When I asked for something to drink, I was told my stomach needed to be rested. Not one part of me rested the entire night.

"Finally, a Doctor Cheng came by early this morning and told me I could go home, as long as my morning blood work came back okay, and I could hold down some breakfast. I actually begged for something for my headache and back pain, and he said he'd write an order for ibuprofen. That was about seven thirty."

"So did it help the pain?" Darcy asked.

"I think about an hour went by until someone gave me a pill, disconnected all the tubes, and rolled me into the hallway where I could see a clock. It was almost nine and I was still waiting for someone to draw my blood and bring me the breakfast the doctor said I had to hold down before they'd let me out of here."

"Why didn't you just get up?"

"I tried to get up, but I just couldn't. My back and leg hurt so badly I had to lie back down immediately. Then, it was so horrible, Darcy. Some ambulance attendants came racing down the hall with someone on a stretcher with bloody bandages on their head, followed by more attendants with what appeared to be children on stretchers. Later, a nurse told me their car was hit by a truck, and a child died.

"That child on the stretcher looked to be about the size of Quinn. That really got to me. I stopped worrying about being cold, hurting, and neglected. I just tried to think about how lucky I am to have you and two beautiful kids. When I saw those injured people, I realized my misery would all be over soon, but another family would be shattered forever."

Darcy wasn't used to hearing Sean sound so emotional. She felt tears welling up in her eyes to think of her family destroyed in a car accident. She quickly erased the thought and asked Sean if his pain was any better.

"Not that I can tell. The older nurse finally did return with a blanket so I'm not quite so cold. Like everyone else here, this nurse seemed upset. I guess you never get used to seeing so much tragedy.

"After all the commotion, she tried to help me. She didn't know anything about my phone but she loaned me hers so I could call you. I wonder if my phone got left in the ambulance. She got things going with the blood work. Right after that, they brought me a tray with some dry toast, jam, and tea."

"So, were you able to eat without throwing up?"

"Well, that's the other ridiculous thing here. My nausea was gone until they gave me the ibuprofen and now it's back, and I don't think the ibuprofen has done anything for my headache or back pain. I told that to the nurse and she said she'd tell Doctor Cheng, but my guess: he's busy trying to save lives.

"When she told me my labs looked okay and they were going to let me go, I decided the best thing I could do is just get out of here. It could take hours for them to get around to my problems. I don't know how these people can even work here. I'm only a patient and I couldn't stand the stress and exhaustion I see in these nurses' faces."

"Then let's get you out of here."

With Darcy's help, Sean again attempted to sit up, but he still found that sitting made his pain unbearable. He lied back down while she struggled to get him into the shorts and shirt he'd asked her to bring.

Minutes later, they heard a ruckus at the end of the hall. Ryan and Arthur were trying to get past the admitting clerk, but an 'only-immediate-family-rule' sent them to the crowded waiting room. Sean stayed lying on his gurney and Darcy stood by helplessly.

Finally, a young nurse came along with a wheelchair.

"I really think I can tolerate walking better than sitting," Sean protested.

"Sir, it's hospital policy that you leave in a wheelchair."

"Please, sitting hurts my back something awful. Couldn't the hospital, just this once, allow me to walk? Please?"

"I'm sorry, Mr. Garmen. I'll ask Doctor Cheng if he can write an order to bypass hospital policy. I'll ask him as soon as he's not tied up."

"No, don't do that. He's terribly busy. Don't bother him. I'll take the chair."

Darcy was horrified to observe Sean holding back tears as he hoisted himself from the stretcher into the chair while the young nurse turned to his tablet and proceeded to tell the Garmens about the possible signs of worsening head injury.

"Your skull fracture should heal over time. Don't exert yourself. Due to the concussion, you might have headaches, dizziness, poor concentration, trouble sleeping or trouble staying awake. Sometimes people become excessively emotional or indifferent. You can use acetaminophen, ibuprofen or naprosyn for the headaches. Return to the ER immediately for blurred vision, vomiting, or altered consciousness. Consult your personal physician if your headaches aren't improved in the next ten days. You can return here to get the stitches out of your forehead in five days. Keep the wound clean, dry, and covered."

"Okay, but the ibuprofen hasn't helped my back pain and the other nurse said she'd talk to Doctor Cheng about it?"

The nurse looked through some screens on his tablet. "I don't see anything here about back pain. Do you want to wait for Doctor Cheng?"

"I'll be fine" Sean lied. He gritted his teeth and signed the discharge documents while Darcy went to get Arthur and Ryan. The nurse pushed the wheelchair to the curb where Sean managed to hoist himself into the van.

Though Ryan drove gingerly, the ride was rough. Once home, they set Sean up on the living room couch. After struggling to get him up two steps to the front door, the stairs to the bedrooms seemed insurmountable. While Ryan helped Sean to get the day-old vomit shaved and showered away, Darcy reclaimed her kids from the Keegans.

Arthur tried to reach an orthopedist that had once helped him with a shoulder problem, but the doctor's receptionist said he didn't accept WhiteGuard insurance anymore. Another doctor they knew couldn't see him for a month. Despite working the phones until five, they couldn't find a doctor on the WhiteGuard provider panel who could see him within the week.

Sean looked miserable and Darcy looked scared. Ultimately, it was Ryan who said he knew where they could get some good pain medicine.

"I just have to track down my wayward brother Corey."

Chapter Ten

It had been four weeks since Eva Rodeki had started using her wedge cushion and she was marveling at the steady improvement in her back pain. The cushion did make her uncomfortable the first few days, but after about a week, she started to notice some improvement. After another week, she realized she was uncomfortable without the cushion. She was using it in her car and home as well as at the office. Just as Eva contemplated sending Doctor Donilski a thank-you gift basket, Doctor Winslow started badgering her about WhiteGuard's plan to dump him.

When she arrived early for her appointment, there were five people crowded into the small waiting room. Tonya handed her just two forms to complete, one about pain and one about her activities and mood.

Eva pursed her lips as Lisa Banks claimed that the butt wedge cushion wasn't helping, and her pain was worse. As she lied through her paperwork, she pondered what other remedies could be coaxed out of Doctor Donilski.

Seated across the room, Eva noticed a middle-aged man holding the paper pile for new patients. He used his writing arm guardedly. The woman seated next to him asked the man if he had a frozen shoulder. He shook his head yes.

"I could tell," the woman said, "because I had one too. Couldn't do anything for months. Just combing my hair was a challenge. My doctor sent me to a physical therapist and a shoulder specialist. Then I saw a chiropractor, but the shoulder wouldn't budge.

"Then a cashier in a checkout line saw me struggling with the groceries and she told me about Doctor Donilski. She said he put an acupuncture needle in one spot in her arm for a minute and she could suddenly lift her arm for the first time in months. The doctor here did the same thing to me, and I was able to raise my arm in a minute."

The woman raised the arm to demonstrate. "It was miraculous," she said.

"So, if your arm's fixed, why are you here?" the man asked.

"Bad ankle" the woman replied. "Sprained it last winter and it still hurts. Doctor Donilski is treating it with platelet-rich plasma. I've had one treatment and it's really helping, so I'm back for another.

Just then, Doctor Stef came out and introduced himself to the man with the frozen shoulder, while Tonya brought the lady with the ankle problem to another treatment room.

Eva's attention turned to the young woman who sat across from her. She frequently opened and closed her mouth.

"Have you seen Doctor Donilski before?" Eva asked.

"I'm seeing Doctor Nagel. She said they could fix my jaw, but we couldn't get authorization from my insurance company. Then my grandmother said she'd pay cash if the doctor here could help me."

"What happened to your jaw? Eva asked.

"I did a face plant on my snowboard a few years ago. My jaw got dislocated and an ER doctor stuck his thumbs in my mouth and jerked it back into place. But it's been hurting ever since. It's too painful to chew so I have to cut my food up like a baby. A dentist had me wear a night splint for months, but it didn't help. My grandma's friend had a jaw problem like this, and the doctor here fixed her."

While Eva digested that testimonial, the man with the frozen shoulder reappeared and handed his chart to Tonya.

"That arm's looking a lot better," she commented. "You couldn't reach the counter when I gave you those papers."

"Look at this," the man boasted, raising his arm up over his head. "I haven't been able to do this for four months. I can't believe this. All he did was twirl an acupuncture needle on this spot for a minute, like that woman said." He pointed to the back of his forearm. "Just please tell me this shoulder won't freeze up again."

Tonya was obviously used to giving directions. "Sometimes Doctor Stef has to repeat the treatment, but hardly anyone comes more than twice, except for the poor concrete guy who goes around with a heavy hose on his shoulder all day. Just do the exercises described on this paper and maybe you'll be cured."

Eva was thinking her job was getting harder by the minute. She was witnessing evidence of treatment outcomes that were hard to believe. Lisa Banks was thinking Doctor Stefan Donilski was a sorcerer. Eva Rodeki was hoping he could cure her.

Donilski gave Lisa a piercing look. "So, Ms. Banks, did you really use cushion when sitting?"

"I really did. I used it for six weeks straight except for weekends when I was out doing chores," Eva lied. "I couldn't see any difference except maybe it made my left hip hurt. My back pain is just as bad and the ibuprofen's bothering my stomach. I don't know what I'm going to do if I can't get some relief."

"Did you read papers about acupuncture Tonya give?"

"I did." Eva said truthfully, "but I don't think I can afford it if my insurance isn't going to pay for it. They will pay for pain medication, which is what I was hoping a pain doctor would prescribe. Besides, if the left pelvis is shorter than the right, how is acupuncture going to fix that?"

"You want my help or not?" Doctor Stef shrugged. "Acupuncture help whether you use cushion or not use, but you need give cushion more chance because you correct; acupuncture not change size of pelvic bones.

"I give pain medicine if you insist, but I guarantee, you just have more pain. Pain medicine work if take all the time. Skip even one dose and pain comes back worse than without medicine. Insurance companies stupid. They pay for what doesn't work. I give free acupuncture treatment when insurer pay for visit. You decide if help or not."

Eva had already decided she would consent, if for no other reason than curiosity. Any doubts she had were arrested by the patients she observed in the waiting room. What she hadn't factored into her charade is what Doctor Stef's hands told him as he reexamined her back.

"Interesting, Ms. Banks, you think cushion not helping. Muscles on long side torso less spasmed. Vertebrae less rotated. I'm surprised you think pain not better."

Caught in her lies and uncertain as to how she could continue to execute WhiteGuard's plan, Eva decided to throw the conniving Lisa Banks under the bus.

"Please let me try the acupuncture. Maybe I could use my cushion more faithfully. Sometimes I'm so busy, I forget about it. I'll be a better patient. I promise. Please don't give up on me yet."

It took less than two minutes for Donilski to place about twelve fine needles around her ankles, knees, and back. Some of them she hadn't felt at all. The ones in her ankles caused a zinging sensation that was only momentarily unpleasant. Doctor Stef advised her that she was supposed to get that feeling, which meant that the needle was contacting the energy in her body. He called this energy "chee," spelled Qi, according to the papers Tonya had given her. Once the needles were in place, some were connected to electrical wires that caused a thumping sensation.

Doctor Stef also turned on a heat lamp over her back, telling her that in better circumstances he'd heat the needles by burning a herb called moxa. "We not use moxa in this strip mall. Smell too much like marijuana. Someone call police."

Twenty minutes later, he turned off the current and the lamp and took out the needles. "Not get up too fast. First time acupuncture can make dizzy."

Eva arose from the table slowly, immediately noticing a feeling of relaxation as though she'd had a few glasses of wine. Not only did her back feel better, but she felt so good in general, that she couldn't suppress a smile. It wasn't lost on Donilski.

"You got dorfed." He smiled back and knowingly shook his head. "Acupuncture release endorphins in brain; make feel like high. This normal response, strongest with first treatment. You wait another twenty minutes and I check reflexes before you drive. Be okay in twenty minutes. Notice full benefit of acupuncture by tomorrow."

If I'm going to feel better than this tomorrow, Eva thought, this really is magic. She could not remember feeling so relaxed and free of pain for years.

Chapter Eleven

Corey Tobler claimed he didn't have any pain medicine for Sean. He offered to bring some weed to smoke that the Garmens graciously declined, in spite of Corey's insistence that it would reduce Sean's pain and help him sleep.

Sean had used marijuana socially when he was younger and before Quinn was born, but he'd decided that as a parent, he'd never be so irresponsible as to jeopardize the welfare of his family. In this state, marijuana was still illegal. Besides, he knew how maddening Corey's drug use was to Arthur. Upsetting Arthur, beyond being injured, was the last thing he wanted to do. Still, he knew he needed something for the pain to be able to return to work. As he was, he could barely move.

Darcy and Sean were so healthy that they didn't have a family doctor, just a pediatrician for the kids. All the WhiteGuard providers they tried to call after Sean was discharged from the hospital couldn't see him for weeks to months, so they wound up going to a local urgent care center that accepted their insurance.

Although Sean's concussion symptoms had quickly resolved, his back pain remained intense and made it difficult to sit. He wound up standing in the urgent care waiting room for almost an hour before he got to see a doctor, who seemed as detached and robotic as the laptop he carried around.

Sean told his story and "Robodoc" said he'd have to see the imaging results from Mercy Hospital. After faxing release forms and waiting another hour, the Garmens were again told that the x-rays didn't show anything. Sean got a one-minute exam. The bottoms of his feet were stroked, his knees were tapped, and each of his legs was lifted.

"Does this hurt?" he was asked as he winced with pain on the right side.

"Hurts like hell, especially when I try to sit. I could not find a comfortable position to sleep in."

With Sean standing, Robodoc lifted the back of his shirt, touched his back, and pronounced that he must have pulled some muscles. Sean was given a prescription for high strength ibuprofen and a muscle relaxing drug. He was told to ice his back and see his regular doctor if he wasn't better in a week.

The muscle relaxer made him sleepy and dizzy. He couldn't take it in the daytime. The ibuprofen bothered his stomach. His pain level stayed the same. Finally, he got in to see a family practitioner named Dietrich Horsley.

Doctor Horsley examined Sean for two minutes, repeating what Robodoc had done, but also watching Sean walk and bend. Unlike Robodoc, Horsley seemed genuinely concerned; especially because Sean reported negligible improvement from lying on the couch for the week, zonked from the medicine, and hurting too much to go to work.

Horsley recommended that Sean start physical therapy and wrote him a prescription for Tylenol with codeine, so he'd be able to tolerate some exercise. It took Darcy another day to find a physical therapist on WhiteGuard's panel of preferred providers and another week to get WhiteGuard's approval of the treatment plan before someone touched Sean's back.

The young therapist had only been in practice for six months when she met Sean Garmen, but her instincts told her that this young, fit, motivated guy was in trouble. Despite the considerable effort he was making to exercise, the muscles of his back, hip and thigh seemed more spasmed each time he limped in. She was so concerned; she sent a report to Doctor Horsley suggesting an MRI and sending Sean to a specialist.

Five weeks after his twisting fall on the staircase, Sean got in to see Doctor Leonard Millany, an interventional anesthesiologist. Millany's office was posh. His waiting room featured an enormous glass case containing a collection of impossibly carved ships in glass bottles. Millany was impeccably barbered and manicured. He wore black scrubs.

Millany interpreted Sean's MRI as normal. He did the same minimal exam performed by the last two doctors, briefly touching Sean's lower back and declaring there was a lot of muscle spasm. He believed that the nerves to the hip and leg had been stretched by the twisting motion of the fall. He recommended a series of nerve blocks with steroid injections to calm down the irritated nerves. Sean could be scheduled for the first injections as soon as WhiteGuard approved the treatment plan.

It was Darcy that brought up the issue of Sean's pain medicine. She said the codeine that Doctor Horsley was prescribing wasn't doing much more than constipating her husband. "Isn't there something better he can take for the pain?"

"Let's stop the codeine." Doctor Millany advised. "I'm sorry, but all the narcotic pain relievers cause constipation. You have to eat a lot of fruit and fiber. Drink a lot of water. Use acetaminophen and naprosyn together instead of codeine, and as soon as we get WhiteGuard's approval, we'll get this pain taken care of."

The Toblers noticed that Sean was in more pain after stopping the codeine. Subsequent to his week of lying on the couch, he had returned to the garage to see what he could contribute. It was especially difficult for him to climb in and out of the two-seaters he needed to test drive, or bend over an engine. He could work on the underside of a car that was elevated on the hydraulic lift for about twenty minutes before his pain level would have him needing to lie down for a few minutes.

After a few weeks, the crew worked out a regimen where Sean diagnosed the car's problem, and the others did the labor. This slowed them down and Arthur worried it would hurt his referrals. Other mechanics sent the Toblers work because they were not only good, but fast. Luxury car owners demanded expedient service.

Arthur struggled with the option of hiring another mechanic. First of all, finding one as talented as Sean was almost impossible. Secondly, Arthur wanted to see Sean recover. He was young and strong, and according to his doctors, he'd only pulled some muscles. He had a great attitude and he seemed determined to get past his injury. Thirdly, earnings were already down from the weeks of slower work. Paying another mechanic would be beyond his means unless he fired Sean.

Arthur also hesitated because Corey seemed invested in Sean's recovery, and he was pulling his weight around the garage for a change. There was a silver lining to Sean's misfortune. If Corey worked at full capacity and Sean could recover, Arthur wouldn't need another mechanic. Besides, finding a good mechanic took time. Finding the time to do the recruiting was challenging because they were all working extra hours to compensate for Sean's limitations.

After deciding against a new hire and waiting another month, Arthur started to doubt the merits of his decision. Sean wasn't improving. He came to work every day and did all that he could, but if anything, his posture was more stooped, and his pace was getting slower. Throughout his ordeal, he'd somehow maintained his sunny disposition and kept his patience with demanding customers; but now, uncharacteristically, he was becoming sullen and irritable.

Chapter Twelve

Unseasonably cold winds were blowing across the Midwest. Normally, Eva Rodeki's back pain would have been worse on such a stormy day, but instead it felt better than she could remember. Just as Doctor Stef had predicted, acupuncture's benefits were more noticeable the day after treatment; and there were no unpleasant side effects.

Eva was astounded that a few minutes of needling had done more for her back pain than all of the years of aspirin, Tylenol, Advil, Ben Gay, back belts, magnets, ice packs, heating pads, massages, the ridiculously expensive firm mattress that worsened the pain, yoga, Pilates, and reiki. There were also the prescription drugs, physical therapy, chiropractic adjustments, and steroid shots she had endured. She wondered how she was going to explain this to Doctor Winslow when she hadn't even admitted that she had a bad back in the first place.

Eva reviewed the files of multiple patients being treated by Stefan Donilski. She suspected that those who were being prescribed narcotics were already dependent on narcotics before they came under his care. He was doing a lot of nerve blocks, but he wasn't billing for procedures that the insurer didn't cover.

Eva also analyzed reimbursement data for two doctors who had recently filed complaints against Donilski. They were both interventionists who stuck steroids in just about every back and neck they encountered. Yet, more than half of their patients were still showing up in the system as being on chronic medication.

It also appeared that if steroid injections didn't fix the pain, the interventional doctors sent the patients back to their referring physicians or sent them on to surgeons. Either way, many of those patients were still requiring pain management.

In a head-to-head analysis, the physicians who were willing to accuse Doctor Stef of inappropriate treatment, were indirectly costing WhiteGuard more than Doctor Stef, not only because they were being reimbursed more; but also, because their patients were more likely to wind up having surgery.

It wouldn't be the first case of professional jealousy Eva had seen in her years of reviewing provider performance. Competition for patients with decent insurance drove some physicians to undermine competitors.

Eva found it hard to believe that CLUJ's accountants hadn't drawn the same conclusions. Donilski was costing the insurer less than other pain doctors. Eva guessed that he'd come into WhiteGuard's crosshairs because, unlike the doctors who were afraid of competition, he was training other doctors to provide more services to more patients. With life span increasing and more people refusing to just suffer in silence, insurance companies were terrified that pain management was going to devour profits. A physician teaching other doctors how to manage pain was a serious threat.

Eva also realized that Doctor Stef's use of alternative treatments made it easy for the insurer to target him. Anytime insurance companies could label a treatment as "investigational," they could make a case for not covering it. It didn't matter that acupuncture has been around for at least five thousand years and seems to be the longest surviving system of healthcare in existence, as Eva had just learned. There just isn't a lot of published research that confirms its effectiveness.

Insurance companies only reimburse for what the industry considers "proven" treatment. Proof of a treatment's effectiveness and safety requires trials which are costly to conduct. Without capital, pharmaceutical companies and device manufacturers can't properly run trials to demonstrate the merits of their products. They also can't pay lobbyists to get their products in front of the government agencies whose approval is needed to bring the product on the market. If there isn't a product to market, there's no return to investors.

Acupuncture can't return profits to investors because there's no device or drug to sell. Its effectiveness rests almost entirely on the practitioner's knowledge and skill. Consequently, there's limited published research about its results, so insurers can claim it's unproven.

Eva's positive experience with acupuncture overrode her long-ingrained belief that treatment needs to be based on published research. The overtaking of every aspect of health care by business interests had become despicable to Eva.

For a while, she tried to avoid Doctor Winslow. Eva also returned to Doctor Stef for more acupuncture on the pretense that she was still trying to trap him into prescribing narcotics. However, his manual examination of her back on her return visits belied any attempt on her part to claim that the cushion and the acupuncture weren't helping. She had even decided that she'd pay cash to continue to see him once she informed Doctor Winslow that she hadn't been able to catch him doing anything out of bounds. After three visits, she felt remarkably improved, while Donilski was only being compensated for visits and not for the treatment that was actually helping Eva.

It was right before Thanksgiving when Henry Winslow confronted Eva about framing Donilski.

"Look, I've tried every trick I know to get him to start me on narcotics or recommend some treatment that Lisa Banks doesn't need, but he's not taking the bait. He is unconventional, but I can't catch him stepping over any boundaries or cheating us in any way. What I saw going on in Donilski's practice was legit, and this doctor is helping people who aren't finding help elsewhere."

Wanting to escape her entrapment duty, Eva suggested Winslow send in another ringer. She mentioned that Patrice Kramer from the credentials office had asked her for a referral for elbow pain. "Why don't you have Patrice check him out? Maybe she can get something you can trip him with."

Doctor Henry Winslow heard an alarm bell go off in his head. His job depended on getting rid of these pain doctors, and he was totally unprepared for what Eva Rodeki had to say about Doctor Stefan Donilski. Eva was his best weapon and not only had she failed, but she was defending this doctor.

The idea of sending Patrice in seemed worth considering though. She wasn't the knowledgeable nurse that Eva was, but she was pretty good at snow jobs. Anytime she had to get on the phone to tell a physician that his credentials were unacceptable, she did a great song and dance routine. Henry rarely had to follow up and confront the physician himself. It was worth trying her out as a ringer.

Henry wouldn't send her in with her real problem though, the painful elbow; that was too straightforward. He'd coach her to give a history for intractable migraine headaches, the diagnosis that most physicians felt inadequate to help, and from which two-thirds of sufferers never obtained satisfactory relief, even with care by a neurologist like Donilski.

Chapter Thirteen

Sean was scheduled for his first steroid injection the week before Thanksgiving. He couldn't take anything for pain that day because it was important that he be able to report whether the injected anesthetic relieved his pain.

Doctor Millany had explained that Sean would be in a fluoroscopy suite so that placement of the needle could be done with real-time x-ray guidance. If the injected anesthetic knocked down the pain, then the doctor would know he was targeting the right nerve and a steroid would be injected into the same area to calm inflammation.

Finally, Sean's day to hopefully get some relief arrived. He positioned himself on his belly on the fluoroscopy table and the doctor inserted a needle into his back. A second later, the doctor got called out of the room because another patient was having an emergency. Sean could hear the excited voices of the doctor and his assistant in the next room talking about an allergic reaction. They called for an ambulance.

By the time Leonard Millany came back to the fluoroscopy suite, Sean had been lying in a flexed position with a needle in his back for almost fifteen minutes. Being afraid to move, anxious about what was happening next door, and stuck in that position for so long, his pain was aggravated. He told Millany he didn't think he could lie in that position any longer, but the physician coaxed him into just bearing with it for a few more minutes. His reward could be great pain relief.

So, Sean gritted his teeth and waited for the numbing shot to take effect. When he reported that his pain was still there, Millany advised him there was another nerve that could be responsible for the pain, so as long as they'd gone this far, it only made sense to inject the next area and see if that erased the pain.

Again, Sean reported that he couldn't feel any difference and the position was killing him. Millany persuaded him to allow him to do one more shot. "Got to numb the nerves above and below the suspected problem," he insisted. "Otherwise, all of the time and effort we've already invested could be for nothing, while the third nerve block could do the trick."

Ten agonizing minutes later, Sean complained that his pain was no better, so the physician postulated that Sean was probably just uncomfortable from being in the flexed position for so long. To expedite things, he'd just give the steroid injection in all three places because there was still the hope that the steroid could help, even though the anesthetic hadn't.

Sean was desperate for help, so he acquiesced. By the time the procedure was over, he felt like his right leg was weak and numb, but the pain he had come in with that morning persisted; only now it seemed worse. When he finally got off the procedure table, his leg was so rubbery he couldn't walk, so he was rolled out to the waiting room in a wheelchair. Sitting made him hurt even worse and sitting in a wheelchair embarrassed him and resurrected his worse fears. He was told that the leg would wake up soon and then he could go home.

"I can't go home like this. I need to see Doctor Millany for help with this pain."

"I'm sorry," the receptionist said. "We had a little emergency here this morning and it's put the doctor behind schedule. It might be a while if you want to wait as he's injecting another patient right now. If you can't wait, I'll have him call you at home when he's finished."

Sean knew he couldn't stand the pain sitting in the wheelchair, so Darcy wheeled him out to the car where he hauled himself onto his back on the back seat. Darcy had to lift the dead leg for him. No position felt comfortable, and his sense of helplessness made him angry.

After they'd been home for a few painful hours, Darcy called Millany's office and told the receptionist that Sean's leg was starting to come alive, and it was burning like hell. He was getting zero relief from the Tylenol that had been advised, and his pain seemed infinitely worse. She asked for the doctor to please call in some pain medicine so Sean might be able to sleep and return to work.

The receptionist assured Darcy that she would give the doctor the message. She apologized that he was still catching up after the emergency. She confirmed the Garmens' pharmacy phone number.

After trying to settle Sean on the living room couch and watching him grimace and groan, Darcy went to pick the kids up at the Keegans. Caring for three dependents had become a demanding job. A friend of Darcy's said she could baby-sit, but the woman had a toddler and an infant of her own. Darcy feared it would be too much for her to also deal with Quinn and Frieda. Frieda was walking now, and she needed constant supervision. Quinn was even more of a handful. There was absolutely nothing he didn't get in to, from cake batter to motor oil.

As it turned out, Stan and Emily Keegan had practically adopted the Garmens. They'd never had children and they'd recently sold the bakery they'd owned for forty years. As retirees, they were bored, and they both took delight in helping their young neighbors. Stan Keegan enjoyed showing curious Quinn everything in his patio garden. Emily Keegan was thrilled that the kids loved the pretty cookies that came out of her oven. Darcy was relieved to have competent babysitters just a few doors away.

Darcy also appreciated how helpful the Toblers had been. Arthur insisted on paying Sean his full wage even though he wasn't working at full capacity. On most days, Corey Tobler had been taking Sean to and from work in the van where he could lie down. The arrangement strengthened Corey's and Sean's long-time friendship.

What Darcy didn't appreciate was that they were all running around and jumping through all kinds of insurance hoops just to try to get Sean the care that he needed, but Sean wasn't getting better. Now, it seemed like he was getting worse.

Doctor Millany did not call back and did not call anything into the Garmens' pharmacy. When Darcy tried to reach his office, she was advised that the doctor had to leave the office early to check on a hospitalized patient. The Garmens guessed it was the person who had the emergency earlier in the day. When neither she nor her pharmacist had heard anything by late afternoon, she called the office again. She wound up begging the answering service to have the doctor call in some pain medicine.

By eight that evening, Darcy still hadn't heard from Millany or her drug store, while the look in Sean's eyes said he was scared. Although he was obviously trying to minimize his pain, it was very apparent to Darcy that he was feeling worse than he had been in weeks, and he admitted that he was having a different kind of pain in addition to his typical pain. Darcy couldn't see how he was going to get through the night. She started calling everyone she knew to see if anyone had medicines stronger than Motrin or Tylenol, but Sean and Darcy's friends were healthy young people. None of them used prescription pain medicine.

Doctor Horsley wasn't comfortable prescribing anything because he "wasn't sure what medicines Doctor Millany had given during the procedure" and he "didn't want to mess anything up."

Ultimately, it was Corey Tobler who said he knew where he could get something strong. Darcy was so worried about Sean she told Corey to get whatever he could get his hands on. By the time he showed up at nine thirty, even Sean was so desperate for relief that he was willing to accept whatever Corey had to offer. But when Corey told the Garmens he'd scarfed some Oxycontin, they both had second thoughts. They'd heard bad things about this drug. Darcy also worried that Corey had maybe bought it on the street. Who knew whether it was the real thing or something toxic.

Corey insisted that it had been prescribed for the father of a friend who had pancreatitis. The friend gave him two ten-milligram pills. Corey said that was a low dose.

"Just don't cut in half." He went on to explain, "it's a time release pill and if you cut it, you'll get twelve hours' worth of medicine all at once. That's how people get into trouble with this drug. I've known guys who abuse it. The big high comes when they crush it and get the whole dose all at once. No one gets hurt if they just swallow a ten-milligram pill. That stuff you hear about on the news, people killing themselves, is when they take an eighty-milligram pill.

"Trust me, Sean, Old Buddy, you know I'd never hurt you. I've never seen a guy look like he's in this much pain. You know if I didn't care, I wouldn't be here now. Just give yourself some relief tonight and get your doctors to treat you with something else tomorrow. You shouldn't have to suffer like this."

While Corey's arguments were persuasive, both Darcy and Sean remained reluctant to have him try Oxycontin. But when Sean tried to get up to use the bathroom and Darcy saw him holding back tears as he hobbled to and from the couch, it was she who decided he needed to at least try one of the pills. He agreed.

Chapter Fourteen

Winter wasn't being kind to the medical director of WhiteGuard Health Insurance. Henry Winslow's son Adam had to drop out of his third semester of medical school when he was diagnosed with testicular cancer, shortly before Christmas.

"Curable," they were assured, though it had already spread. The testicle was removed the day after Christmas and Adam started a course of chemo that would delay resuming his studies until the following fall. He'd also have to repeat the semester he lost, so Henry would have to cover additional tuition.

Adam returned to his mother's home to battle his illness which magnified Henry's sour relationship with his first ex-wife. Gloria had spent the past decade in a relationship, but she wouldn't marry the man because collecting alimony checks from Henry was her ongoing revenge. So, while Henry paid the bills, it was Gloria and her man-friend who acted like the loving parents.

Gloria still lived in what was once his handsome home, while Henry flew back and forth from his measly apartment and stayed in cheap motels. The flight time from Chicago to Atlanta was only an hour and a half, but it took two hours at both ends of the journey to get to and from the airport. At least Gloria's partner wasn't around when Henry visited, but everything in his old house had the feel of the other man who'd taken his place in his family.

January brought another unwelcome surprise. Henry's daughter Jill, a college senior, announced she was getting married in June. She wanted a traditional wedding with Henry walking her down the aisle, despite their strained relationship since that fateful day she'd witnessed him cheating on her mother.

For the year he was married to his gold-digger receptionist, Jill had wanted nothing to do with Henry, but after his second divorce, there were visits. There were birthday celebrations and holiday dinners that made Henry feel like he at least still had one daughter. Henry's older daughter still wanted nothing to do with him, but his baby had figured out how to work the situation. Jill converted his guilt into a trip to Europe her junior summer, a car for graduation, tuition for an ivy league college, and now a wedding for just a hundred and fifty guests.

As if all that wasn't enough to drive him to misery and the poorhouse, the woman he'd been dating for the past twenty months was pressuring him for marriage. Barbara Smagley was a successful mortgage broker, never previously married and no kids. She was smart and attractive, and it was especially pleasant to hang out with her in her well-appointed condo, which was infinitely nicer than Henry's digs.

But the last thing Henry wanted to do was get married again. Why spoil a nice relationship with more financial obligations? Besides, as much as he liked Barbara as a companion, he wasn't in love with her; but he also didn't want to break it off. It had been years since he'd been in a comfortable relationship, and he wanted to maintain it the way it was. He relished having someone to go to dinner with, watch a movie with, and sleep with when he was in the mood. He had no desire to share laundry, car maintenance, and bankbooks.

For the time being, he could forestall Barbara's pleas for commitment using his distress over Adam's illness as an excuse, but Adam would be better in a few months and Barbara wasn't going to wait forever. Fourteen years younger than Henry, she was bound to go looking for someone more available. Damn if it didn't seem like every woman he'd ever known was there just to manipulate him.

Meanwhile, Henry was having no luck ensnaring Doctor Stephan Donilski. Not only was Eva Rodeki singing his praises, but Patrice Kramer also came away from her visit without the goods. In fact, she confessed to Henry that she had a genuinely positive experience seeing one of Donilski's associates, a Doctor Ernest Krauss.

After Patrice had given a dramatic account of debilitating migraine headaches that only responded to fentanyl, Doctor Krauss conducted the most comprehensive history and physical examination Patrice had ever had. He also did an extensive psychological evaluation. They should have anticipated that, knowing he was a psychiatrist.

Doctor Krauss advised Patrice that he wanted her to try a new migraine preventive medicine, but it could take some time for the drug to start working. Patrice begged him to just prescribe her some fentanyl while she was waiting for the new medicine to kick in. Her headaches were downright cruel.

Doctor Krauss offered sympathy, but he was adamant that migraine sufferers avoid using pain relievers, even over-the-counter drugs. He claimed that the biggest problem with frequent use of pain relievers was rebound headaches as soon as the medicine wore off. Instead, he wanted Patrice to give up caffeine, supplement her diet with enzyme Co-Q 10, vitamin B2 (riboflavin) and magnesium, and come for acupuncture treatments.

Henry was surprised to find information that supported Krauss's treatment plan. When he'd last reviewed migraine management, he'd only read about medications.

Patrice returned one more time to beg Doctor Krauss for something to make her headaches more bearable. Doctor Krauss patiently explained to her again why pain relievers should be avoided. He also taught her a self-acupuncture technique for management of the headaches. She confessed to Doctor Winslow that she had no poison arrows to sling at this affable physician. Everything he had done to try to help her fictitious persona seemed appropriate, and he spent more time with her than he was compensated for.

No sooner did Henry run out of options for framing Donilski, he was informed that Donilski was now training another physician, a family practitioner who'd been on WhiteGuard's panel for years. CLUJ was going to hear about that from someone and Henry realized that he better be the one to deliver the bad news.

While he was still trying to frame that message, Eva stopped in to tell him that she'd just learned that another pain practice was expanding. Two physicians just added a physician assistant to their staff to accommodate a growing patient base.

Henry reasoned that CLUJ would have to understand that referrals to pain clinics were going to continue to increase. Maybe some business owners might actually care about their employees in pain, and would switch their company insurance policies to another company that wasn't discriminating against pain patients.

Ever since a legal case in California was settled against a physician who had failed to provide adequate pain control for a patient, doctors started to fear being sued for not providing pain medicine, and many became more liberal about prescribing. As a result, more people with pain problems were seeking and gaining access to narcotics.

Unfortunately, drug abusers and profiteers also gained better access to narcotics, for which law enforcement blamed doctors. Somehow, they expected doctors to be able to distinguish the legitimate pain patient from the con artist, even though some of the most sophisticated people on the planet were easily taken in by conmen like Bernie Madoff and Sam Bankman-Fried. It's a rare human being that never gets duped.

So, around the turn of the millennium, doctors became vulnerable to malpractice suits for not prescribing narcotics, but also vulnerable to prosecution for prescribing narcotics to patients who misused or sold their drugs. Just as doctors were being put in the damned-if-you-do-damned-if-you-don't position, the pharmaceutical industry came up with multiple new narcotic formulas, like long-acting morphine, slow-release oxycodone, and quick-acting fentanyl lollipops. Not only were third-party payers having to absorb the exorbitant cost of these new drugs, but they were also having to pay for the frequent doctor visits required by legal regulation of narcotics.

Henry gave CLUJ his whole dissertation as to why the proliferation of pain services was inevitable.

CLUJ responded that "pain management is a giant black hole sucking the profits out of the insurance business." He let Henry know that if he and his staff couldn't find a way to put the brakes on this trend, he'd find a medical director who could.

It was a Friday in late January when CLUJ threatened Henry with his job. After Henry returned to his apartment and found a phone message from his girlfriend Barbara, canceling their dinner date, he decided to do what he hadn't done for years. He walked from his apartment to a local pub and had a few drinks.

It wasn't enough alcohol to make him inebriated he reasoned, but it was enough to make him a little less cautious and coordinated than he might otherwise have been. Sleet had fallen while Henry ate a steak sandwich and sucked down two bourbons at the bar. A few steps after leaving the tavern, he slipped on an icy sidewalk, and went down hard on his buttocks.

Chapter Fifteen

Sean's pain was no better after his nerve blocks and steroid shots. When Doctor Millany finally called back the day after the procedure, and Darcy explained that Sean was so miserable that he couldn't go to work, the doctor responded that it could take a few days for the steroids to work, and they should just be patient.

In response, Darcy told the physician that a friend had given them some Oxycontin which had made the night bearable for Sean, but now he was in serious pain again. Reluctantly, the physician agreed to call in a different analgesic to get Sean through another day or two, just until the steroids kicked in. He said that federal law wouldn't allow him to call in Oxycontin, but he could call in a weaker opioid.

Vicodin took the edge off Sean's pain, but he ran out of it two days later. He still couldn't appreciate any benefit from the steroid shots. If anything, he felt worse.

He returned to Millany the following week. The physician was concerned that Sean's muscle spasm had increased, and his right leg seemed weak. He explained that on rare occasions, the injections could irritate the nerves, but a short course of oral steroids would take care of it.

When that didn't work, Doctor Millany started Sean on a drug called gabapentin, a medicine designed to treat epilepsy, but discovered to also calm down irritable nerves. "We'll start you on a low dose and gradually increase it until we see a good response. It could take a few weeks."

"I have to get back to work," Sean complained. "Can't you give me something for the pain until this other drug starts to work?"

So, Doctor Millany prescribed a few more Vicodin and Sean resumed working and attending physical therapy. But WhiteGuard

Insurance Company restricted coverage for physical therapy for back pain to twelve visits, and on the twelfth visit, a young therapist watched her patient limp out the door in worse condition than when he started, and certainly not for lack of trying. The stoic young mechanic had worked hard at doing the exercises that she had prescribed; they just weren't helping despite his determination and effort.

Five weeks after the nerve blocks and four weeks after Sean had started taking the "nerve quieter" gabapentin, the only changes he'd noticed were a ten-pound weight gain, worse fatigue, and the feeling that it was hard to think.

At first, Doctor Millany blamed the weight gain on holiday goodies, but later he admitted that weight gain was a side effect of gabapentin, along with fatigue and mental cloudiness. He and Sean agreed that he wouldn't tolerate a higher dose, but because stopping it abruptly could make the brain and nerves more irritable, Sean was instructed to slowly taper it down for another few weeks and put up with the side effects.

Doctor Millany also recommended a trial of trigger point injections, a different procedure than the last steroid shots. This time, instead of placing steroids around the nerves to the painful right leg, the steroids would be injected into some of the spasmed muscles with the hopes that they could relax.

So, after waiting for approval from WhiteGuard, a desperate Sean underwent the procedure. Other than causing soreness at the injection sites, the injections did nothing to relieve his pain.

Sean went to see a chiropractor that one of his golf buddies recommended. Two adjustments later, he was still deteriorating, and Darcy watched his disposition sour.

Although he continued to try to put on a brave face and work, the Toblers could also see his deterioration. It was even getting painful to watch him.

Arthur was losing sleep over whether to try to keep him on, or just start the search for another mechanic. There was no way he could continue to pay Sean and hire someone with some experience. In February, Arthur sat his sons down and told them he thought he'd have to let Sean go.

Corey slammed on the brakes. "Wait, Dad! I know of a doctor who can help Sean. That jerk he's been seeing has done nothing to help him. How can these doctors watch this man deteriorate and not see the futility of their treatments. Maybe if the poor guy can get some real relief, he can get back to working better."

Ryan echoed Corey. "You can't just let him go, Dad. He's got a wife and two little kids. Besides, he's the best damn mechanic you'll ever find. We've got to try to save him. Let's see if another doctor can help Sean before we just quit on him."

"This doctor you know Corey, is he in the WhiteGuard book?"

"Who cares, Dad? We'll just pay out of pocket. Ryan's right. We can't afford to lose Sean. It'll cost us more if we lose customers because we don't have someone with his expertise. This doctor knows how to manage pain."

Arthur wondered how Corey knew of such a doctor; but on second thought, he didn't want to know. His kids were right though. If Sean could be saved, that was the most humane thing to do, as well as the best thing for their business.

Arthur just hoped that saying yes to Corey's proposal wasn't giving license to Corey's mixing it up with narcotics. He knew Corey smoked weed and had been doing cocaine. He just hoped he wasn't doing pills too. He had to admit though: Corey had really come around in the garage since Sean's injury. Maybe he was maturing and keeping his nose clean.

Sean did seem irreplaceable. He was so intuitive about high performance cars, that he had become legend amongst dealers from Ohio to Nebraska. Even Detroit auto execs referred to the Toblers. If Sean were forced to go it alone, the Toblers maybe couldn't even compete. After mulling it over, Arthur decided his best option was to let Corey's doctor try to save Sean, and to not ask Corey any more questions.

"I'm trusting you, Corey. Get Sean an appointment with this doctor and let him know I'll pay for it if WhiteGuard won't. You're right. He's too valuable and we've got to help him and his family. That's the best thing for us too."

Chapter Sixteen

Doctor Henry Winslow didn't realize how injured he was until the day after his fall. The alcohol masked the pain at the time he fell, and he'd managed to get up, walk home and plop into bed. But by Saturday morning, he could hardly get out of bed.

Intense pain was shooting from his back down his left thigh. His neck felt wrenched, and he had a wicked headache. He speculated that he'd hit the back of his head and also suffered a concussion, but it was the obnoxious pain in his back that worried him.

With his boss making impossible demands, his kids treating him like an ATM, and his girlfriend seemingly pulling away, Henry Winslow had thought things couldn't be worse. Realizing he might be seriously injured gave him a whole new perspective.

"Just buck up," he told himself as though he was talking to one of his back surgery patients; but when he finally found the courage to ignore the pain long enough to get out of bed, "bucking up" seemed like stupid advice, useless and insulting.

With a mirror, he saw his backside was bruised, but the pain was too intense for there not to be something more serious going on. When he tried to sit and pain shot down his leg, he wondered if he'd blown a disc.

For a few moments, he thought about relieving the pain by going out for a drink. Like many sufferers of essential tremor, Henry had learned that his hands shook less if he consumed alcohol. That's when he started to drink during the day and get himself into predicaments. Recovery had been one of the hardest things he'd ever done.

Memories of his alcoholism were sobering. He stopped thinking about going out for a drink. If he was going to avoid the bourbon demon, he was going to need some strong pain medicine. The over-the-counter pain relievers he had taken weren't making a dent in the searing pain that was shooting down his leg and around to his groin. Yet over-the-counter analgesics were what he used to recommend to his patients.

It was early afternoon before he reached Barbara. She usually spent Saturday mornings at the gym and grocery shopping. Either she wasn't answering her cell phone or wasn't taking calls from him. When Henry finally did reach her and explained that he was hurt, she came to his rescue. He wrote a prescription for Percocet in her name. He didn't want to write for a controlled substance for himself, and he certainly didn't want WhiteGuard to know that he needed a painkiller. After all, it had become his primary job to stop the insurer's outlay for patients in pain.

By the time Barbara got to his apartment, filled the prescription, and before the drug started taking the edge off, Henry was more physically miserable than he'd ever been in his life. He couldn't even sit to eat the Chinese take-out that Barbara had picked up on her way back from the pharmacy.

"Thankfully, I'll have Sunday to recoup before I have to go back in to face CLUJ on Monday," Henry told Barbara as she was leaving. I'll be past the acute pain by then.

As the evening wore on, Henry found himself almost feeling glad that he hurt too much to leave his apartment, because his desire for a shot of bourbon was getting stronger. He would not succumb to alcohol again. He promised himself that.

The pain was hard to bear though. He took another Percocet and went to sleep.

Chapter Seventeen

Sean waited two weeks for an appointment with Doctor Judd Fleishman, the pain doctor recommended by Corey Tobler's friend. First, he had to get a referral from his primary care physician, Doctor Horsley. Then he had to wait for WhiteGuard to deny the referral, so that he could get some out-of-network benefits, since Doctor Fleishman wasn't on the WhiteGuard preferred provider panel.

Doctor Horsley was distressed to see Sean getting worse in spite of the treatments by Doctor Millany. Although it made him nervous to continue to prescribe Tylenol with codeine for so long, he felt it was about all he could do. Sean repeatedly complained that the medicine did little to help him, no matter how much of it he took, but Doctor Horsley was uncomfortable prescribing anything stronger.

Admittedly, Horsley's training in family medicine hadn't prepared him to deal with persistent back problems or pain management. He had merely learned to send backache patients to physical therapists and send them on to surgeons or pain specialists like Millany if anti-inflammatory drugs didn't help.

Horsley's patients had taught him that the procedures done by pain specialists were helpful only for some. Many continued to seek medication to alleviate persistent pain. Yet, even most of the so-called pain specialists didn't like to keep prescribing narcotics. They instead subjected patients to non-surgical procedures and still, half of these patients continued to complain of intolerable pain. It seemed absurd that more than anything else, patients came to Horsley's office seeking pain relief and it was the complaint he felt most ill prepared to handle.

Sean Garmen's case especially disturbed this primary care physician. Unlike many other patients who kept complaining of pain, Sean was younger, healthier, and more motivated to get better. A lot of Horsley's pain patients had diabetes or other painful diseases, or they suffered from neurosis or depression. Some had substance abuse problems. Some hated their jobs, or were seeking attention from a spouse, or relief from a difficult child or parent.

Sean on the other hand, loved his job and seemed devoted to his family. He usually came in with his wife or mother who were distressed about his suffering. Even more concerning was that every time he came to see Doctor Horsley, this young, personable mechanic seemed more crippled. He'd lost his fitness. His movement and posture were impaired. Doctor Horsley consulted Doctor Millany who opined that Sean's back looked healthy on imaging. He had nothing else to offer. Neither did Doctor Dietrich Horsley.

As many times as Horsley called WhiteGuard, he couldn't get to speak to the medical director. He only got to talk to some chatterbox who knew nothing about relentless back pain and quoted rubbish from a call center script.

The so-called patient advocacy specialists offered only platitudes and deferrals. Often, he'd be put on hold for so long that he'd have to hang up. Having to fill out forms, argue with ignorant clerks, and plead for assistance, instead of being able to talk doctor-to-doctor, was an outrageous abuse of his professional role.

All Horsley wanted for Sean Garmen was some additional coverage for physical therapy. If he couldn't cure his pain, at least he could try to keep the man from becoming more crippled. He vowed this would be the last time he'd play the role of advocate. Why had it become his job to battle the beast? Doing so compromised his time, efficiency, and personal income. He'd studied to be a healer, not a beggar.

The only thing that Dietrich Horsley had ever heard about Judd Fleishman was that he was a pill pusher. His patients often wound up on high dose narcotics. Yet when Sean came in requesting a referral to Fleishman, Doctor Horsley not only felt personally incompetent, but believed that he had to give the young mechanic a chance to get any relief available. He reluctantly wrote up the referral and called WhiteGuard multiple times until someone finally said that Sean's case was under review, whatever that meant.

Horsley wondered if it cost more for the insurer to take his frequent phone calls then to actually help the patient. Ultimately, he concluded that whatever it took, he'd continue to try to help this unfortunate man. The despair in the faces of Sean Garmen and his loved ones compelled him to keep trying; even if it meant advocating for this guy to see an ill-reputed pill pusher of a doctor like Judd Fleishman.

Chapter Eighteen

Although he was trying hard to hide it, Eva Rodeki could see that her boss was in pain. She'd even caught Henry swallowing pills one afternoon after accidentally leaving papers in his office and then popping back in to retrieve them. She hesitated about inquiring if he was alright, but caught with a bottle of Percocet in his shaky hands, Henry volunteered that he'd slipped on the ice last week and had some wicked back pain.

The nurse in Eva felt sympathy for him. Her alter ego was almost gloating to think there was justice in his injury. For the past year, he'd been imposing restrictions on pain care for WhiteGuard's insured, and it seemed only fitting that he should now be in pain himself.

Eva was hoping that Henry's accident might bring about a change in his beliefs about pain. She was desperately clinging to hope that somehow, she could still influence the system. It was that hope that enabled her to keep working at this distasteful job, even though it forced her to stoke the machine that prohibited patients from accessing care that might actually help them.

Eva was sick over being involved in an audit of Donilski's practice. One of WhiteGuard's tactics for dumping doctors was to accuse the practitioner of over-billing, or what the industry liked to call "upcoding." Since all health care providers must use a cumbersome numeric system to quantify the complexity of their patient's problems and the level of care administered, and since the criteria for applying many of the codes is vague, it was easy to accuse a doctor of utilizing a more complex code than the insurer was inclined to pay.

WhiteGuard would notify the doctor that they disagreed with his coding, and that the doctor owed them money for using the wrong code in the past, for which he had already been reimbursed.

Physician groups all over America were suing insurance companies for this practice, but most individual physicians couldn't afford the legal fight. Appealing these decisions required hiring arbitrators and attorneys. The process could take years and it sucked time and energy out of clinical duties. Many physicians found it more practical to just negotiate the extortion fees down to an affordable level and then withdraw from WhiteGuard's panel of preferred providers.

In cases where doctors tried to navigate the appeals process because their coding was *not* erroneous, they'd wind up spending their time fighting with the insurer instead of seeing patients. CLUJ considered it a win-win.

WhiteGuard was now demanding to see notes on two-hundred-sixty patients who Donilski and his colleagues had treated over the past fourteen months. Eva knew that Doctor Stef and his colleagues actually spent more time with patients than they charged for. But she also knew that Doctor Stef's medical records were hand-written, brief, and difficult to read. It would be easy for the auditors to claim almost anything they wanted about billing improprieties.

Eva felt badly to think that Donilski's office was in a frenzy now, trying to review and copy all the information that the insurer demanded. Staff morale and their time to see patients would be compromised. In the end, WhiteGuard would "downcode" most of those charts based on Doctor Stef's illegible scrawl, and demand that he pay back tens of thousands of dollars for upcoding, plus penalties and fines. If he didn't withdraw from the insurance "partnership" on his own, they'd boot him from their panel so WhiteGuard patients would have to pay out of pocket for his services. Revenues gained from the process would go to bonuses for their executives.

As both a victim of and an accomplice to corporate greed, Eva disrespected Doctor Winslow for his role in formulating WhiteGuard's attack on pain doctors. She wanted to see him get a dose of his own medicine. Simultaneously, the compassionate nurse in Eva didn't want Henry the person to suffer.

"Have you seen anyone for your pain?" she asked.

"Been trying to manage it myself," Henry confessed. "But I'm getting to the point where I probably do need an MRI to make sure I didn't blow a disc or two. The pain isn't following the pattern of just one bad disc. Eva, you've talked to so many patients about the doctors around here. Who would you recommend?"

Eva could almost hear the opposing shouts of the devil and angel sitting on her shoulders. The angel was yelling Donilski. He'd certainly helped her. The devil said to send Henry to Doctor Maynard Burke, known in some circles as an outright surgical predator. No matter what the patient complained of, Burke would find something to operate on. Burke was also the most handsome, charming man in the Midwest, a true con artist. Even when patients had horrible outcomes from his unnecessary surgery, they almost never complained. Burke also had electronic medical records that elegantly justified everything he did.

Older primary care physicians almost never referred patients to him. However, because Burke went out of his way to befriend young interns on hospital rounds, he always had a fresh supply of new doctors who thought he was Maynard Marvelous.

If anyone should have been getting booted off WhiteGuard's panel of participating physicians, it was Maynard Burke. But under the direction of CLUJ, Doctor Winslow, and the rest of the profit-motivated masterminds at WhiteGuard, surgeons weren't being targeted. If the patient wasn't cured by surgery, these doctors passed the patient back to their primary care doctors to deal with the aftermath. WhiteGuard was more concerned with the costs generated by physicians who kept seeing the patients, than with the doctors who quickly got rid of these patients.

Eva was pretty sure that Henry didn't know about Burke's reputation, since surgeons weren't on CLUJ's hit list. She also rationalized to herself that if anyone could avoid unnecessary surgery by a knife-happy orthopedist, it was another knife-happy orthopedist. Having worked at the same hospital as Henry back in his operating days, she knew that he also never hesitated to perform surgery, a tendency that intensified when his two ex-wives were demanding alimony.

From her conversations with patients, Eva also knew that Maynard Burke did an excellent job of impressing patients with his beguiling personality and attentive pre-surgical routine. He was masterful at making patients believe that he was the most caring doctor in the world.

Justice wasn't just seeing that Henry Winslow was injured, but seeing him get the kind of inappropriate care that so many other back pain patients fell victim to. Henry believed that he had ruptured discs, which he considered a surgical problem.

The angel's voice got outshouted. Eva suggested that Henry have his back pain evaluated by orthopedic surgeon Maynard Burke.

Chapter Nineteen

Doctor Judd Fleishman hadn't always been a liberal prescriber of narcotic pain medicines. During his medical training in the 1980s, there had been little mention of these old drugs, except for the management of postoperative pain.

Even during his internal medicine residency in a big city hospital where sickle cell anemia patients in crisis could be heard screaming all night, few received narcotics. The mentoring physicians counselled that these patients were most likely drug addicts and that giving them narcotic pain relievers would just fuel their addiction. They were hospitalized so they could be administered high volumes of intravenous fluids to break up the blood clots in their fingers, and toes. The chief hematologist believed that since these patients would rarely live past the age of thirty, there wasn't much sense in having them spend what little time they had seeking narcotics.

While it made sense at the time, Judd was now repulsed by this prejudicial, ignorant view about pain management for a population who spent many days of their short lives in sheer agony.

During the first two decades that he practiced medicine, Judd Fleischman was conservative about prescribing narcotics. Unless his patients had cancer eating at their bones, he'd only prescribe a few days' worth of Tylenol with codeine for burns and other injuries. Like most doctors trained before the millennium, he was terrified of causing addiction. It had been strongly ingrained in him that the risk of addiction was a more serious consideration than severe, unrelenting pain.

It was shortly after the millennium that Judd Fleishman's views about pain were drastically changed. In 1999, his wife of eighteen years suddenly developed trigeminal neuralgia. Also known as Tic Douloureux, this poorly understood condition causes severe facial pain. In a period of a few weeks, his wife went from being a highly functional wife, mother, piano teacher, and church organist, to being a tortured soul, unable to smile, talk, or eat without excruciating pain.

After seven months of inadequate medication and other unsuccessful treatments, including gamma knife radiation of her face, Judd's wife was reduced to skin and bones. Unable to work or sleep, she refused a gastric feeding tube. In hospice care, she was finally given enough pain medicine to allow her to die in peace.

That same year, Judd's brother Conrad, an electrician, was in a head-on collision with a pickup truck that smashed Conrad and his compact car to pieces. Over the next year, Conrad recovered from multiple fractures of his arms, legs, ribs, and pelvis, but he continued to complain of severe, unremitting neck pain and headaches.

"Your neck looks great on x-rays," his doctors kept telling him. "It's just a bad whiplash. Give it time. Do more physical therapy. Take some more Advil." Judd kept giving his brother the same advice.

"What about something stronger for the pain?" Conrad asked repeatedly.

"You don't want to get hooked on narcotics," Judd would answer. "Try to find a good masseur. Whiplash pain is mostly from muscle spasm. You need to learn some relaxation techniques."

"But I can't even turn my head. I've tried all kinds of massage, yoga, even hypnotism. The headaches make it hard to concentrate. Working on ceiling wiring with my arms overhead is getting to be impossible. My employer and insurer say whiplash doesn't qualify for disability benefits. What am I supposed to do?"

Judd offered his best words of encouragement in his last telephone conversation with Conrad. Later that week, his brother was fatally electrocuted. Judd was left to wonder whether pain had caused Conrad to make a mistake, or lack of help with pain had caused his brother to take his own life.

Judd vowed at Conrad's grave that he'd never again listen to a patient plead for help with pain and not offer the best help available. Addiction might be an undesirable side effect, but addiction was better than death.

Subsequently, Judd Fleischman took every available course in pain management he could find. He studied pharmacology. He subscribed to journals about drug addiction. He also started to prescribe narcotic pain relievers to those patients in his internal medicine practice who appeared to be in need. He was astounded by the results. Judd saw lives turn around. He watched blood pressures go down. He observed improved dispositions. Some sedentary patients started to exercise. Some came off their antidepressants. Some stopped coming in for colds and other little annoyances that they had previously been unable to tolerate. It was too late to help his wife and brother, but gratifying for Judd to know that he was preventing premature aging or suicide in others.

Being willing to prescribe narcotic pain relievers had its downside though. Con artists, who suffered from addiction or made their living selling drugs to addicts, frequently sought him out. It was always difficult to distinguish the legits from the phonies. One of his most deceitful patients turned out to be an elderly woman with a prosthetic leg. She kept cocaine in her prosthesis and got caught selling drugs to high school kids.

Too many times, local police had contacted Doctor Fleishman because someone he refused to treat, or discharged for medicine misuse, had forged prescriptions in his name. He'd often slept poorly, worrying about law enforcement blaming him for bad behavior by patients.

Judd was also treated by former colleagues as though he'd crossed over to the dark side. He could feel their disdain when he attended meetings at local hospitals.

They dissed him for writing scripts for strong painkillers for someone who merely had whiplash. Patients confided that other doctors were calling him a "drug pusher" and a "pill factory."

Judd also wound up dropping off of insurance panels. Insurers were haranguing his patients over the narcotics prescriptions, and he was spending more time appealing their decisions than taking care of people. It was a constant battle. He finally gave up and changed his practice to a self-pay operation.

He only had to think of his wife, brother and his long-suffering patients who had shown such a positive response to pain management, to console himself that he was doing the right thing. The risks of legal trouble, reduced income, and being ostracized by an ignorant medical community, didn't trouble him as much as watching pain kill people.

Still, he did what he could to protect himself from the con artists. He maintained an office with no street visibility. He kept his phone number out of directories. He didn't maintain a website. He only accepted new patients who were referred by other physicians and whose records were forwarded by the referring physician. Hand-delivered medical records were rejected because of the possibility that the con artists would present falsified histories and x-rays, manufactured by web-based phony document creators.

When Judd Fleishman received Sean Garmen's referral, he was surprised it came from a Doctor Horsley, a physician he'd never heard of. He wasn't surprised to see that Horsley was treating Garmen with Tylenol with codeine.

Physicians with no pain management training didn't understand that this was one of the least effective narcotics available. Almost every other narcotic pain reliever could be adjusted upward to a point where it was effective. Codeine, however, stops working at a moderate dose level. It doesn't matter how much more codeine the patient takes; higher doses won't help. Extra pills can only increase the risks of liver damage from the acetaminophen.

Judd had also come to appreciate that one of the biggest paradoxes in pain management was that over-the-counter pain relievers could cause organ damage. Aspirin, ibuprofen and other anti-inflammatory medicines could cause stomach ulcers. Ibuprofen can poison the kidneys. Aspirin causes hearing damage. Prescription Vioxx caused heart attacks and got pulled off the market. Tylenol, the most recognized brand name for acetaminophen, can cause liver damage, especially in the presence of hepatitis, or alcohol consumption. So many over-the-counter medicines contain acetaminophen, that it was common for patients to not know they were taking it.

High doses of opioid pain relievers, on the other hand, didn't seem to cause any organ damage. Unlike over-the-counter pain relievers that people can use without restrictions, most narcotic pain relievers don't ravage livers, kidneys, or hearts. In use since ancient humans discovered opium from the poppy plant, these medicines are highly effective for relieving pain.

The risk of using opioids is that they cause dependency. Paradoxically, it's accepted that diabetes sufferers depend on taking insulin several times a day, and many other medical conditions from allergies to heart burn to high blood pressure require daily pills for control, but the risk of people chronically needing opioids to relieve their pain is viewed differently.

At least Sean Garmen's records suggested that he wasn't abusing his medicine, but he was being prescribed more Tylenol with codeine than was good for his liver. That the prescription was of no substantial benefit was evident to Doctor Fleishman as soon as Sean came hobbling into his office.

Chapter Twenty

By the time Henry Winslow got in to see Maynard Burke, his pain was considerably worse. Being medical director of WhiteGuard hadn't earned him an earlier slot in the surgeon's busy schedule. That made Henry think the guy must really be good.

While waiting the two weeks for an appointment, Henry had done everything doctors with his training would have advised their patients to do; but even with the hefty doses of Percocet he was taking, he was unable to tolerate stretching exercises. In fact, he couldn't find any physical activity that wasn't painful.

When ibuprofen proved useless, he put himself on a high dose of prednisone, but he still got no relief. He could manage to work only by raising his computer to standing height and not getting in and out of chairs.

CLUJ however, demanded his attendance at multiple meetings that required him to sit for hours. He found he could only get through his duties by taking larger doses of Percocet, far more than he would have ever prescribed for his patients.

Henry rationalized that it was better than drinking alcohol, but he also worried that just as alcohol addiction had once consumed him, he could now be on his way to narcotic addiction. Worrying about addiction along with worrying about his job, his son's cancer, financing his daughter's wedding, and being sexually unavailable to his girlfriend, all aggravated his craving for a drink. By the time he got into see Doctor Burke, he was depressed and exhausted from the pain and anxiety.

"Not to worry," Doctor Burke said reassuringly. "With my standing in the hospital, I can get you an MRI today, and if need be, I'll get you on the OR schedule by next week. We'll have you feeling better in no time. If you can get to my hospital office tomorrow morning at six, I'll meet you before I start my first case. We can go over the MRI together. Do you need anything for the pain while we're getting this diagnosed?"

Henry wasn't about to admit that he was taking huge doses of Percocet written in Barbara's name, but it would certainly be more ethical and less risky if another physician was prescribing for him. So, he admitted that he had tried various medicines but got the best relief from some Percocet that a friend had given him. "It just doesn't last very long, and my workdays are very long."

Burke was normally very stingy with analgesic prescriptions, but thought it was in his best interests to be especially accommodating to the medical director of the insurance company that provided most of his reimbursement. So, Henry left with a generous prescription for a longer acting form of Percocet, the much-maligned, slow-release form of Percocet, Oxycontin.

However, the dose that Burke prescribed was the lowest available, and in the weeks that Henry had been self-medicating, he had already needed higher doses. By the time he dragged himself to see Burke the following morning, he was desperate.

"Not good," Burke said when Henry joined him to look at his MRI. You've got quite a few bone spurs on your lumber vertebrae that are probably pressing on the nerves to your leg. Your discs look pretty shrunken. You must have worn your back out all those years you were bending over an operating table. I think we can get rid of that pain if we clean those spurs off. What do you think?"

Henry didn't know what to think. He was surprised there were no disc ruptures to explain the sudden, high-level pain. The bone spurs hadn't developed overnight.

Doctor Burke theorized that when Henry fell, his vertebrae got slightly repositioned and that's why the bone spurs were now poking the nerves. That made sense. Then there was the fear of narcotic addiction. Henry couldn't take that risk while waiting for time to ease his pain. Besides, Burke had come recommended and the man had such an air of confidence about him that Henry felt he was in good hands.

He signed the consent forms.

Chapter Twenty-One

Within a week of seeing Doctor Fleishman, Sean's pain had been reduced to a tolerable level. He was far from being pain free, but compared to the intense pain he'd suffered for the past few months, he felt like a new man. Though his work pace wasn't what it had been, he was ecstatic to be back on the job.

The biggest difference was at night. Although he was still inclined to lie down as soon as he got home from work, and he preferred to eat standing up, he was finally able to sleep for most of the night. That alone had made a big difference in his attitude. He was more proficient at work, and he was better able to tolerate playing with Quinn and Frieda. Moreover, he could finally engage in some lovemaking. It was a welcome positive change, but it wasn't just Doctor Fleishman's medicine that had Sean feeling better.

It was the marijuana Corey was providing him at the end of their workdays that had made Sean relaxed enough to ignore the pain and enjoy his wife and children. It was the marijuana that took away the nausea and itching caused by the pain medicine. It was the marijuana that enabled Sean to finally sleep at night. If he took his opioid pain relievers at night, they just kept him awake. It had become a vicious cycle of pain, no sleep, more pain, more medicine, no sleep, until "Doctor Corey" came to his rescue.

Corey had been after Sean to smoke weed for his insomnia for weeks. "I know you, Sean Garmen, the perfectionist. Wheels always turning in that brain of yours. You're the mechanic's mechanic who loses sleep about the timing on someone's old Ferrari, or you're pondering why a Jaguar isn't purring.

"I watch you, Sean. You're fighting the pain all the time. I see it in your eyes. How is it that you're willing to stick all those toxic pharmaceuticals in you, but you're afraid of Mother Nature's nightcap? Go figure! Lie there in pain all night and see if I care, or try this joint. I got it from the parts guy at Lexus; it's premium indica for sleep.

"Meanwhile, I can't sleep worrying about you making a mistake on the Lamborghini in the garage this week, because you can't sleep. Damn you, Sean! You can't go on this way and you're making the rest of us nervous."

Corey had caught him in a vulnerable moment. Sean had suffered really bad insomnia during the first few weeks that Doctor Fleishman had him try various pills. He'd been irritable and his concentration was suffering. He'd dropped a wrench on the hood of a multi-million-dollar Bugatti that had resulted in some costly labor. He was humiliated, but Arthur just swept the error aside and told him he appreciated him, even if it cost them a day's income.

Sean also felt guilty that his kids seemed annoying when they just wanted to play with him, and he was feeling more and more distant from Darcy. He'd also started to develop pain on the other side of his back and down the left leg. He'd mentioned it to Doctor Fleishman who said that he was probably just over-using his uninjured side to take the stress off the injured side. He should try not to limp.

It had been a somewhat slow day in the garage. Ryan left early and Arthur had gone to pick up a part for an Austin Healy for a collector who frequently sent him business. Corey and Sean had just solved a transmission problem for a '97 C5 Corvette and were cleaning up when Sean took two tokes of Corey's weed. That night, he slept better than a baby.

During the several weeks in which he had been having that evening joint, Darcy suspected nothing. She was uncomfortable enough that Doctor Fleishman was prescribing one opioid in the daytime, another one at night, something else for angry nerves, and something else to relax muscles, but she was happy with the changes in Sean's mood and sleep. She believed that Fleishman's prescriptions were responsible.

Sean reasoned that he didn't need to worry Darcy by letting her know that he was now also smoking marijuana twice an evening; once before leaving the garage for home, and once before bed when he'd go out to check on something on his perpetual Mustang project.

Chapter Twenty-Two

Two weeks after surgery, Henry Winslow had the same exact back pain he had before Doctor Burke scraped bone spurs off his lumbar vertebrae, but now, he also had some new pain. He thought the post-operative pain should surely have gone away at this juncture, or at least improved. Doctor Burke agreed to see him back early in the morning in his hospital office. The ever-smiling Burke thought he was healing just fine.

"You're not thirty-five years-old anymore. It takes a few more weeks for things to settle down when you have surgery at this stage of life. We had several different lumbar levels to treat. You can't expect to be as good as new. Let's get an approval from your insurance for more physical therapy and we'll carry you through some additional rehabilitation and taper your medication. We want you to rehab completely."

"How easy is it to get WhiteGuard to pay for extended physical therapy?" Henry sheepishly inquired. He knew better than anyone that WhiteGuard's policies had made it close to impossible for the insured to get extended PT. After all, Henry had written those policies.

Maynard Burke laughed. "Surely not hard for WhiteGuard's medical director. But if you're worried about violating company policy, why not just pay for the therapy yourself? This therapist gives cash discounts." He handed Henry the business card of a massage studio.

"These people aren't physical therapists," Henry protested.

"They are the best though," Burke responded enthusiastically. "A physical therapist named Jim Sweeny prescribes and bills for the services, and he trains massage therapists to do amazing body work: tendon releases, nerve glides, muscle balancing, posture training, and pain control techniques. The therapists there are especially talented, and they've helped a lot of people. You should really give them a try."

Before Henry could protest further, Burke was out the door. As if he didn't have his own job to go to, Henry had to wait another fifteen minutes for Burke's assistant to get the surgeon to write prescriptions for physical therapy and more Oxycontin. His brow furrowed as he looked at the prescription.

Just as he needed a bigger dose of the pain reliever, Burke had cut his dose in half. When he complained to the assistant, he was told he'd have to reschedule to discuss the issue with Doctor Burke. The surgeon had reportedly left the office to start an OR case.

Henry was furious by the time he got to WhiteGuard. He was outraged that Burke had reduced his medication after he'd specifically complained that he had persistent pain that his medication was not adequately controlling.

What's more, Burke had done this with the casual comment that Henry needed "complete rehabilitation" as if he was an addict, and not someone who was working long hours while dealing with tremendous pain. It wasn't like he was some bum sitting home getting high. Hell! He was responsible for decisions that impacted the health care of hundreds of thousands of people.

As a recovered alcoholic, Henry knew the difference between being in pain because of addiction and just being in pain, and since Burke's surgery, he was in a lot of pain. Damn that Maynard Burke, a lousy surgeon, and a real wise guy! "Go get your pain massaged away." Talk about adding insult to injury!

With his back screaming, his pride smoldering, and rage churning his innards, Henry glanced at the schedule on his desktop: meetings all day long. There were meetings with the case review team, the hypertension committee chairman, the chief financial officer regarding his budget, and a lawyer defending against a couple who were suing WhiteGuard for denying qualified care for their prematurely born son. CLUJ had also scheduled Henry for a working lunch with the pharmacy manager.

As he poured over piles of case notes, Henry's cell phone rang. His daughter Jill apologized for calling him during work, but she didn't want him to get upset when he saw some bills from the wedding planner.

Then his cell phone was ringing again. It was ex-wife Gloria. She was probably going to remind him that she'd been very patient waiting for her alimony check when he was recovering from back surgery, but she really needed it now. He'd get around to mailing that check later. He let her call go to voice mail while he looked for his pain pills.

It felt like a meat cleaver had been thrust between his hamstrings when he reached into the pocket of the jacket he had slung over the back of his chair. When the cleaver sunk into his gluts, his shaky hands dropped the vial containing his last six Percocet on the carpet. He got down on all fours and found all of the pills but one. Then the door pushed open, and Eva Rodeki walked in.

"Are you okay, Doctor Winslow? I knocked twice. When you didn't answer, I came in to check on you."

Henry was so flustered, his shaking hands couldn't get the pills back into the container. Once he did, he couldn't get up off the floor. As Eva stood there gaping at him, he was suddenly overcome by crushing chest pain that took his breath away.

Chapter Twenty-Three

Darcy Garmen couldn't decide which was worse: Sean in pain or Sean on drugs. Either way, he was not the man she'd married. That cheerful, energetic, athletic guy was gone. The person who'd taken his place was a moping, hunched over guy who was always tired and cranky. He had little patience for his children and zero interest in anything at home except his Mustang project, which Darcy now knew was a cover-up for smoking weed.

Damn that Corey! He was a rotten influence from the get-go. Sean would never have started with weed if Corey hadn't egged him on; and he wouldn't be taking all that other stuff that Doctor Fleishman was prescribing either if it hadn't been for Corey.

Even worse, it seemed as though Corey was now their only friend. When Sean was first injured, friends dropped by frequently, offering to help and wishing a speedy recovery. But after Christmas, they came by less often. Sean's golf buddies were already starting to play, but after hearing that Sean still wasn't up to it by early Spring, they stopped calling. Darcy's friends also seemed less available. They were probably tired of hearing about her husband's health problems. If it weren't for Sundays with her mother-in-law, Darcy would have felt like she didn't have a friend in the world; except for that damn Corey. He was there almost every other night.

'Working on the Mustang,' how stupid of her to believe that. She'd caught the two puffing on a pipe when she went out to the garage one night in search of Quinn's missing shoe. Corey had the audacity to ask her if she wanted a toke.

"Someone in this house has to be a sober parent," she'd snapped.

She knew as soon as she'd said it that she'd cut deep. She could see the guilt and hurt on Sean's face. He immediately put the pipe down and told Corey to go. Then he came to her in Quinn's room and went through his son's favorite nighttime routine. "Vroom, Vroom! The Mustang zipped down the highway."

Darcy could see the proud father Sean used to be. He apologized repeatedly for being injured, for being cranky, for being in pain, for not confiding in her about smoking with Corey, and for not showing her how much he loved her. He begged her forgiveness. He pleaded with her to understand that without weed, he'd be much worse. Then, he'd said he'd give it up. He didn't want to do it anyway. It made him feel like an unhealthy person, not to mention a criminal. He swore he'd taken his last toke.

After eleven days of Sean being weed-free, it was Darcy who called that damn Corey. "I can't believe how miserable he is," she confessed. "He's not sleeping again, and his mood is just so down. I told him all weekend I was wrong, and he should call you, but he wouldn't do it.

"Corey, I'm scared of him smoking weed, but I'm more scared of seeing him like this. I know Doctor Fleishman is trying to help and he can work better, but now I see the irritability from the pain medicine that was there when he first got on those drugs, and before he started with the weed. There's a huge difference when he's smoking. He can't go on the way he is, and I can't go on living with him like he is."

She couldn't believe she heard herself say that; let alone to that damn Corey, as though he was her closest friend. She had said it however, and it was true on some level. It was something she'd never want to confide in Rosemary. Sometimes, she felt like she was hanging in there for Sean because losing him could mean losing the only mother she'd ever had.

After saying that to Corey, she had to admit to herself that it was no fun living with Sean anymore. He was of no help in their household or parenting duties. He stretched out in his recliner and watched TV whenever he wasn't "working on the Mustang." He had no desire to go anywhere or do anything but work and lay around. He'd let Quinn engage him in rough play only to become irritable with his son when his pain was aggravated. He paid no attention to Frieda who in turn ignored him. He was even grouchier with his mother. He made no effort to call friends, other than that damn Corey.

Corey to the rescue again, or was Corey the cause of all their trouble? Darcy couldn't make up her mind. Arthur, Ryan, and Corey had been like doting parents to Sean when he first got hurt. They had also supported him through months of being disabled. No one else had found them a doctor who was willing to treat the pain. Whatever Corey's reasons were, Darcy had to admit that he really cared about Sean, but having Sean hang out with Corey was a different matter.

Corey was all about partying and hooking up with the bored housewives who brought their sugar-daddies' Audis in for broken taillights. He dated women who considered cars to be fashion accessories. Darcy also knew that Corey did cocaine, which scared her more than fraternizing with fast women. In Sean's condition, extra-marital sex didn't even seem like a possibility, let alone a threat. Corey couldn't corrupt Sean that way. Or could he?

Corey was a persuasive cuss. Apparently, it was Corey who'd talked Arthur into keeping Sean on the payroll. It was Corey who'd persuaded Sean to go beyond his original doctors and use narcotics. Corey was the guy who talked tennis club ladies into the back seat of his Lincoln Towne car. And now, it was Corey who had persuaded them both that it was in Sean's best interests to smoke weed.

That damn Corey! How curious that she felt like he was the only person with whom she could share her feelings.

Chapter Twenty-Four

The ambulance ride from the WhiteGuard building to the emergency room at Mercy Hospital was quick. Fortunately, Henry's chest pain came on after rush hour, or he might have spent a lot longer in the swaying vehicle that reeked of antiseptic and echoed with radio chatter and rattling oxygen tanks.

By the time they got to the ER, Henry's chest pain was mostly gone, but the pain in his back and leg continued to howl. He knew they'd probably give him morphine for the heart attack, and he was pretty sure he'd just had one; so, he continued to clutch his chest with the hopes that the morphine would kill the pain in his back and leg.

Shortly after a technician hooked him up to a cardiac monitor, a gray-haired ER physician told Henry he was being managed for a heart attack until serial cardiac enzyme reports came back from the lab.

Henry waited on a cot surrounded by monitors, screens, and a curtain. Feeling utterly alone, he was stunned by the surprise entrance into this tiny space by Eva Rodeki. Like the good nurse she was, she immediately assessed what was in the IV bottles dangling over Henry's gurney.

"I'm sorry you're dealing with these health issues, Doctor Winslow. The personnel office didn't seem to know who we should call in event of an emergency. Is there someone we should notify or to whom you've given Power of Attorney?"

"Whoa, whoa, whoa! Power of Attorney is still mine," Henry protested to emphasize that he still had all his faculties. He simultaneously realized that he was totally unprepared for being sick or injured, let alone disabled. Maybe he should have married Barbara when she was badgering him. Now she didn't seem too interested in having a partner with a bad back and a Percocet habit.

Momentarily, he thought his son Adam should have Power of Attorney, but that seemed crazy when Adam himself was on chemo for cancer. It dawned on him how alone in life he was, how there wasn't anyone to call, anybody who cared, and no one that would come.

Barbara might come, but he really didn't even want her to know that now he was an old guy having a heart attack. He was alone in an emergency room, and he would be perceived as the codger with no family. Even worse, he was in terrible pain, and he needed more medicine to be able to work; but he knew that the doctors in the ER would only address his heart attack, not his aching back. For that, they'd tell him to follow-up with his regular doctor, even though, he theorized, it was the terrible pain in his back that caused him to have the heart attack.

Just as he was overcome with self-pity, it occurred to him that he wasn't actually alone. Eva Rodeki was sitting there on a stool at the side of the stretcher. It looked as though she was genuinely concerned, but he reasoned she'd probably been sent by CLUJ to ascertain whether WhiteGuard needed a new medical director.

Henry was worried about his job. He'd recently taken a week off for his back surgery and a week off before that, for his son's cancer surgery. Then he was scheduled to be away in June for his daughter's wedding. He could just envision CLUJ sending out advertisements for his job. He had to persuade Eva that he was going to be back fast. This busy colleague of his wasn't visiting him because of her big heart. She was at his bedside because she was a dutiful soldier in CLUJ's obedient army.

He tried to look comfortable and relaxed as he added "No need to worry my family for this little bout of chest pain. They're worried enough about my son Adam's cancer. Besides, the ER doc was in here and said my EKG looked okay; they're just waiting for my enzymes. Let's not get worked up about Power of Attorney just yet. You let CLUJ know he doesn't need a new medical director either. I'm still on the job."

More wishful thinking than a lie, Eva told herself. She had observed this doctor stumble, fall, and get back up more than once in his personal life and career, and she knew he really didn't believe he was at the end of the line. He had such a strong survival instinct that he couldn't recognize the signs. How else could a physician be a hatchet man for CLUJ if he didn't go around wearing blinders?

For Henry Winslow, the signs were all there, flashing in florescent orange. Eva summarized them to herself: back injury, worse after surgery, heart attack, dependency on pain medication, lack of family support, lack of good physicians on the WhiteGuard panel to help him recover from whatever Doctor Burke did to him, and CLUJ for a boss. His downward spiral was spinning fast.

People in Henry Winslow's situation become disabled victims of relentless pain and Henry was getting a hefty dose of the lousy state of health care that he had helped to create. It wouldn't be long before CLUJ *was* looking for a new medical director; someone who could really knock those proliferating pain doctors out of the game; someone whose heart was still on the job.

Eva felt as guilty as she did sorry about the future of Doctor Henry Winslow.

Chapter Twenty-Five

Though Sean's mood and sleep were better with Corey's weed, Darcy was worried about his physical deterioration. He was getting more stooped, and his legs looked thinner. When he was standing, he'd shift his weight from side to side so often it was distracting. He avoided sitting whenever possible. He spent a lot of time in the bathroom because his pain medicines were constipating.

When Darcy looked at a picture of Sean holding newborn Frieda on her computer, he looked so much younger and healthier. She wondered how he could have aged so quickly. But what disturbed Darcy the most was not being able to see a happy ending. If Sean was getting worse after all those injections and all the medication he was on, where was the hope that something was going to make him better?

The doctors had repeatedly said to be patient; these back pain episodes can last for months. No one had said what happens if you didn't get better after so many months. When she really thought about it, none of the doctors had even given a good explanation as to what was wrong with Sean.

First, they'd said 'muscle pull,' then 'pinched nerves,' then it was changes in his posture due to muscle spasm. They all said his back looked healthy on imaging, nothing to surgically fix. So, if there was nothing that wrong with him, why was her husband so crippled and consumed with pain?

Darcy started to wonder why the doctors weren't doing more to figure it out. Just giving medicine didn't seem like an answer. In fact, it seemed like a cover-up because they really didn't know what was wrong with him. Worse than that, maybe the medication was delaying better diagnosis and treatment.

As she looked at that picture of Sean from almost two years ago, she realized she had many questions. An Internet search provoked more questions. The web was full of doctors, chiropractors, and other practitioners advertising their back pain treatments. It was also full of bloggers who had tried all the treatments and were still looking for answers. The most discouraging blogs were from sufferers who were worse after surgery. Then, there were the blogs of people who were cured by a cleansing diet, or by meditation, or by wearing a copper-infused corset.

There were endless advertisements for expensive mattresses, magnets, nutritional supplements, and shoe inserts, all guaranteed to take away pain, but there was nothing that Darcy could see as a real potential remedy for the declining condition of her husband. Perhaps their only hope was finding a better doctor.

Looking at the ratings of doctors on the web was also confusing. Doctors were either loved or hated, but whether they knew anything about a case like Sean's was impossible to discern.

Who really knew how good a doctor was anyway? Wasn't that something her health insurance company was supposed to be doing? They wouldn't reimburse someone who wasn't competent, she reasoned; but then why weren't they reimbursing Dr. Fleishman? He was the only one who was trying to help Sean.

Darcy wasn't sure why on this lovely spring day, she'd suddenly lost hope. Up until now, she'd awakened every morning thinking that this is the day when Sean will start to feel better. She had believed that whatever he'd hurt was going to heal, and that this whole episode was just a temporary setback in their lives. She'd counselled herself daily to be patient, to let the recovery come with time, to trust the doctors and their medicines, and to look forward to the future when Sean would be his old self again.

Now, feelings of despair were taking over. Suddenly, Darcy started to think that Sean wasn't going to get better, that she might be dealing with a permanently crippled partner. The more she read about chronic pain, the more hopeless she felt. There were thousands of people in the web world whose whole lives were about relentless pain that doctors couldn't fix. Of the many that blogged their sad stories, an alarming number of people hadn't even had the good fortune to find a physician like Doctor Fleishman, who was at least willing to prescribe pain medicine.

Darcy read of people who traveled hundreds of miles to get help with their pain, only to arrive one day and find their doctor's office had been closed because law enforcement thought the physician was prescribing too many narcotics. Darcy found the stories too depressing. She logged off and gathered up Quinn and Frieda to get some fresh spring air.

The Garmens lived a few blocks from a neighborhood park. As she watched her children play, Darcy stewed about what she had just learned. At least Sean has Doctor Fleishman, she consoled herself, but what if he wasn't available? Whatever else was going on with Sean, he was much better able to function with Doctor Fleishman's prescriptions than without.

As much as they both hated that he was on narcotics, reading other peoples' accounts of pain that wasn't adequately treated made her realize that things could be worse. Still, she had to find out whether she should really give up hope that Sean could get better, because up until now, it was hope that was keeping her going.

Lost in thought as she pushed Frieda on the swing, she didn't actually see Quinn fall from the ladder of the slide, but she saw immediately that he had a broken arm. A bone was poking through the skin, and he was screaming.

Chapter Twenty-Six

"Only a very mild heart attack, maybe just some angina," the ER doctor said when Henry's labs came back. He'd notified the cardiologist on call. Doctor Nanette Tremont normally would have had Henry follow-up in the office, but she said she'd come in and see him in person. It wasn't because she was worried about him as a patient. It was because she was curious about this physician who had peddled policies with which she was furious, especially WhiteGuard's rates of reimbursement for in-hospital consultations.

Nanette Tremont had been a cardiologist for seven years and she'd quickly built a sizeable practice. Then, just when her earnings were good enough to finish paying off her student loans and bring in a junior partner, WhiteGuard had slashed reimbursement rates. The compensation for doing a consult in the hospital was so low, it was insulting.

Doctor Tremont wished she could just stay in her office and trust emergency room personnel to take good care of her patients. However, ERs were now tending to be understaffed and suffering from high employee turnover. Nanette couldn't always tell who was managing her patients. Sometimes, it was an inexperienced nurse practitioner. Nanette hoped to give the WhiteGuard medical director a piece of her mind.

"So, what do you know about this Doctor Winslow?" Nanette Tremont asked the ER physician as she studied his EKG and labs, "other than he's medical director of WhiteGuard."

"He told me he was an orthopedic surgeon, but he had to quit due to hand tremors. The tremors look like you wouldn't want him operating on you. Poor guy!

"He keeps complaining of back and leg pain even though he's on a morphine drip. I've increased his dose because I suspect he's kind of tolerant. He's been on opioids since he had back surgery a few weeks ago."

"It figures WhiteGuard would have a surgeon as medical director," Doctor Tremont remarked. "I've yet to meet an orthopedist who understands anything about cardiology. All they know is cut, saw, hammer, drill, screw that new joint into place, and dump the patient back on the primary care physician. This is the kind of physician a big insurance company hires to make medical policy? It's beyond absurd. I suppose that even if I told this guy he can't go back to work, WhiteGuard would just hire another surgeon who doesn't know what it's like to take care of patients on an ongoing basis.

"Anyway, I agree with you. If this poor bastard even has a heart, it probably will recover well. His EKG is already better. I'll go take a look at him.

"You are a lucky man," Doctor Nanette Tremont told Henry Winslow after examining him. "Looking at your tracings from the ambulance and this new one, I think you probably had a clot in the main coronary artery, but it broke up quickly. The muscle cramped and gave you pain, but I'm optimistic it got its blood flow back soon enough to avoid significant damage.

"We'll check your cardiac enzymes again later today to see whether they've stabilized. I'd like to keep you overnight." Nanette added, "if that's not an insurance problem." She pierced her lips to keep from sneering.

"You mean admit me or just monitor me here in the ER?" Henry inquired. "I'm a physician you know, I could monitor myself at home, as long as you can help me control my back pain. I had surgery recently."

"So, I'm told; seems like the pain has been a major problem for you. What did you have done?"

"A few weeks ago, Doctor Burke scraped some spurs off my lumbar vertebrae, but the pain that sent me to him is still there. Now, I also have new back pain. Instead of getting better, it's been getting worse and it's hard to tolerate at times, even here now on the morphine," Henry confessed. "But I think with an adequate prescription, I could get by if you'd discharge me. I really need to get back to work."

Nanette almost lost her composure when she heard Maynard Burke's name. It was miraculous when that guy's surgery did actually help someone. However, the fact that an orthopedist like Winslow would even have subjected himself to back surgery, suggested that he was dealing with serious pain.

"What was going on with your back that made you see Burke?" she asked.

"I took a hard fall on an icy sidewalk in January. I'd have thought I would have recovered in a few weeks, but I got steadily worse despite exercise and anti-inflammatories. Even steroids didn't help. The pain goes up my back, down my leg and sometimes it stabs me and takes my breath away. I'm just miserable sitting, which is what I have to do all day. My imaging showed degenerative arthritis and we thought some big bone spurs were pressing on the lumbar nerves. Now I'm not so sure. Not only didn't the surgery help the original pain, but I have a whole new, different kind of pain. It's been hard to manage."

Nanette found her anger at WhiteGuard giving way to sympathy for Henry, another victim of an unscrupulous surgeon. He wasn't the first patient she'd seen who'd had a heart attack from the stress of intense pain.

"Have you consulted a pain specialist?" she asked, trying not to give away her disgust with Doctor Burke and the big insurers who continued to reimburse him.

Nanette also knew that WhiteGuard was making it difficult for patients to get any kind of benefits for pain management. She was caring for several cardiac patients who'd complained that their new health insurance policies specifically denied coverage for chronic pain. One of those patients had recently killed himself, presumably because of pain which he could no longer afford to treat or stand to live with.

Henry wasn't even thinking about insurance issues. He hadn't considered going to a pain specialist and now it was dawning on him that there might not be any around who would even want to take care of him because of WhiteGuard's policies.

"As a physician, I've been trying to take care of the pain myself. Is there someone in particular you refer pain patients to?"

"Funny you should ask," Nanette replied. "It's difficult to find pain services that my patients' insurance will pay for. It's come to the point where I just refer them back to their primary care doctors. That's a poor solution because those doctors don't want those patients. Very few feel competent to provide pain management and those that do, have more patients than they can handle.

"Between the poor reimbursement rate and the fear of regulatory agencies holding them accountable for drug abuse, most physicians simply won't write prescriptions for narcotics anymore, or they provide the patient with so little medicine that the patient winds up in my office with uncontrollable high blood pressure or a heart attack. These patients are paying the ultimate price for a health care system that is more concerned with costs than patient outcomes."

Nanette felt some of her anger melt away as she tossed her barbs at Henry. She had come to attend to him specifically because she wanted to communicate her outrage with WhiteGuard's policies, and from the look on Henry's face, she'd scored without giving him another heart attack. So, maybe he had a heart after all, and now it was her duty to provide the best care a heart could get in this flawed system.

Nanette was conflicted about what to do with Henry clinically. If she didn't help him out with what he claimed was severe back and leg pain, she risked adding more stress to his already stressed heart. So, just disconnecting him from the morphine and sending him home seemed risky.

The minor heart attack he'd had wasn't severe enough to justify admitting him to the cardiac care unit. Nanette had a few patients who got stuck with fantastic hospital charges because WhiteGuard had refused to cover the costs of what they said was unnecessary intensive care. It had taken her many hours to argue with the insurer so that the burden wouldn't fall on sick people. She wondered if WhiteGuard would do that to Henry Winslow.

Like most doctors, Nanette felt inadequately prepared to help someone in Henry's situation. While it was common practice to treat a patient having chest pain due to a heart attack with intravenous morphine, Nanette had no experience managing pain that wasn't related to the heart. And managing someone like Henry, who seemed tolerant of morphine, was way out of her comfort zone. For lack of a better alternative, she dumped Henry's non-cardiac problems back onto the emergency room physician.

"I'd like to keep him here until we can recheck his enzymes. Text me the results. You ER folks need to take care of his back pain. If the heart looks good after twelve hours, he can be discharged. I want to see him in the office next week with blood pressure records."

Doctor Tremont quickly dictated a report and left.

Chapter Twenty-Seven

Quinn was in no condition to walk and when Darcy tried to pick him up to carry him, he screamed as though she was killing him. His screams started Frieda crying, and now Darcy was stranded three blocks from home with two screaming children and no one around. She was grateful for her cell phone. She dialed 911.

Quinn screamed for the entire fourteen minutes it took for an ambulance to arrive. Even after his arm was splinted, he shrieked with every bump in the road.

"Can't you give him something for the pain?" Darcy asked as she watched her little boy cry inconsolably.

"Sorry," the ambulance attendant explained, "but we can't carry controlled substances on these rigs. There are too many criminals out there who might hold up an ambulance. As soon as we get to the hospital, they'll get him something strong. Poor little guy, I think he broke both forearm bones. We'll be there in about ten minutes if there's no traffic. Just let him squeeze your hand with his good hand when we hit bumps. Who can we call to help you out here with the children?"

Darcy wanted Sean to meet them at the hospital and she hoped he wasn't out test-driving a car. She needed to have him come take care of Frieda. Sean's injury had taught her that they would likely be in the ER for a long time.

With Quinn and Frieda both crying hysterically, and Darcy's arms engaged in trying to comfort them, an attendant in the front seat made the call for her. Fortunately, Sean was in the garage and said he'd meet them at the hospital. The Keegans weren't home, Rosemary was working, and Darcy really didn't know who else she could impose upon to take Frieda home.

There was another ambulance pulling up to Community General when they arrived, so they had to wait to get near the ER doors. The ambulance attendants carefully moved Quinn's stretcher, but not without making him scream. Their procession waited as another stretcher hurried towards the entrance carrying an unconscious young girl. Darcy saw an attendant from that ambulance show a nurse a baggie full of pill bottles.

Just when she thought she'd have a long wait to get past the reception desk, someone came and quickly moved them from the waiting area full of adults to a room where there was another screaming child. Moments later, a clerk came in the room to take Darcy's insurance information. He wasn't interested in Quinn.

The other mother told Darcy that no one had come to assess her daughter for at least ten minutes, even though the child had knocked a pot off the stove and had burns on her face, shoulder, chest, and hand. They waited while their children cried.

After another few minutes, a petite young woman in lavender scrubs appeared. She introduced herself as the assistant triage nurse. She appeared too young to be a nurse, let alone a supervisor. She first went to the bed with the little burned girl, took vital signs, and said the doctor would be along shortly.

When she came to Quinn's bed and looked at his arm, Darcy became alarmed by the look of concern on the young nurse's face. When she wrapped a blood pressure cuff around Quinn's good arm, he cried out as though it also hurt.

"What about something for pain?" both mothers asked in unison.

"Oh definitely" the nurse replied, "as soon as we get the doctor in here."

"How long will that take?" the other mother asked before Darcy could spit out the same words. "My baby's been screaming for an hour."

"I'll get her in here just as soon as possible. I'm so sorry we're so busy this afternoon," were her parting words as she literally ran out of the room.

Over the crying of their kids, they commiserated. Darcy told the other mother about the teenager who looked half-dead who she'd seen on their way in. She suspected the girl's situation was more life-threatening than their children's injuries, and that's why they were waiting. As she recalled Sean's account of the auto accident victims when he was in the ER, she consoled herself that as bad as Quinn's injury appeared, at least she wasn't going to be burying him, as the parents of the teenage girl might be doing.

Finally, a physician appeared. She apologized for their wait. Darcy asked if the overdosed girl was going to make it. Privacy rules couldn't contain the doctor's sad expression as she avoided answering the question. Darcy and the other mother became silent.

The physician carefully assessed the little's girls burns and finally, she got to Quinn. She felt everywhere on his head, legs, and torso for areas of tenderness, explaining that she wanted to take as few x-rays as possible. As she was hurrying off to the next emergency, she announced that she was going to call for an orthopedic surgeon and get both children hooked up to IVs to treat their pain.

Long before Quinn got his first dose of pain medicine, Sean arrived at his son's bedside. He was horrified when he saw the arm, but not surprised to see how slowly things got done in the ER. Finally, a nurse came into the room and started an IV in Quinn's foot because when they touched his "good" arm, he cried as loudly as when they touched the bad one. He screamed some more with the IV insertion. Then an x-ray machine was rolled into the room and the little burned girl was moved elsewhere. After x-rays were taken, the narcotic finally allowed Quinn to drift off to la-la land.

Half an hour later, the doctor informed them the left arm was probably just sprained, and the knees just bruised; but the fractures of the right arm were serious. She wanted the range of motion of other arm joints to be assessed under anesthesia. An orthopedist was coming to consult as soon as he finished up in the OR.

"Is the orthopedist on the WhiteGuard insurance panel?" Darcy asked. Her budget was being decimated by an ever-growing pile of medical bills. The thought of having to pay out of pocket was almost as scary as the possibility of surgery, but Quinn's arm was scarier.

The ER doctor explained that unless the Garmens had their own orthopedist who they'd like to call, the ER could only avail itself of the specialist who was on the call schedule for this shift. "Most of our staff physicians take WhiteGuard," she offered. "I feel very strongly that your son's fractures need to be managed by an orthopedist."

The Garmens waited another hour for the orthopedist to finish up in the OR and come to the ER. Finally, a handsome, middle-aged man in surgical garb entered their cubicle and smiled at them. He spent a few seconds looking at Quinn and the x-rays. He then removed his gloves to shake Sean and Darcy's hands and warmly introduced himself as the orthopedist on call, Doctor Maynard Burke.

Chapter Twenty-Eight

Eva Rodeki was feeling profoundly guilty as she drove back to her WhiteGuard office from Henry's ER bedside. She cursed herself for sending him to Maynard Burke, but consoled herself that it was Henry who decided to have this surgery. With Henry's knowledge and experience, he should have sought a second opinion or at least investigated other options. But then, she considered that he'd come to her for advice, and she hadn't suggested other options, and Henry had apparently never heard the gossip about Burke. The guilt gnawed at her.

Eva felt even worse about having to meet with CLUJ regarding Henry. She'd barely put her butt cushion in her chair when his secretary called to say that Mr. Udall wanted to see her immediately. She wound up sitting idly in his outer office for twenty minutes. From within, she could hear his booming voice along with the voice of Clinton Sperling, head of WhiteGuard's legal department. Audible snippets suggested they were arguing about how many more attorneys were needed.

Eva knew that there had been a recent rash of lawsuits against the insurer and Sperling's staff was swamped. There was a cluster of wrongful death suits, and the family of a deceased, disabled child had hired the most powerful law firm in the Midwest. There were also suits by providers over reimbursement issues. A large multi-specialty group, accused of fraudulent billing, had hired a nationally prestigious law firm.

Just that morning, Eva was advised that numerous angry patients were complaining about Doctor Nagel being dropped from WhiteGuard's panel. Jennifer Nagel was the pediatrician Doctor Donilski had hired and trained in his techniques. Her patient following had grown rapidly.

WhiteGuard dropped her on a technicality regarding a specialty change and had just informed the patients. One angry caller accused WhiteGuard of discrimination because he knew of nurse practitioners and physician assistants with less training who were practicing pain management. They were still on the panel.

Eva surmised that it was Donilski's rapid expansion that put Doctor Nagel in the crosshairs. Donilski's practice was the insurer's number one target at the moment, so Nagel was doomed by association. Eva felt outraged by WhiteGuard's treatment of this doctor. Specialty accreditation was a favorite discriminatory tool of third-party payers, and in Eva's opinion, the wrong specialties were being accredited.

Anesthesiologists and psychiatrists, along with rehab specialists (physiatrists), had somehow managed to hijack the specialty of pain medicine. Physicians from primary care and other specialties were considered ineligible for certification without fellowship training. However, fellowship programs were so competitive that few could qualify.

Both in Doctor Stef's waiting room and in her interviews of patients who were being used to dig up dirt on Donilski, Eva had only heard good things about his associates, Doctors Krauss and Nagel. Some said that Jennifer Nagel was the most caring doctor they'd ever met; not surprising for someone whose career had evolved from helping crying babies to helping crying adults.

Still, Eva doubted that Nagel could win a discrimination suit. There were too many insiders who wanted to keep other doctors out of their turf, and WhiteGuard would have no problem finding such doctors to testify against the pediatrician.

As she listened to CLUJ and the attorney arguing, Eva was also reminded that one of the most experienced WhiteGuard attorneys had recently quit in the middle of a major case, because he could no longer defend policies that were grossly unfair to patients. She wondered how low the morale must be for the rest of the legal team.

Finally, Clinton Sperling emerged from CLUJ's office, head and shoulders sagging. They exchanged knowing nods to each other as Eva was beckoned in.

Eva wondered if Henry's situation had triggered CLUJ's current hissy fit. Although it was Sperling's lawyers who had to defend WhiteGuard in court, it was Doctor Henry Winslow who had to justify the medical policies to the lawyers. If CLUJ were to lose Henry now, those lawsuits might be harder to defend, and CLUJ might be deprived of his fall guy.

Eva knew that CLUJ could find another lap dog doctor who'd serve the stockholders if Winslow was gone. Many a physician would put personal gain above patients' best interests.

Feeling like she had to give CLUJ a realistic opinion about Henry's situation, Eva considered the impact on WhiteGuard. Telling CLUJ that his medical director was fine, if he really wasn't, would make her appear incompetent as a nurse. But telling CLUJ that Henry was probably in a major state of decline would be unfair to Henry. Ultimately, it was Eva's guilt about contributing to Henry's miserable situation that compelled her to try to protect him, at least for now.

"Doctor Winslow is one tough bird, Mr. Udall. He did have a mild heart attack, but I'd be very surprised if he didn't pull through it just fine," she lied.

Chapter Twenty-Nine

Sean and Darcy stared at their phones and watched the minutes creep by. Doctor Burke had explained that he'd anesthetize their son in order to meticulously examine him for other injuries. Then he'd realign the broken bones, and re-x-ray the arm to see if the bones would hold their position in a splint. If so, he'd apply a cast and they could take Quinn home in a few hours.

"However," he went on to explain, "with a bad fracture like this, there could be powerful muscle spasms that will pull the broken bones out of alignment. If that occurs, I'll have to pin the bones together, so they'll stay in the right position and heal properly. Otherwise, Quinn could wind up with a deformed right arm. Then we'd have to rebreak the bones and realign them with more hardware. If I do have to pin the bones together, we'll be in the operating and recovery rooms for maybe two hours, and Quinn will have to stay in the hospital overnight."

Darcy and Sean were impressed with how caring and informative Doctor Burke was. He also exuded confidence. They signed consent forms, kissed their son good-by, and were escorted to the family waiting room. A half-hour later, a nurse came to tell them that surgery was proceeding.

As they waited, Sean paced the floor. Darcy spent the time entertaining Frieda and calling Rosemary, the Keegans, and Corey to tell them of their situation. She even called her father and stepmother in Colorado with the hope that they'd show more interest in their grandson than they'd ever expressed regarding Sean's injury.

Darcy's father sounded genuinely concerned. He promised that he and Noreen would come visit them over Memorial Day weekend. He was sorry they hadn't ever met granddaughter Frieda, but they were all tied up with another business start-up that Noreen's brother was undertaking.

Two very long hours later, Doctor Burke came to the waiting room to tell them the surgery was successful and that they would be able to see Quinn in the recovery room as soon as he was awake. He showed them x-rays on a tablet as he explained how he installed plates on both bones and screwed the broken ends to the plates to keep them in proper position.

"We need to give Quinn some strong antibiotics. There's a high risk of infection because the skin wound created by the broken bone was contaminated with playground dirt. He'll be going home tomorrow on two antibiotics. Kids don't need much for pain. Tylenol should work just fine. Also, perhaps a year from now, the plates will have to be removed because as Quinn grows and his arm bones get longer, the plates will become problematic." Finally, he asked if the Garmens had any questions.

Darcy only paused a second before asking, "do you also treat bad backs?"

Doctor Burke seemed genuinely interested as Darcy expressed her worries about her husband. He listened attentively as she poured out their frustrations about the lack of a consistent diagnosis and Sean's failure to improve over time.

Doctor Burke watched Sean walk, sit, and bend. He checked the strength and reflexes of his legs and told the Garmens that he wouldn't be charging them for this consult, because they were such a nice young couple, and because they already would be having a lot of expenses with their injured child. He had such a fatherly air about him.

"Back problems are a specialty of mine," Maynard Burke assured the Garmens. "Right now, and for the next few days, our focus needs to be on Quinn, but here's my card so Sean can make an appointment to see me in the office where we can do a more comprehensive evaluation.

"I can see Sean's really suffering, so I'll try to get him in quickly. Meanwhile, perhaps you can release your x-rays and records from other doctors to me. It would be my privilege to have the opportunity to help you with this terrible pain."

Chapter Thirty

Eva was both right and wrong about Henry's prognosis. The heart attack didn't seem to impact him to any noticeable degree. He returned to work the next day. He explained to Eva that the cardiologist advised serial blood pressure readings, and Henry asked Eva if she'd be willing to take blood pressures for him. He had a machine to do it himself, but he didn't trust the erratic numbers he was getting.

Henry was apparently too embarrassed about his failing health to go to the employee medical clinic. Since Eva already knew about his heart attack, he felt comfortable with her, and she was an experienced nurse. He wondered how much gossip there had already been about his ambulanced exit from the building.

The relationship between Eva and Henry changed once the blood pressure routine began. Although these company people had seen each other almost daily for a few years, in meetings and hallways, there conversation had never gone beyond the job. Now, it seemed that Henry felt that Eva was his confidant. With each visit, their conversations became more personal. They both had three children, a son sandwiched between daughters. They were both single. They both hated what they had to do for WhiteGuard, but they needed their jobs.

Eva listened far more than she talked. She closely guarded her secret about knowing Henry in his days of drinking and divorces. Being the self-absorbed soul that he was, Henry never asked Eva anything that would have divulged that history.

Even without this daily interpersonal interaction though, Eva could see that Henry's back trouble was getting the best of him. He fidgeted in his chair at meetings. He limped when first getting out of a chair.

Sometimes it looked like his left leg was on the verge of collapsing under him. At the end of the day, he'd look exhausted.

His blood pressure was highest when his pain appeared to be more severe. Eva could also discern when his pain medicine was wearing off, because these symptoms would look worse, and he'd become anxious. She could see it in his eyes, his breathing, and his tremulousness.

Henry on the other hand, tried to be stoic. Even when he looked to be in agony, he pretended there was nothing wrong, up until one stormy April day, about two weeks after his heart attack, when even Eva's old backache was surfacing.

Observing that Eva was rubbing her back, Henry brought up the subject of his personal battle with pain. He even confessed that he'd been writing prescriptions for himself in a friend's name, because he didn't have a physician that would do it for him. He'd been acting as his own doctor for years, and had never connected with any community physicians since becoming medical director.

"What does Maynard Burke say about you having so much pain this many weeks after surgery?" Eva asked.

"That bastard thinks I'm doing great" Henry replied. "He cut my pain medicine back and told me to go see some stupid massage therapist. How did he get to be the esteemed doctor you recommended anyway?"

Eva hoped her face wasn't flushing or paling as she responded that most patients loved Doctor Burke. "But you of all people know back surgery. It's a fifty-fifty proposition. Almost half of our insured who are using pain management services are failed back surgery patients. I'm truly sorry you didn't turn out to be in the half that gets relief. Did Burke send you to Jim Sweeny's practice?"

"Yeah, you know about them?" Henry was sorry he hadn't asked Eva sooner.

Eva sighed. "I hate to tell you this, but Sweeny got dropped from our panel last month. Remember our decision to drop physical therapists whose employees didn't all meet the new credentialing criteria? I think it affected three practices and Sweeny's was one of them. I have a report on my desk that there were over two dozen calls from angry patients who could no longer go to those therapists.

"But if you self-pay, there's no reason why you couldn't go yourself."

"There's plenty of reason," Henry snapped. "It would look ridiculous if WhiteGuard's medical director is seeing a clinician disapproved of by WhiteGuard. I'd be humiliating myself and the company."

"You're right," Eva admitted. "How stupid of me. But it's really a shame, Henry, because Sweeny's clinic did seem to help some of our most hopeless cases. Sweeny's from South Africa and some therapists wouldn't work for him because his methods are unconventional. I've spoken with a few patients who said that what Sweeny's clinic did was more beneficial than what conventional guys did.

"I recall one failed back surgery patient, a pharmacist, telling me that Sweeny's people worked one-on-one with him to get rid of the kinks and realign his posture and movement. The clinic he'd gone to before had one therapist barking orders at multiple patients on exercise equipment simultaneously. The only hands-on treatment he got there was when the therapist came by to pat him on the shoulder and tell him what a good job he was doing."

"So, who would you tell a patient like me to see now?" Henry asked. "And please, someone on the WhiteGuard panel. I know there's not too many left and I have to confess, I'm starting to regret that; but surely there's someone on our panel who has something to offer. I'm not returning to that bastard Burke, and I can't keep writing my own prescriptions."

Eva didn't want to be responsible for more trouble for Henry, and thought it better to tell him of several options and let him decide. "Well, there's Doctor Millany or the Valley Spine Care Clinic. Also, I've had some good feedback about a new rehab doctor we credentialed in January, a Doctor Alan Crenshaw. There are a few other physical medicine practices in the WhiteGuard book, but I don't hear much about them. Some specialize in neuro rehab for patients with strokes or traumatic brain injury. One is doing pulmonary rehab for COVID victims. Most do orthopedic rehab."

"Who would you go to if you were in my situation, Eva?" Henry asked.

Eva felt like she owed Henry the truth. "You probably don't want to hear this, but based on what I know, I'd go to Donilski. He's not off the panel yet. Apparently, he's filed an appeal about the upcoding, so maybe he'll be around for a while. I think he's an exceptional clinician."

Chapter Thirty-One

Sean was able to get in to see Doctor Burke in a week. Burke repeated the brief exam he'd done in the surgical waiting room and looked at Sean's imaging studies. Like the other doctors, he thought Sean's back looked healthy on x-ray and MRI. He didn't think the new symptoms were coming from the back. So, he took Sean to his office x-ray to take films of his hips and tailbone.

"We've found the problem," he announced as he pulled the images up on a computer. "See this here? This is the coccyx, what most of us call the tailbone. See how it curves in here, almost like there's a fishhook on the end of it.

"Here! Look at this x-ray." Burke put somebody else's pictures on the screen next to Sean's. "See how this person's tailbone is much straighter than yours. Of course, not everyone has the same shape tailbone, but one as curly as Sean's is much more likely to cause trouble if it's traumatized. What I think has been happening here, is that when Sean took that staircase fall, it jammed the tailbone into some of the nerves that come out from under it. It also might have loosened its connection to the sacrum, the bone above it that anchors our buttock muscles, the gluteals or gluts as they're commonly called.

"If the tailbone is wobbly, the local muscles will try to stabilize it by contracting. It's like when Quinn broke his arm, and the muscle spasm pulled the bones out of alignment after I reduced the fractures. The gluteal muscles that anchor on the tail bone are large powerful muscles. When they spasm, they pull on other structures in the back and leg. They also can press on the sciatic nerve sending pain down the leg. That's why Sean has been getting worse instead of better."

"So, what's the solution?" Sean asked.

"Very simple," Doctor Burke replied. "We just get this whacked up, wobbly fishhook tailbone out of there. No more muscle spasm trying to stabilize it. No more irritation of nerves."

"You're talking about surgically removing it? What are the risks of doing that?" Darcy asked.

"Minimal," Burke replied matter-of-factly. "Much simpler than what we just did for Quinn. The procedure only takes about a half-hour, though the patient is in the OR longer than that because it requires general anesthesia. Of course, you can expect to have a sore bottom for a few weeks after surgery, but that's normal. Sitting might be uncomfortable for a while."

"Sitting is miserable for me now." Sean responded. "How come none of the other doctors made this diagnosis?"

"Well, it's an uncommon problem and a lot of doctors don't recognize it or look for it. Pain like this usually does come from the low back, so the tailbone isn't suspected; and, although it's standard procedure to take pictures of the low back, the tailbone isn't generally included in those pictures.

"It also wasn't seen on your MRI because that imaging technique doesn't look at bones very well. MRI is good for looking at soft tissue like discs and the spinal cord and nerves. X-rays are still the gold standard for looking at bones.

"See? Look here!" Burke pulled Sean's original films back up onto the screen. "This older x-ray you brought from when you were first injured ends at the sacrum, just above the tailbone. So, no one saw your fishhook until we took these more specific x-rays today."

"Well, I'm glad someone finally looked for it. Have you done a lot of these operations?" Darcy asked.

"Probably more than any other surgeon around. I do about a dozen of these cases every year." Burke looked down at his shoes and then directly into Darcy's pleading eyes. "I have extensive experience doing this procedure and some of my patients' lives have changed dramatically because of it. Pain from a wobbly tail bone can be awful, and there really isn't any other way to help a patient in this situation, except to remove the coccyx."

Darcy and Sean were elated. At last, they'd found someone who had really looked for the cause of his pain, and finally, there was some hope that Sean could get out of pain and off the narcotics. They also appreciated how gentle Doctor Burke had been with Quinn who was running around in his cast like nothing ever happened.

Sean eagerly signed the consent forms. Darcy's sense of hope returned when Doctor Burke's office called them later that afternoon to report that they had secured a spot on the operating room schedule for the following week.

Chapter Thirty-Two

When Henry decided to disregard Eva's advice and check out WhiteGuard's physician files himself, he concluded that Doctor Leonard Millany had been a pain specialist longer than anyone else on their panel. He couldn't believe Eva had recommended Donilski. She was just a nurse anyway.

Henry's research reminded him that the procedures that doctors like Millany were doing weren't around when he started to operate on backs. When community hospitals were first acquiring MRI equipment back in the mid-1980s, Henry was still in med school. It was exciting that spinal discs and nerves not visible on x-ray could finally be seen. It was then believed that bad-looking discs were the cause of pain.

Only after decades of failed back surgeries and more MRI data, did doctors come to appreciate that back pain isn't always diagnosable by this technology. It's now understood that many people who have bad-looking discs on MRI do not have pain.

The typical surgical patient has a bad disc between the fourth and fifth lumbar vertebrae. That disc is especially vulnerable to stress because that's where the lower back curves out towards the butt. The entire upper body rests on that curve.

Surgically removing that bad disc can relieve pressure on nerves to the back and legs. However, its removal can also make the neighboring vertebrae unstable, which can also cause pain. Surgeons have managed spinal instability by pinning the wobbly vertebrae together. Unfortunately, patients who've had their lower backs fused with hardware can wind up overusing their upper backs and hips, which can also cause pain.

As the risks of surgery have become known, the approach to back pain has become more conservative. Doctors have mostly been injecting steroids into painful structures to calm inflammation. If one treatment gives temporary relief, the patient may undergo a series of injections, though repeated steroid shots have their own risks.

If patients get pain relief from steroids injected around irritable nerves, but only briefly, doctors sometimes try to put the nerves out of commission by blasting them with radio waves, (a procedure called radio-frequency ablation, RF for short). RF may require repetition and sometimes the nerves grow back angrier.

Doctors once tried to shrink bulging discs by injecting them with meat tenderizer, (MSG). It worked, but also caused some fatal allergic reactions. WhiteGuard was currently reimbursing doctors for heat-shrinking discs with a procedure called IDET, (intra-discal electro-thermo-coagulation). Some surgeons were getting paid to replace bad discs with synthetic replicas. WhiteGuard was *not* reimbursing regenerative specialists for injecting bad discs with stem cells and other biologic treatments.

Doctor Leonard Millany was being reimbursed for implanting electrical switchboxes, (spinal cord stimulators or SCSs), to block pain signals to the brain, and little pump devices to deliver narcotics directly to the painful area. Henry worried that such treatment wouldn't work for him because he was already so tolerant of narcotics.

Henry was also nervous about procedures with unknown long-term results. The first patients to undergo new, experimental treatments for bad backs are often dachshunds. The long backs of wiener dogs are especially prone to intervertebral disc disease. The next patients to try out new procedures are typically very desperate people. Henry was hoping to not have to be a human guinea pig. Perhaps, he just needed more effective doses of the pain medication he was already on in order to do his job.

As Henry reviewed Leonard Millany's profile, he became concerned that the pain doctor didn't seem to prescribe much pain medicine. Had he looked further back into Millany's history, he would have seen that Millany had prescribed lots of narcotics when he first opened his practice. But as insurers started reimbursing for the new high-tech procedures because they were cheaper than surgery, Millany changed his game.

Performing procedures paid a whole lot better than writing prescriptions. It also enabled pain doctors to switch from repeatedly listening to the complaints of chronic pain sufferers as they returned for monthly refills, to seeing patients a few times and then sending them back to primary care doctors once the procedures were done.

Doctor Millany's staff moved some patients around to accommodate the WhiteGuard medical director. Millany labored to keep a straight face when he heard that Maynard Burke had done Henry's surgery.

From his years of experience in this small city, Leonard Millany had learned not to criticize his fellow physicians, no matter how awful they were. If he communicated that a patient had received poor care from another provider, it would hurt his referral base. It wasn't uncommon for Maynard Burke and other surgeons to tell disappointed patients to go see what Leonard Millany could do for them if they had persistent pain after surgery.

As Leonard Millany looked at Henry's MRI, he saw no reason for Burke to have removed bone spurs. They were a normal finding in people Henry's age and unlikely to have been the cause of pain. In fact, he didn't see why Henry was having as much pain as he was. He was convinced however, that the pain must have been bad enough for Henry to have consented to the operation.

It was all too common for patients to have pain that MRIs failed to explain, and Doctor Millany had a procedure in his tool bag for just that situation. So, Henry consented to undergo a discogram, whereby fluid is injected into the discs, one at a time, to see if any of them cause pain.

The discogram is done under fluoroscopy, a real-time x-ray that allows the interventionist to see the needle's position. No sooner did Millany turn on the fluoroscope, he saw that Henry's fourth lumbar vertebra was fractured and collapsed. He surmised that when Burke scraped spurs off the bone, he traumatized it. No wonder Henry was in so much pain. He was walking around with a broken back.

So, Millany proposed doing another minimally invasive procedure called kyphoplasty. This involved inserting a catheter into the collapsed vertebra and then threading a balloon through the catheter. If inflating the balloon successfully re-expanded the bone, then a special acrylic cement would be injected into the balloon in attempt to build the bone back up to its normal size.

Henry was elated to think that his suffering could be relieved, and Doctor Millany scheduled him for a kyphoplasty at the end of the week.

Chapter Thirty-Three

On the night after his tail bone was surgically removed, Sean Garmen looked like a maniac. His heart rate and blood pressure were dangerously high and climbing. Despite having used the maximal doses on the patient controlled analgesic pump that Doctor Burke had ordered, and having been given a sleeping pill, Sean was unable to sleep.

When supervising nurse Michelle had looked in on him, he was clutching the sheets with tight fists, shaking, sweating, and vomiting. Nothing she had tried to do for him had given him any comfort. Michelle was so concerned that she put in a call to Doctor Maynard Burke at one in the morning.

"Damn that Judd Fleishman," Burke told Michelle from the comfort of his bed. "That pill pusher puts these people on such high doses of narcotics for garden variety back pain that we can't give adequate medication when they come out of surgery, and they really need it. But is Doctor Fleishman there in the middle of the night to take care of them when they're post-op? Not that guy. When there's real pain, the good pain doctor is nowhere to be found. Just give Mr. Garmen some Tylenol and if his BP is really that bad, get who's ever on-call for cardiology. I'm not getting involved with a blood pressure problem." Burke hung up.

Michelle grimaced when she saw that Nanette Tremont was the cardiologist on-call. Tremont was a dedicated doctor, but the cardiologist had been in this situation before and was not inclined to mop up messes made by Maynard Burke. Like other doctors whose patients had suffered poor outcomes from Burke's surgeries, she would say that the patient had been "Burkecized." When Burke's cases went south, he was masterful at manipulating things so that the patient would believe that someone else was the cause of their problems, not the charming orthopedist.

Michelle got anxious when even the on-call hospitalist seemed to be avoiding this Burke patient. In despair, she called Nanette Tremont. Miraculously, Tremont was already in the hospital, seeing a critical patient in the ER. When she heard it was a Burke post-op patient, she hesitated, but when she heard that the twenty-nine-year-old man's systolic blood pressure was two-hundred seventy, she agreed to see him. Though she'd sworn she'd never get involved with another Burke case, she couldn't ignore the danger for this young patient, or Michelle's distress. Michelle was known throughout the hospital as the nurse who always knew what the patient needed.

Sean could hardly unclench his hands enough to even point at where he hurt. Not only was his bottom in agony, but his head was pounding, and his vision was blurry. Shortly after he gave consent for the cardiology consult, a blood pressure medication was administered though his IV. It hardly made a difference.

It appeared to Nanette Tremont that unless Sean's pain level could be reduced, he was going to burst some blood vessels. She maneuvered to get a home phone number for Judd Fleishman, who was flabbergasted when the cardiologist explained why she was calling him at one-thirty in the morning.

Doctor Fleishman had no idea that Sean Garmen had seen Maynard Burke and subjected himself to this surgery. He'd seen Sean for his monthly refills about two weeks ago, and the subject never came up. Judd became incensed when Nanette explained the post-op pain medicine that Burke had ordered. Though Sean's records clearly indicated he was on oral opioids pre-operatively, Burke had ordered the equivalency of less than that for postop pain control.

Judd Fleishman squeezed his phone in anger. Sean needed three times the dose that Burke was giving him. Burke miscalculated the conversion from oral medication to intravenous administration. The idiot had effectively put Sean Garmen into an acute state of narcotic withdrawal. He was outraged by Burke's stupidity and inhumanity.

Fleishman advised doses for the analgesic pump and within a few minutes, Sean's blood pressure started coming down. The sweating, shaking and nausea gradually lessened. Nanette ordered a cardiac enzyme panel to make sure he hadn't had a heart attack. She advised him to return to her office with blood pressure readings after hospital discharge.

Chapter Thirty-Four

Henry's kyphoplasty was done on Friday, so he'd have the weekend to recoup. He'd become increasingly anxious about losing time from work, though he did everything he could on his laptop.

Whenever he was back in the office, he had to attend meetings. As hard as he tried to delegate to others, numerous issues had to come before him personally as medical director. When he returned to work on Monday, he would be expected to meet with representatives from multiple departments and make numerous decisions.

Henry was grateful that Doctor Millany had agreed to write pain medicine scripts for him. Although the interventionist had pretty much gotten away from doing any ongoing medical management, he was sympathetic to Henry for having had to walk around with a broken back for weeks while carrying on his professional duties.

Millany was also sensitive to Henry's situation of not being appreciated by other community physicians. It was well known that WhiteGuard had hassled quite a few pain doctors to the point that some had closed their practices or dropped off the insurer's panel. Millany's office had been plagued with requests for consults by desperate patients who needed prescriptions. They were told that Doctor Millany wouldn't manage their meds. Any doctor could do that. Doctor Millany had unique skills and equipment that other doctors didn't have and that kept him busy enough.

However, in the case of WhiteGuard's medical director, it was in Millany's best interests to make an exception. Even though Henry's narcotic dose seemed quite high, Leonard Millany reasoned that his practice would have a better chance of nhot being targeted in WhiteGuard's war against pain doctors if the company's medical director depended on him for pain management. Since Henry's original pain hadn't been alleviated by Burke's stupid surgery, Henry's pain could turn out to be chronic, even if the kyphoplasty relieved the pain of the fracture.

The day after his procedure, Henry was already noticing some difference in his pain. The original pain was still present in his back, butt, and leg, but the more intense pain that had been plaguing him since shortly after Burke's surgery was a little better. He was amazed that the stabbing and aching that drove him into Burke's clutches in the first place seemed so much more tolerable, now that the crushing pain of the fractured vertebra was alleviated. He also felt a huge sense of relief that a respected doctor was prescribing for him, instead of illegally writing prescriptions for himself.

Barbara didn't even know that Henry had continued to write prescriptions in her name. He'd persuaded a neighborhood pharmacist that his girlfriend was afraid to pick up the prescriptions herself because of a recent rash of pharmacy hold-ups. Oxycontin was such a coveted and expensive item in the drug abuse world, that addicts were going to desperate means to get it. There'd been several reports of Oxycontin thieves breaking into closed pharmacies or holding up pharmacists at gunpoint.

The local police chief did a TV spot to warn people to make sure they weren't followed when leaving a drug store. Some people with little white pharmacy bags had been attacked in parking lots. The police chief also advised stripping labels from drug bottles before discarding them. Addicts were combing the city dump to find labels that gave the patient's name, address, dose, and refill status. They'd then try to call in a refill, or they'd rob the patient's home.

Henry's pharmacist didn't question that a petite woman like Barbara would feel safer if her physician boyfriend was picking up her prescriptions. Doctor Winslow seemed like a solid citizen and the prescriptions were a good part of his earnings. He didn't give it too much thought until Doctor Henry Winslow showed up with a prescription for the same dose written in his own name by Doctor Leonard Millany. He scowled as he scrutinized Barbara's account.

Henry sensed the pharmacist's suspiciousness. He could have kicked himself for not going to a different pharmacy. This little old-fashioned drugstore was a short walk from his apartment, and he found it much easier to walk there then to walk to the garage, get into his car, and drive to a big chain pharmacy. Also, some pharmacists had given him looks of disapproval. This pharmacist had never made him feel like a criminal, until now.

"I've recently had surgery and now Doctor Millany's just done a procedure on my back." He pulled up his shirt to show the kyphoplasty bandage, knowing that the scar from Burke's operation was also apparent. "I was really hurting, so I tried Barbara's prescription which helped more than I ever would have imagined; so, Doctor Millany wrote the same script for me."

He couldn't tell if the pharmacist believed him or not, and an enormous wave of anxiety overcame him. He told the druggist he'd come back for the prescription later on, and he hobbled outside as quickly as he could to call Barbara to warn her that the pharmacist might be calling her to check out his story.

Chapter Thirty-Five

Ten days after his tailbone surgery, Sean limped into Doctor Judd Fleishman's office for prescription refills. He wasn't aware that during his post-op ordeal, Doctor Fleishman had been consulted by the cardiologist and knew about the surgery and post-op fiasco.

"Why didn't you check with me before you went to see Doctor Burke?" Fleishman asked. If anyone in the community appreciated what happened to Burke's patients, it was a physician who treated chronic pain. Doctor Fleishman's practice was full of people who had succumbed to useless operations and wound up with worse pain than they had before surgery. In fact, Judd had another patient in his practice who'd had their tailbone removed by Burke, because they'd been told that all their troubles came from a curly coccyx. The surgery caused worse pain.

Judd had gone so far as to check on the incidence of coccygectomy (tailbone removal) at Community General Hospital through a friend with access to records. He learned that while other orthopedists never or rarely performed this surgery, Maynard Burke was averaging three to four cases per year. And that was just at Community General. Burke was also on the surgical staff of Mercy and City Central Hospitals. Judd had no way to get to the records in those facilities, but he imagined all the hospitals loved Burke for keeping their ORs busy.

Sean explained to Doctor Fleischman how Doctor Burke had been wonderful when Quinn broke his arm, and how he'd been so generous as to evaluate him just after Quinn's surgery, without even charging them.

"Did Doctor Burke do a rectal exam?" Judd asked.

"Huh? Why do you ask that?"

"You probably didn't realize that when I first evaluated you, Sean, I specifically checked your coccyx when I did a rectal exam. I pushed and pulled on the tailbone to see if it was wobbly, and I asked you if it was tender." Judd looked back at notes from his initial exam, and they clearly indicated that he had done that, while also checking the prostate, as any good internist should. Sean's tailbone was neither mobile nor tender.

Sean remembered that Dr. Fleishman had done an extremely thorough physical at this first visit, but he didn't remember the tailbone part.

"Do you know how Burke decided it was the coccyx causing your problem?"

"He took a special x-ray and showed it to us alongside someone else's x-ray." Sean replied. "He said it was so curly it looked like a fishhook."

"Are you having any trouble peeing?" Judd asked.

"As a matter of fact, it's been hard to get my stream going. Pooping is also extra difficult. Is that from the surgery?"

For a moment, Judd debated whether to just drop the subject or show Sean the absurdity of what Burke had done. His anger with Burke won out. He took out an anatomy atlas that showed different shapes of the tailbone.

"A curly tailbone is one of four common shapes. The variation in the shape of the sacral and coccyx bones causes the variation in the shape of the buttocks. Some people's rear ends protrude out like a shelf. Some people have flat butts.

"I don't have your x-rays here, so I'm not at liberty to say that there wasn't something abnormal about your tailbone, but unless your pain is gone, I'm concerned that Doctor Burke may have removed a normal coccyx. Most physicians would recommend against such a procedure unless your tailbone was tender or wobbly, and that would only be discernable by manually examining the bone."

Judd showed the Garmens two other pages in an anatomy atlas. One picture showed the nerves that come from the spinal cord on their way to the bladder. He explained that those nerves could have been damaged by tailbone removal.

Another picture showed that most of the muscles that form the pelvic floor also attach to the tailbone. Judd explained that the pelvic muscles contract to start the process of emptying the bowel and bladder, and that those muscles could also have been injured by the surgery. Finally, he explained that any injury would hopefully be temporary and that the nerves and muscles could make a full recovery.

Sean and Darcy didn't want to believe that the kindly Doctor Burke had done an unnecessary surgery, but Sean had to admit that his original pain was as nasty as ever, and now he had more pain. He could only sit if he wound a towel up into a doughnut and put his tail end in the donut hole.

If Doctor Fleishman was right, the Garmens were in a quandary regarding Quinn's fractured arm. Darcy told Fleishman that Quinn was still in his cast and that the long-range plan called for surgical removal of hardware in about a year. As she revealed this, she watched Judd Fleishman's upper lip curl.

"Is this malpractice, Doctor Fleishman? I really don't know how to handle this, especially with Doctor Burke taking care of our son."

Judd wasn't sure what to do himself. He had once reported Burke to the state medical board and about six months later, he'd received a response that his concerns had been carefully evaluated and disciplinary action wasn't indicated. Judd didn't know if Burke had friends on the medical board, whether the board didn't care about overly aggressive surgeons, or whether his complaint was dismissed because, after all, he was that doctor who was writing all those narcotic prescriptions.

After that, Judd decided that he himself was too easy a target for some other disgruntled doctor who didn't like to see patients on narcotics, so he resolved not to wave his name in front of any regulatory agencies in the future.

Now, another Burke victim was suffering, and Judd was wondering if Burke had also done unnecessary surgery on their child. Little kids didn't have big powerful muscles to pull the broken bones apart. He'd have to research if Quinn really did need hardware fixation.

"Well, before I make any judgments, why don't we have your and Quinn's medical records and imaging released to me, so I can see what's going on and give a valid opinion. In the interim, let's increase your pain meds a bit to get you through the recovery period. We'll re-evaluate next week."

Chapter Thirty-Six

As per usual, Barbara Smagley went to the gym on Saturday morning and turned off her cell phone. Henry had to reach her before the pharmacist called to ask her about the prescriptions. If she didn't confirm that the prescriptions were hers, the pharmacist would have no choice but to report Henry to authorities. Otherwise, the pharmacist could also be criminally charged for not reporting his suspicion of prescription fraud.

Predictably, Barbara didn't answer her phone, so Henry left a message. The quickest way for him to get to her in person was to call for a cab to take him to the gym. As the cabbie drove, Henry kept frantically punching in her number. He left several more messages begging her to call back immediately.

When they arrived at her health club, Henry felt even more panicked when he didn't see her car in the lot. Either she hadn't gone to the gym or had already left. He was trying to call her again when out of the corner of his eye, he saw a man and woman getting into a Jeep across from where the cab was idling. No wonder he couldn't find her car. She'd come to the gym with someone else, someone who looked like a new boyfriend.

Henry jumped out of the cab as quickly as his pain would allow, and yelled her name, but he was a second too late. The Jeep pulled away. If he could have run, he would have chased it; but in the condition he was in, he had no chance.

Having observed Henry's predicament, the taxi driver pulled up closer to where his fare had limped to. Henry pulled out a twenty-dollar bill and thanked the driver for saving him a few steps. "There's more where this comes from if you'll follow that green Jeep that just pulled out of here," Henry said.

The driver looked alarmed. "I don't want any trouble, Mister."

"This won't be high speed," Henry responded as he tossed another twenty at the driver. "I just need to catch up with the people in that car. I'll make it worth your while if you don't lose them."

The cabbie hit the gas pedal and Henry tried calling Barbara again. Now he was getting the message that her voice mailbox was full. It gave him some hope that at least the pharmacist hadn't reached her yet either, but he wondered if the voice mailbox was full because the pharmacist had left a big message, along with all the messages he'd left.

Three blocks from the gym, the cab driver was able to maneuver behind the Jeep. "Now, what do we do?" he asked.

Henry hadn't thought of that. Since the pharmacist had given him that look of disbelief, he hadn't had time to think. For lack of a better plan, he directed the driver to just follow them while he contemplated his options. At the next red light, he could see Barbara and the man fairly well. They seemed to be having an animated conversation.

He hoped the man was just a friend or neighbor, but it wouldn't have surprised him to learn that Barbara was dating someone new. He'd seen little of her lately, although they still spoke on the phone. Shortly after his back surgery, she'd taken vacation time to visit her mother in Arizona. They'd spent a sexless weekend together when she got back; just around the time his back pain was starting to worsen.

He never told her about the heart attack. He lied about being unable to meet her for dinner on the day he was hospitalized. The weekend after that, she claimed she had plans with her niece. Henry wondered which of them was the bigger liar.

When he'd called her to tell her he was having the kyphoplasty procedure this Friday, she agreed to have dinner with him on Sunday, tomorrow. Maybe her gym buddy was just a friend.

At the next red light, Henry thought he saw Barbara using her cell phone, but he couldn't be sure. He could only hope that she was picking up her voice mails and that she'd answer his message before she'd answer one from the pharmacist. As he pondered what he'd do next, the Jeep turned down a side street. The cabbie followed it to a private driveway where Barbara's car was parked. With what little speed he could muster, Henry exited the cab and hobbled up to the Jeep.

"I'm a friend of Barbara's," he stammered, as an athletic looking man got out of the car and eyed him suspiciously. "I've been trying to reach her on her cell phone about something really important. I knew she'd have it turned off when she went to the gym, so I've been trying to catch up with her."

The man replied, "She's on the phone right now, something about a pharmacy problem."

Chapter Thirty-Seven

Even with supplemental pain medicine, Sean had a miserable week. His leg, back and now his butt were all just screaming. In as much as he'd managed to go to work most of the time since being injured, he was now finding it almost impossible to do his job. On top of all the back and butt pain, he was so constipated his belly hurt.

The Toblers remained supportive. They could see he was suffering. Arthur insisted that he take a few days off, even though the garage was exceptionally busy that week. To make matters worse, Ryan Tobler's wife Chloe, who managed the phones and helped Arthur with scheduling, ordering parts, and accounting, also needed time off.

Ryan and Chloe had been trying to start a family for three years and they were ecstatic when she finally got pregnant. But in her fifth month, she started spotting. Her obstetrician advised strict bed rest, the same day that Arthur told Sean to stay home and use his energy to heal.

Meanwhile, Darcy was overwhelmed trying to assist Sean and Quinn at home. Her little boy, who had a cast covering his entire right arm, needed help with everything and so did Frieda. Sean was of no help with anything, and he'd become so cranky that Darcy couldn't stand to be around him.

When her mother-in-law came to visit on Sunday, Rosemary could feel the tension permeating their environment, and she sensed that Darcy needed a break. She decided to take a few days off from her job as a dental practice manager to care for her son and grandchildren, and she encouraged Darcy to go help the Toblers out by taking on Chloe's duties. Arthur spent that Sunday showing Darcy around the office. Rosemary spent the next three days taking care of Sean, Quinn, and Frieda.

By midweek, Darcy felt like a new woman and Rosemary was on the verge of insanity. Darcy loved working at Toblers compared to being a housewife and nursemaid. Rosemary couldn't fathom how Darcy tolerated being trapped in the house with a toddler, a disabled four-year-old, and a grouchy man who could do nothing but limp around in pain and sit on the toilet. She hated seeing her son so miserable.

When Sean's appointment with Doctor Fleishman came up that Wednesday, it was Rosemary who accompanied him, while Darcy worked for Arthur. Fortunately, the Keegans were available to baby-sit Quinn and Frieda. The pairing of miserable, crippled adults with rambunctious, little kids wasn't a good combo in Fleischman's waiting room.

It was especially fortunate that the children were not with Sean and Rosemary for that visit. As was typical, they sat in the waiting room with other patients, as Doctor Fleishman tended to run late. They had been sitting there for about ten minutes when four men in suits stormed into the office with guns in hand. A tall, older man told the patients he was from the Federal Drug Enforcement Agency and that Doctor Fleishman's practice was being closed.

One of the other men ordered the receptionist to shut down her computer and hand it over. Within minutes, the two other men who had barged into Doctor Fleishman's inner office were leading the physician and his assistant out of the suite with their arms handcuffed behind their backs. Doctor Fleishman looked terrified as they marched him out the door.

The tall agent told the patients they needed to find another doctor. Doctor Fleishman wouldn't be practicing anymore. He ordered them to leave immediately.

It was Rosemary who spoke up. "Why?" she asked the federal agent. "What has Doctor Fleishman done besides help people like my son here, who's in terrible pain and needs his medicine?" Another patient in a wheelchair echoed her question.

"Doctor Fleishman's prescriptions have killed people," the agent responded. "Now, I suggest you leave immediately." He motioned to the door with his gun and the shocked patients rolled and limped out the door as the pale, trembling receptionist was scrambling to hand over whatever the other agent demanded.

The small group of patients and their partners gathered in the lobby, each of them hoping the others could suggest an alternative. Without their prescriptions, they would be facing withdrawal, and anyone who had ever experienced abrupt narcotic withdrawal would do whatever they could to avoid going through it again.

"We are so screwed," said the man in the wheelchair. "I used to live in Montana and the Feds did this to a wonderful pain doctor there." Everyone in that state, including the federal senators and congressmen tried to defend that doctor. Even the state medical board said he was a highly ethical doctor who had never violated any laws or regulations. But, because two of his patients had died from overdosing themselves, some federal prosecutor decided to take the doctor down. All we could learn from reporters who were following his case was that it takes a long time for an investigation like that.

"Meanwhile, I went all over the state trying to find another pain doctor, but no one would help me. They were too scared. I wound up moving here because my sister, who has bad arthritis, said she had a good pain doctor here. I bet all the pain doctors here will be scared now too."

"The same thing happened to a pain doctor in Virginia," another patient said. My daughter-in-law was going to a doctor there after she got banged up in a car wreck, and they threw that doctor in jail because some of his patients were selling their medicine and someone died.

"It's ridiculous. If a guy shoots himself with a gun, they don't arrest the gun dealer. If Phyllis Fat Ass finds the local baker's muffins so delicious that she gains a hundred pounds eating them and has a fatal heart attack, they don't throw the baker in jail. What if Speedy Petey buys a souped-up sports car and finds that going ninety miles an hour makes him feel so good that he just keeps speeding, until he crashes and kills a whole family? The car dealer won't get blamed. But if someone misuses a doctor's legitimate prescription to off themselves, they arrest the doctor.

"I'll tell you what's happening here. The Feds can't get the drug lords, but the doctors are sitting ducks. If some federal prosecutor hasn't made enough drug busts, he looks to see who's prescribing the most narcotics and goes after some poor physician who's only trying to help people."

"So now what do we do?" Rosemary inquired of the group. "Do any of you know a doctor that can help us?"

"Fat chance of that," said the other patient. "I've had three back surgeries and I got worse after each one. I think I've been to every specialist in a hundred-mile radius of this city, and Doctor Fleishman's the only one I ever found who was willing to write me prescriptions for an adequate amount of medicine. All the rest of these pain doctors just wanted to keep sticking steroids in my back. Until I met Doctor Fleishman, I was ready to kill myself. He literally saved my life."

"We're screwed," said the man in the wheelchair again. "You'll see. As soon as the word gets out about Doctor Fleishman, every other doctor around here will be scared to prescribe narcotics. I have just enough medicine to get me through the night and tomorrow morning, I'm heading over to the methadone maintenance clinic at Mercy Hospital. I much rather have to go there every morning and line up with the heroin addicts than try to live with my pain."

"What causes your pain, may I ask?" said Rosemary.

"A Goddamn stupid surgery," the man responded. "I had terrible back pain, and I was so desperate for relief that I let a maniac surgeon in Iowa remove my tailbone. He damaged the nerves to my legs so badly that now I can't walk."

Chapter Thirty-Eight

Barbara Smagley was mortified to see Henry tapping on the window of the Jeep. As she continued to sit in the front seat and talk on her phone, she motioned for him to wait. Henry thought he was going to have another heart attack waiting, unable to hear what she was saying through the closed car window. Finally, she put the phone down and got out of the car.

"What on earth is going on here, Henry?"

"I'm so sorry to intrude." Henry answered. "I've been trying to reach you all morning. It's important or I would never have come after you like this. I just missed you coming out of the gym, but saw you leaving, so I followed. This is awkward. I'm really sorry, but I've got to talk to you."

Barbara remained angry. "What's so important that you tailed me like this?"

Henry glanced at the man who Barbara was with and said, "I need to speak with you in private. Please, Barbara. I'm sorry but it's urgent."

Barbara nodded to her companion, and he made his way towards the house. "What's the matter, Henry?"

Now that he finally had her attention, he didn't know what to say. "It's complicated," he mumbled. "Could we please go for a cup of coffee or something?"

Barbara had never seen him look so flustered. Henry was a man who didn't let his feelings show, even when circumstances would provoke some display of emotion in most anyone else. He was clearly distressed, and she deduced that whatever had made him chase her across town must be of some consequence.

"I could use a cup of joe myself," she conceded. "Let me just go tell my friend, and why don't you get rid of the taxi that's waiting for you. We can take my car to that coffee bar on North Street."

As Barbara drove, Henry tried to think of how he was going to explain that he'd been writing fraudulent prescriptions in her name. Barbara was all about honesty and integrity. She would be furious to know that Henry could be facing felony charges, and that she could be perceived as an accomplice. She had, after all, filled that first Percocet prescription in her name herself, the day after Henry had fallen on the ice.

Henry was also struggling with how he was going to ask her about her gym buddy. Maybe he was just a friend, but he was a good-looking guy who appeared more age-compatible with Barbara, and his residence wasn't so close to her condo that carpooling to the gym made sense.

Still, losing Barbara to another man wasn't nearly as upsetting to him as getting arrested and losing his medical license for writing fraudulent prescriptions for a controlled substance. He had a frightening mental image of himself in a jail cell, writhing from narcotics withdrawal and from the severe pain in his back and leg.

As Henry wallowed in his dilemma, Barbara's phone rang. "No wonder you didn't have it," she said. "Can you have the other pharmacy transfer it over to you? Thanks for helping me out with this."

Before Henry could ask, Barbara explained that she had called her doctor for a renewal of her allergy eye drops. This spring's pollen was ferocious. Apparently, her doctor's office had phoned the prescription into the wrong pharmacy. So, she'd run around Friday after work thinking her doctor forgot to phone it in. She didn't bother Henry with it because he was having his kyphoplasty. Finally, her druggist had contacted her doctor's office and learned of the mistake, so now the problem was solved.

"Then you didn't get a call this morning from the pharmacy in my neighborhood?" Henry asked, almost holding his breath.

Barbara scrolled through her phone. "Well, I see some voice mails from when I was in the gym that I haven't listened to yet. Why do you ask?"

Henry exhaled relief. If he could persuade Barbara to lie for him, maybe he wouldn't be going to jail after all. His heart stopped racing. At least the cops weren't coming for him this moment, but he still had to face the task of telling Barbara what he'd done, and that she might also be at risk.

Chapter Thirty-Nine

It looked like the man in the wheelchair was right. Sean was able to get in to see his primary care physician the day after Doctor Fleishman's arrest. As Sean told Doctor Horsley the story, Rosemary watched the doctor grow anxious.

"I'm so sorry," Horsley said, "but the doses that Doctor Fleishman was prescribing for Sean are way outside of my comfort zone. It's ridiculous that primary care doctors like me don't get more support for managing pain. Instead, we get hassled and cheated by third party payers, threatened by law enforcement officials, manipulated by profiteers who masquerade as pharmaceutical scientists, bamboozled by con artist patients, and humiliated by the media who feast on the scourge of addiction. Moreover, I feel really crappy about being not being in a position to help a patient like you.

"I'll tell you what I can do. I can write a small prescription for these medicines so Sean doesn't have to experience acute withdrawal, but we must also immediately find a pain specialist. Either we find a doctor who will prescribe more, or we send Sean to a detox program to help him taper down."

Sean's explanation that he didn't think he could work without pain medicine didn't alter Horsley's resolve to not become his pain doctor.

The following day, Sean seemed more miserable than ever. He took as little of his medicine as possible in attempt to ration his supply. The words of the man in the wheelchair kept echoing as he, his mother and his wife tried to find an alternative provider. Darcy, who was back on home duty, called Doctor Burke to see if he would help them out, but Burke's office said the best they could do was move Sean's and Quinn's post-operative appointments up from two weeks away to next week.

Darcy asked if she couldn't just at least speak with Doctor Burke. She was sure he'd understand. The receptionist said that Burke is looking at too many bones to have time to practice medicine over the phone. They'd just have to come to their appointment to discuss the matter.

Rosemary returned to work and asked one of the dentists if he could help. He agreed to prescribe some Vicodin for a few days, just until they could find another doctor. He wasn't willing to write for the stronger pain relievers that Sean needed. He had been Rosemary and Sean's personal dentist for many years, and he knew Rosemary would never have made this request if the situation wasn't desperate, but he had strict limits on his prescriptions for controlled substances.

Sean called Doctor Millany who said he'd be happy to see him again and re-evaluate him, but he couldn't take over prescribing his pain medication. Sean made an appointment anyway, with the hopes that if Millany would just see him, he'd be more sympathetic.

Rosemary and Darcy called every other physician they could find in the WhiteGuard book who listed themselves in specialties related to pain. But either they were told that the doctors didn't do medication management, or that they weren't accepting new patients, or that the first opening in their schedule was months away.

After the first few calls, the Garmens learned to not even mention that Sean had been a patient of Doctor Burke's or Doctor Fleishman's. It seemed that some doctors balked about seeing a patient who'd been under the care of either. The story of Dr. Fleishman's arrest had made the news, but Doctor Burke's name also seemed to provoke chilly responses.

Miraculously, Rosemary's long time family doctor returned her call at the end of the day. After she explained the situation, he reluctantly admitted that Burke had a reputation for doing unnecessary surgeries.

Rosemary didn't have to ask why other doctors in the community knew this but stayed silent. After working in a dental practice for more than twenty years, she knew all too well that only under extraordinary circumstances would dentist A ever file a formal complaint against dentist B; even though the dentists in her practice would frequently comment about some poor patient who had unnecessary or inappropriate care from another dentist.

The biggest offender in their community was a young dentist with a dazzling smile. He was a smooth talker who reportedly did more reconstructive procedures in a week then most dentists did in a month. Patients didn't complain about his work, but some who came to Rosemary's practice complained that they couldn't afford "Doctor Smiley" anymore. Riverside Dental Clinic had more reasonable prices.

Rosemary had discussed the matter with the senior dental partner long ago. Her boss explained that it wasn't 'honor among thieves' that kept the next dentist quiet. It just didn't do the patient any good to tell them they'd wasted their money elsewhere. Ratting out the last dentist mostly undermined patient confidence in the whole profession, and made patients less willing to do work that was really needed.

Besides, the typical exploitive dentist was charming, so patients were un-inclined to report them to professional boards, even if other dentists did. In essence, the profession lacked an effective way to police itself. Rosemary's instincts told her the same was true for physicians.

Rosemary's doctor agreed to see Sean to see if he could help. He was an old-school internist who believed that addiction was a worse affliction than chronic pain, but he was also compassionate. Rosemary hoped that when he saw Sean, he'd realize that her son did need the medicine.

Their visit concluded with her doctor making a referral to the University Pain Clinic, a two-hour drive from their town. There was a seven week wait to get an appointment. They would put Sean on the list for cancellations. It was all the doctor could do with Sean's doses being so high.

Chapter Forty

Barbara responded to Henry's predicament with tears and rage. The conversation that started in the coffee shop ended with Barbara leaving him stranded there. But, if the pharmacist did call her, she'd lie. She had to as Henry explained, or she could also be charged with prescription fraud.

At least they agreed on the details of what she'd say if investigated. She'd taken a bad fall. She had banged-up knees, a sore neck, and a severely sprained wrist. Her orthopedist boyfriend had been taking care of her.

Henry was so relieved that the prescription issue might be behind him, that it took a few hours for the end of the relationship to sink in. He wondered which was the primary factor; Barbara having someone new come into her life, or his not having agreed to marriage back when he was still a healthy man.

He took a long look at himself in the mirror. He thought his face was still handsome. He still had great teeth and a full head of lustrous silver hair, but he appeared older than when he last critically looked at himself. Certainly, his posture looked older. Being of sub-average height, he'd always carried himself very upright. Now he looked stooped and shorter. He tried to get his back straighter, but that just caused him to bend his knees and look even shorter.

As his mirror image frowned back at him, Henry realized he was hurting in both old and new ways. He was supposed to have taken it easy all weekend. Doctor Millany had remarked that he hoped he had a good book to read, because he should stay lying down as much as possible for the first twenty-four hours after kyphoplasty. Even the walk to the pharmacy was probably more than he should have undertaken, and that walk turned into more walking and getting in and out of cars.

Henry had been informed that a possible complication of kyph-oplasty was the leakage of the cement onto the spinal cord or nerves. Doctor Millany had said it had never happened to any of his patients, even though he had done several dozen cases, but there were some reports of bad outcomes. Millany assured Henry that it was an extremely rare problem, and the procedure could be very successful.

Henry had become so tired of the pain and his drug dependence that he put blinders on to the risks. Now, because he'd been overactive, the possibility of cement leakage terrified him. It seemed worse than getting arrested; so frightening that he dismissed it altogether.

His thoughts turned back to Barbara. She had a right to be so angry. He wondered if after the initial rage passed, she might be amenable to reconciling; maybe they could just be friends. He hated to admit it, but he really needed a friend. Being in a position of authority and being single had made it difficult to socialize with colleagues.

Henry was also regretting that Barbara wouldn't be accompanying him to his daughter's wedding. He needed to have a pretty, younger woman to dance with in the company of his ex-wife, children, and old friends who would be attending the elaborate affair that Gloria and Jill were planning.

Suddenly, he wondered if Eva Rodeki might be willing to accompany him to the wedding, as a friend of course. He'd never thought about her in romantic terms. Not that she wasn't attractive; she was petite and she had fine features. But her hairstyle and clothes were always so businesslike that she lacked sex appeal. On the plus side, she was shorter than Henry, even in his shrunken state. He did know that she was widowed and had children. Funny, he thought, he didn't know anything else about her. But if life had taught him anything, it was to not get involved with coworkers.

Still, he couldn't help but fantasize about Eva. He liked her Southern wit and charm. He also loved the challenge of wooing a new woman. His usual courtship tactics wouldn't work with this woman though. Eva would perceive him as her boss with a bad back, bad heart, and narcotic dependency; hardly a successful, debonair doctor with an important job. Maybe, though, she'd be willing to get away from a cold, rainy spring in the Midwest and spend a weekend in the good old South. He'd ask her on Monday.

When Henry got up to use the bathroom, he experienced severe back pain. He reasoned it was just because he'd been too active when he should have been resting. He took another pain pill and returned to bed, but an hour later the medicine wasn't doing much for him, and he found himself craving a drink.

"Hell," he told himself, "It's Saturday night, my girlfriend just broke up with me, and I'm in pain, whether I lie here or go over to that new restaurant and have a steak and a bourbon."

Then he debated with himself about the stupidity of walking around and drinking again. That's how he got into this mess in the first place. He decided instead that he'd microwave himself a frozen dinner and spend the evening quietly at home.

Just then, his doorbell rang. He hoped it might be Barbara, over her fury, and there with some Chinese take-out. He almost fainted when he opened the door and saw a uniformed policeman.

Chapter Forty-One

Rosemary came back to her son and daughter-in-law's town house on Saturday to see what else she could do to help. Sean seemed worse. Any relief accrued by a week away from bending over and crawling under cars had been expunged by having to taper his medication. He hadn't experienced full-blown withdrawal, but he was suffering insomnia, anxiety, and increased pain.

He snapped at Darcy and the kids for nothing and everything. "Quinn's too loud! You call this mud coffee? How could you put that bad gas in my car, you idiot! Mom, you're suffocating me with your pity. When is it going to stop raining?"

Relief came to Darcy and Rosemary when Corey came by in the late afternoon to have Sean check out a Mercedes. After working on it for two days, none of the guys at the garage could figure out where the click-clack was coming from, and they'd promised the customer the car would be ready by Monday.

Darcy used to resent Sean's job interfering with their family time on weekends. Now, just having him out of the house for an hour was better than fresh air. She wondered if it was really an issue with the Mercedes or whether they were just off to score some weed, or maybe narcotics.

How she wished she could confide in Rosemary about her escalating anxiety over Sean's dependency on marijuana. She didn't for several reasons. Foremost, she knew that Sean was much better smoking weed, especially when it came to being able to sleep. Secondly, it was the absolute wrong time to take away another drug while he was trying to wean himself off narcotics. When weed first became an issue between them and Sean had stopped using it, he was unbearable to be around.

Darcy also feared driving a wedge between Rosemary and Sean. Alcohol abuse was an enormous issue for Rosemary. She'd practically disowned her older son Michael, when she realized that he and his wife partied a lot. Sean and Darcy were the good kids in Rosemary's eyes. Darcy just couldn't see any benefit in spoiling that image or bringing Rosemary's wrath down on Sean when he was already suffering so much.

Darcy talked about her three days working at Toblers instead. "Getting out of the house was exactly what I needed. The Toblers are fantastic, especially Arthur. Even Corey is something special. Despite his bad boy reputation, he's really helping Arthur. He's also the smartest, mechanically and in how he handles people.

"Wednesday, I saw an arrogant woman, dripping with jewelry, giving Ryan a hard time because her BMW wasn't ready. Corey stepped in and had her laughing and thanking the Toblers for working so hard on the car.

"I'm really worried about what Arthur's going to do if Sean can't work. I can see how hard it is for them to keep up without Sean. Arthur showed me how to access their bank and payroll accounts and they're not making it if Arthur draws his salary. He didn't last month. I'm astounded at how generous he's been through this ordeal."

"Did Arthur get someone in there to do the office work yet?" Rosemary asked.

"He has some interviews on Monday. Actually, he asked me if I could maybe come in to help orient someone if the temp agency sent him anyone he thought was worth employing. He's hoping this agency will send better candidates than the lousy mechanics he was sent by a technical temp agency."

"Not surprising," Rosemary responded. "Our office has seen its share of losers from those agencies. It's so hard to get people who are competent and reliable. Even dental hygiene schools seem to have no standards for who they admit for training, as long as the numbskull can pay tuition."

When Sean returned, Darcy thought he was less irritable. Even Rosemary noticed the difference. Darcy surmised that they had been out for a smoke and that it was the weed that had taken the edge off. He would never have lit up with his mother in sniffing range.

"I take it you got that Mercedes problem solved," Rosemary remarked. No matter what else was going on in her son's life, she knew that nothing gave him more pleasure than figuring out what was wrong with an automobile. He was just born to do it. No wonder he seemed more relaxed, she concluded, until after dinner when he became irritable again. Rosemary decided to go home.

Sunday morning, she returned. She and Darcy had given up their Sunday matinee routine weeks before. They didn't like leaving the kids home with Sean, and together, Quinn and Frieda were too noisy for the theater. Today though, she planned to take them all out for lunch, knowing Sean would probably decline. He did.

"I've got a plan," she told Darcy as the kids dug into their french-fries. "I've already talked to Arthur about it. We're going to hire a nanny for you and Sean, and Arthur wants you to work at the garage so he can continue to give you guys a salary and cover your health insurance. He's going to tell Sean to take another few weeks off and either go find another doctor or go to rehab. He'll get another mechanic in there to help, and just consult with Sean on the more challenging cars. Sean can work as much or as little as he's able, but Arthur will encourage him to take the time off to heal."

"That's fantastic, but how am I going to find someone I can trust? My friend Leah hired a highly recommended nanny, and the woman was locking the kids in the closet if they disobeyed."

"I've got you a good person. She's a patient in the dental office, a real sweetheart. Her name's Pauline but she goes by Polly. I've known her for years. She used to be the nanny for a professional family, but their kids got too old to need her. When they were young, she used to bring them in and the youngest child was a handful, a real little hooligan. She was always wonderful with them.

"I called her to see if she could recommend someone, and it turns out she's available and willing, even though I told her it's probably just short-term. I hope you don't mind that I made these arrangements, but you sounded so happy about the few days you spent at Toblers. As I see it, nothing is going to improve if we don't make some changes for all of you."

Chapter Forty-Two

The sight of a policeman at his door made Henry think his heart would stop beating altogether. Then he recognized the policeman; he was Barbara's gym buddy. He handed Henry a shopping bag and told him that Barbara wanted to return things that Henry had left in her condo. Henry felt the blood return to his cheeks when gym buddy left.

The shopping bag contained a bracelet he'd given her for Christmas, a pair of his boxer shorts, and a foil wrapped toothbrush. There was no note, but the appearance of gym buddy in police garb spoke volumes as to why Barbara would bother to return these things he didn't need. Henry wondered if she was as vengeful as ex-wife Gloria.

Eva was surprised by the change of tone in Henry's conversation when he came into her office to get his blood pressure reading on Monday morning. He seemed to be looking at her differently and it made her uncomfortable. He had never previously asked about her weekend. She tried to change the subject by asking him about the kyphoplasty. He gave her an earful about his continuing battle with pain.

The only thing Eva had done on the weekend besides laundry, vacuuming, gardening, and paying bills, was take her daughter shopping for a prom dress. None of this could possibly be of interest to Henry, even if she did feel like divulging it.

His blood pressure was more elevated than usual. Eva suggested he come back at lunchtime to get another reading. She also suggested that he consult with his cardiologist. She then turned back to her computer, but she could feel his lingering gaze as he limped out of her office.

Eva's email was endless; nothing unusual for Monday. The big issue was still the numerous reports of pain patients in a panic over their doctor's office being closed. Dozens of them were begging for or demanding that WhiteGuard refer them to someone to take over their prescriptions or pay for detox. They'd all be referred back to their family doctors.

Even though Judd Fleishman had been disassociated from WhiteGuard for several years, dozens of their insured went to him anyway. They paid his reasonable fees out of pocket, despite paying huge premiums to WhiteGuard for what was supposed to be comprehensive coverage. Now, they were finding that other doctors were unwilling to take on a "Fleishman junkie" and if they did, they charged exorbitantly.

Some of their insured would also learn that their policies excluded benefits for detox and drug rehab. They'd have to finance it themselves, just like they did their prescriptions. WhiteGuard's call center was dealing with some very angry people. Eva prayed there'd be no suicides.

There was also an email from Attorney Clinton Sperling. He was advising Eva and Henry that another patient was suing WhiteGuard because his insurance policy wouldn't cover acupuncture. He was a forty-three-year-old house painter with multiple sclerosis. He'd been getting good relief from acupuncture and believed that it was discriminatory for WhiteGuard to accept his premium payments, but deny him coverage for the only form of treatment that helped.

All Eva could do was email Sperling back a copy of the latest company policy on acupuncture, which stated that there wasn't enough evidence in the literature to prove that it worked. The fact that it worked for this unfortunate man wasn't considered sufficient evidence by Henry.

Eva was actually thinking about calling Donilski's office to schedule another acupuncture session for herself as her alias, Lisa Banks. Just then, Henry came hobbling back into her office for a recheck. His pressure was a little better and his hands seemed less shaky, so she assumed that his pain medicine had kicked in. He was eyeing her again. Still, she was taken aback when he asked her to lunch. She absolutely did not want to get involved with this man, but she didn't turn him down because he was her boss.

Eva presumed that Henry wanted to pick her brain about doctors who he could get pain medicine from. He'd alienated every pain doctor in the community and now he needed one. Poor Henry Winslow, she thought.

They sat down at the far end of the employee cafeteria and made small talk. She kept waiting for him to complain about Doctor Burke, or CLUJ, or his pain medicine. Instead, he invited her to accompany him to his daughter's wedding.

"Well thank you, but I just don't know right now. I'll have to check on the schedules of three busy teenagers."

Chapter Forty-Three

Darcy and Sean were pleased with Polly within an hour of her arrival, as Quinn and Frieda warmed up to her quickly. Darcy spent the morning orienting her to things around the house and the children's routines. She found herself feeling jealous as she observed her kids turning to Polly for attention, and minding her better than they did either of their parents.

Quinn was suddenly doing things with his un-casted arm that he'd previously demanded that Darcy do for him. Even Sean wondered how much of the children's recent misbehavior had been a response to their stress. Polly's patient demeanor was a soothing antidote.

Darcy almost skipped out the door when she kissed the kids good-by to return to Toblers. Arthur was delighted to see her. "I didn't have a good feeling about either of the temp people I interviewed. One had a blank look on her face when I explained how to process orders. The other was about as approachable as a cactus. She'd be no match for the guy who thinks having a Rolls Royce makes him more important than the next guy with highway bling. I need someone at the front desk who knows how to humor these blowhards. You did great when you were here, Darcy. Thanks for coming back."

Sean came to the garage with Darcy because he didn't want to interfere with the kids getting used to Polly being in charge, or so he said. Darcy figured he didn't know what else to do with himself. His only escape from his misery had been working on cars. He was bitterly disappointed when Arthur told him there were only routine repairs that day. He wasn't needed. He was supposed to be taking it easy in advance of his upcoming appointment with Doctor Burke.

Rosemary took off from work to accompany Thny Sean and Quinn. She was grateful for having that kind of flexibility with her employer. She'd started working for Doctor Donovan as a receptionist when he was fresh out of dental school. He helped her get trained as a hygienist. After a few years, his practice had grown enough to bring in another dentist and a year later, he partnered with an orthodontist.

Rosemary progressed from hygienist to practice manager as Riverside Dental Clinic eventually came to employ eleven dentists and dental specialists, five hygienists, six dental assistants, and an office staff of three. Rosemary had a good relationship with everyone there, along with all of the long-time patients. She could take off almost any time she needed, and they'd all cover for her.

Darcy wanted to go with Sean to see Doctor Burke herself. She wanted to look in his eyes when she told him that taking out the tailbone had made Sean worse. Doctor Fleishman was arrested before they could get his opinion, and they were losing sleep thinking that Burke had done unnecessary operations on both Sean and Quinn. But when it became apparent that Arthur really needed her, Darcy acquiesced to her mother-in-law. She knew that Rosemary wouldn't be timid about challenging the legitimacy of Burke's surgeries.

They waited in Burke's office for almost an hour. His receptionist told them he got tied up in the OR. By the time they did get to see him, Quinn had become restless. Burke took a little remote-operated car out of his desk and gave it to Quinn to play with, explaining that he wanted to see how he was using his hands. The child's eyes spun with excitement. Despite his cast, he quickly figured out how to operate it, and Burke pulled out another car, got down on his hands and knees, and for a few minutes, regressed to age four himself.

While Burke frolicked on the floor with her grandson, Rosemary surveyed the diplomas on his wall. The one that rang her bell was a surgical residency certificate from the University of Iowa. Iowa was where the man in the wheelchair had said he'd had tailbone surgery. A vision of Sean in a wheelchair made Rosemary shudder.

When Burke turned his attention from Quinn to Sean, he claimed he never received the message that Darcy had called about Sean needing pain medicine. Sean told him the story of Doctor Fleishman's arrest and Burke seemed surprised at that too. Maybe he was too busy doing surgery to pay attention to the news; it certainly seemed like every other doctor in the community was aware of Fleishman's arrest.

"That's terrible," Maynard Burke claimed. "But I'm not surprised. Prescribing so many narcotics to so many people is bound to lead to some dire consequences. Not good if patients wind up dead."

"What's really not good is Sean's pain," Rosemary countered. "My son doesn't complain, but as his mother, I can tell you he's in agony and he's only been getting worse since you took out his tailbone."

"I'm also having trouble emptying my bowel and bladder," Sean added, now that his mother had validated his misery. "Sometimes, I feel like I'm going to explode."

"These are known side effects from your surgery, Sean. It was all in the consents you signed. Probably just a little inflammation of the spinal nerves, and we should be able to calm that right down with a course of steroids. I'll give you a few Percocets to help you taper down from the narcotics Fleishman had you on. I also want you to start prednisone today, and take a tapering dose for the next ten days. I'll see you back when we bring Quinn back to cut that cast off.

"You'll have to forgive me for not having much time right now. I just came from a long surgical case. and I have some patients waiting." He quickly typed something into his computer, smiled charmingly, and started for the door.

Rosemary sprang from her chair and blocked his exit. "Doctor Burke, my son has had no relief from the surgery you did, and now he has more pain and symptoms than he had before he came here. The least you could do is examine him and help him out with this pain."

"I understand your concerns ma'am, but we really need to see how he's doing after the nerves calm down from taking the prednisone, and then we can do a much better assessment. Now if you'll please excuse me, I have patients to see. My assistant will retrieve the toys and get you set-up with appointments. Sean will be much better after the prednisone. I promise."

Burke smiled. He kissed Quinn on the top of his head, side-stepped Rosemary, and sidled out of the room. They waited another ten minutes for an assistant to bring some papers. Rosemary glanced at the prescription and saw it was for just six pills. "This must be a mistake," she said. "We're not leaving here until Doctor Burke writes a prescription for a reasonable quantity of pain medicine."

The assistant felt Rosemary's fury. She went to inform Burke. From her position in the doorway, Rosemary heard Burke being confronted. "This family says they're not leaving til you write the guy for more drugs. How do you want to handle this? The old woman looks pissed."

Maynard Burke pulled his assistant into another room out of earshot. "Just let them sit there." He looked at his watch. "If they don't get going in about a half-hour, go back in and tell them I got called away to an emergency. If they give you a hard time, just tell them you'll call the police."

"Do you want me to call the police at that point?"

"I doubt you'll need to," Burke said. "If they don't get going, just tell them the police aren't too sympathetic to loitering drug seekers. That usually gets the stubborn ones out the door pretty quickly. If you do have to call the police, ask for Lieutenant Plineo. He owes me a favor."

Chapter Forty-Four

Eva was wrestling with Henry's invitation. He had emphasized that he was only seeking her friendship and he'd arrange separate hotel rooms. She'd be free to do whatever she liked besides attend the wedding. He'd pay all her expenses.

When she asked, "What happened to your girlfriend?" Henry said he'd broken off the relationship because it wasn't fair for a young, athletic woman like Barbara to be saddled with an older guy with a bad back.

Eva had met Barbara Smagley at WhiteGuard's executive Christmas party. She'd thought of her as "Miss Buffness." Henry hoped his explanation would make him seem kind and caring, and make Eva more sympathetic towards him. Then he worried he was being too transparent. Eva was exceptionally perceptive.

The invite meant a free trip home for Eva. Her mother still lived in her hometown, and was too frail to travel, while Eva found traveling with her three kids by air too expensive. She'd drive there for Christmas. Also, each summer, she flew two of the kids back to visit Grandma by themselves, while she had one-on-one time with the third. She wanted to get to know each of her children as individuals without their siblings around. To leave them alone together without Mom would be another educational experience.

Eva worried that the trip would let Henry in on the secret that she'd been a nurse in the same hospital where he used to be a surgeon. Someone who they both knew might approach them at the wedding. Then he'd know that she'd deceived him for all the time they'd worked together. But she wondered, what would be the harm if Henry found out she knew about his past? It would only make him more indebted.

Maybe it would also make him less likely to pursue her, if those were his intentions.

Maybe, there was a benefit to spending some time with Henry. Perhaps she could influence him to resist the demands of the bean counters at WhiteGuard and cut patients a break once in a while. If CLUJ's top people pulled off a subtle mutiny, could the Board of Directors be embarrassed enough to take a more humane approach to health care? Probably not, she fretted.

Maybe Henry was sincere that he just wanted to be her friend. With all of his health problems and now, the loss of his young girlfriend, he was probably in need of a friend. Add in his recent heart attack, and maybe he's afraid to travel by himself. Maybe all he really needs is a nurse.

Then, Eva wondered why he hadn't asked a younger nurse to be his date. She thought about the vivacious redhead in the case review department, recently divorced and on the hunt. There were some others. So maybe, he was really interested in her. That, Eva thought, would be reason to decline his invitation. The last thing she needed was to wind up in an awkward relationship with her boss.

No sooner had she dismissed the whole idea, she started to think about how badly she needed a break. She hadn't taken any time off in months and she'd never spent a weekend away from her kids. At ages seventeen, fifteen and thirteen, they were capable of taking care of themselves. They were good kids, and she believed she could trust them. Her daughter could drive them to their weekend activities since she would have Eva's car. It might be healthy for them to feel a little independent.

Suddenly, an all-expenses weekend away from her otherwise mundane life seemed like a golden opportunity. She and her daughter could shop for gowns together. Henry had said it would be a formal affair and it had been years since she had bought herself something fancy. It was prom season, and she was sure she could find something that would work for her amidst the youthful fashions.

The more she thought about it, the more it seemed like going was the thing to do. Besides, Henry probably wasn't interested in her as much he felt safe with her. She already knew about his heart attack and pill habit. That must be why he didn't want to ask another nurse. Eva wondered if she should tell him about their previous association. It was going to be an interesting weekend.

When Henry came in for his blood pressure reading on Tuesday, he gave her a look of anticipation. He even tried to swagger. After noting his elevated blood pressure, Eva balked.

"I'm really sorry that I don't yet have an answer for you about the wedding. I'm still trying to coordinate the kids' stuff."

Chapter Forty-Five

Darcy loved her job at Art Tobler Auto Tech. The customers and the suppliers were an entertaining cast of characters. It was fun to talk to the joke-cracking Texan who collected taillight covers, and the gabby lady in St. Louis who had hundreds of old hood ornaments.

Darcy came to truly appreciate how knowledgeable mechanics like her husband had to be. There was so much complicated stuff to know about current cars and then, Arthur's mechanics also had to know about vintage cars.

Darcy learned that Arthur was a specialist in British collectible sports cars, especially Triumphs, MGs, and Sunbeam Alpines. Sean also loved MGs. When Darcy first met him, he was restoring a red one. It mostly sat in Rosemary's garage but when it ran, it was a thrill to pilot around curvy country roads.

One of Darcy's daily jobs was combing eBay for certain parts that were hard to find and some that Arthur liked to stockpile. Arthur's knowledge of parts dealers was what originally made him successful. If someone needed a transmission for a 1963 Ferrari, Arthur knew where to find it. Then along came the Internet and everyone who liked to rebuild the classics could locate parts just as easily.

Fear of competition from the dotcoms made Arthur decide to sell two collectible cars that he'd rebuilt over a decade. His timing was lucky and both cars went for top dollar. He used the proceeds to build six more bays on his property near the highway. Arthur's grandfather had bought that property in the 1950s before the interstate was even on the drawing board.

Body-work guys and mechanic assistants kept the bays busy with routine work, while the ace mechanics worked in the main garage.

Tinkering with old machines was a lot more fun than doing ordinary repairs on contemporary cars, but it was the routine stuff that paid their bills.

Darcy was amazed to learn that domestic cars were frequently being made abroad, while the foreign ones were often made in the USA. Online, she communicated with parts dealers from around the world.

What Darcy found most entertaining though, was the interaction between Arthur and his sons. Arthur and Ryan would argue about a car's problem and Corey would have to step in and come up with the final solution. He was also the one that defused impatient customers. If Darcy had a computer issue, Corey could fix that too.

Had she not heard those stories about Corey being a slacker and a party animal, she would have thought he was the heart and soul of the family and the business. Besides, those stories were from when he and Sean first worked together. Corey had probably matured since then. And she had to admit, he was fun to be around.

Then on Friday afternoon, Arthur said he had spent the morning with a tech school student who looked promising. "Only twenty-one, but very smart, and he knows the classics; Kenny, a real honest to goodness car-nut."

Chapter Forty-Six

CLUJ's administrative review meetings started at seven-thirty in the morning and lasted the entire day. Medical staff and patient advocates sat at the farthest end of the board room. The bean counters sat at the conference table with CLUJ at its head.

There was, as always, a continental breakfast featuring sickeningly sweet bakery goods, and very strong coffee. Falling asleep was unforgivable. The sugar buzz was meant to camouflage the tartness of CLUJ's opening remarks.

"Our stockholders are unhappy. In a bear market, these big investors get nervous, and we expect many of them to transfer funding to companies with better profits. WhiteGuard's numbers aren't keeping pace with some of the industry giants who are moving in on our territory."

Eva's temples started to throb. What was coming was a seven-hour corporate business smackdown. Under the table, her hand stroked the bottom edge of her sweater, as she thought about the stray kitten her youngest daughter had brought home last week. It was a perfect clone of her cuddly, old calico and they named it Ditto. Thank goodness she had worn that sweater. CLUJ liked to keep the conference room temperature in the frigid zone.

They heard about increased premium rates for small business owners, redefined benefits for new policy holders, and reduced reimbursements for doctors.

They heard from multiple speakers that the best thing they could do to increase their profit margin was to improve their marketing. The best products and services in the world don't reach the masses unless they are well-marketed. And with good marketing, the worst products in the world can become immensely popular.

It infuriated Eva that health care corporations and pharmaceutical companies were spending more on marketing than on research. Take a pill to offset your bad diet. This drug will let you jump in a lake. This drug will have you dancing.

Eva once counted that her kids saw more than a hundred drug commercials during one rainy weekend of watching TV. She fretted that drug companies amassed wealth by selling their products, while so many sick people were denied access to the actual products they needed for their medical care.

The management team members did get to speak with each other during a ten-minute recess. Eva hid out in the lady's room. She had spent the entire meeting just trying to avoid Henry's gaze. She really didn't want to speak to him.

"They'll be no lunch break," CLUJ announced when they returned from decanting their coffee. "We've ordered in so we can do a working lunch."

If the deli sandwiches didn't give them indigestion, the next few speakers did. They were instructed that the correct way to speak with WhiteGuard's insured was to address them as "health care partners," instead of "policy holders." They were advised about words to avoid. Eva's spirits sank as a speaker lectured them about corporate team spirit.

Finally, they heard reports from each of the departments. Eva spoke about upgraded criteria for provider credentialing, CLUJ's euphemism for "let's kick more clinicians off the preferred provider list."

Henry spoke about changes in medical policies that would eliminate access to treatments that were previously covered. He spoke about evidence-based medicine, the concept that the only legitimate treatments are those that have been proven to be effective in clinical trials.

"There's never been a clinical trial to prove that parachutes save lives," Eva wanted to shout at Henry. "Insufficient evidence" was just a concept that the pharmaceutical industry created to get their hands on the healthcare dollar.

Eva wondered if Henry believed in the hypocrisy of evidence-based-medicine, or if he was just another good soldier in CLUJ's army. She hoped that like her, he was only acting a part for a paycheck, playing a role on a stage where CLUJ was the director.

Eva also wondered if she could still stall giving him an answer about the wedding trip. She hadn't yet made up her mind.

Chapter Forty-Seven

After Burke's assistant took the remote-control cars away, Quinn started to throw a tantrum. As furious as Rosemary was with Burke, she didn't see the likelihood of his coming back to prescribe more pain meds, and it didn't seem worth watching her grandson have a meltdown to keep waiting. After they stormed out of his office, she promised Sean and herself that she wasn't going to let this surgeon get away with hurting her family. She'd hire a lawyer.

For the next few days, Sean faithfully took his prednisone. It did make a slight difference on days two and three, when his dose was high. But by day five, as his dose was going down, the pain level was going back up.

On the seventh day of steroids, Sean was back in the office of Doctor Leonard Millany. Sean and Rosemary explained to him that they couldn't tell if Sean was getting worse again because the steroid level had gone down, or because he had cut his pain medicine dosage down by seventy percent since Doctor Fleishman had been arrested.

Doctor Millany believed that Sean was getting worse because the steroid level was dropping. "The fact that you were better at first, when you were on a higher dose means that steroids will help. But when you take the steroids orally, only some of the dose gets to the targeted tissue. Most of it goes to the rest of the body, where it's not needed. It will help much more to put the steroid directly into the painful area."

Doctor Millany was very confident that Sean's need for painkillers would decline if the inflammation was calmed down. "Also, the injection is easier to do than those we did last fall, because the canal in the sacral bone where the nerves are is easier to get to. We also don't need to do it with fluoroscopic imaging, so it costs less."

Rosemary carefully read the consent form and decided it was worth a try. She didn't really understand all the risks, but she had been impressed by how much better Sean had seemed over the weekend when he was taking the high dose prednisone. It made sense that putting a steroid directly into the inflamed tissue could help. Sean was desperate enough to try anything to get rid of his burning rear end. His original pain didn't even seem so bad since he had been putting up with the new pain that followed Doctor Burke's removal of his tail bone.

The steroid shot wasn't too bad either, but the day after, he felt much worse. He was supposed to return to Burke that day, but he couldn't even get up to go. When he called to cancel and begged for something more for the pain, he was told Doctor Burke wasn't available to call in a prescription.

It was a good thing his mother had hired Polly, because there was no way he could take care of the kids. He was also glad not to have Darcy there. He could no longer stand the look of pity in her eyes. He felt like she resented him at the same time she hovered over him. He hated being a burden, and even though Corey had scored him some Viagra, he hurt too much to even think about sex. He had become useless as a father and husband as well as a mechanic.

He also hated it that Darcy liked going to work so much. It was as though she had stolen his world and the Tobler family away from him. Her efforts to look pretty for work also distressed him. She'd stopped wearing anything but comfort clothes after Quinn was born, and he'd forgotten how attractive she was in high heels.

Then he chastised himself for being jealous. He knew Darcy was a wonderful wife and mother and that her life's plans had also been destroyed. Besides, it was important for her to look nice at Arthur's front desk. Some really high-class people came in there. That thought rekindled his feelings of jealousy.

After Burke's office turned him down, he called Millany's office for more pain pills. The steroid shot wasn't supposed to have made him worse.

Chapter Forty-Eight

Jill's wedding was only five weeks away and Henry was still waiting for Eva to confirm whether she could make it. He wasn't sure he could make it himself, in spite of going for physical therapy three times a week. His pain was better, but his legs felt weak. His newest MRI showed some cement had extruded through a crack in the fractured vertebra and was now impinging on the spinal cord.

After shots of steroids didn't help, Doctor Millany recommended maximizing muscle strength while giving nerves more time to recover. Despite the physical therapy, Henry was feeling weaker. Emptying his bowel had become a monumental task. There were days his belly hurt almost as much as his back.

Eva was starting to have second thoughts about leaving her kids alone for the weekend. Her seventeen-year-old daughter, the perfectionist, had become a basket case about what to wear to the prom. She was still questioning her choice of dresses. She couldn't decide how to wear her hair. Her prom date was flirting with a classmate.

Eva's thirteen-year-old daughter was jealous of the attention that had been diverted from baby sister to prom queen. The two girls were squabbling about bathroom time to the point that baby sister had moved into Eva's bathroom.

Simultaneously, Eva's fifteen-year-old son, who was spending way too much time in both bathrooms, appeared to be in love with a fourteen-year-old girl who looked like a thirty-year-old hooker. He kept finding excuses to go outside and then one of his sisters would spy on him and see him walk past the girl's house. It had started the previous weekend when the girl said hello to him. Now he was texting her all day long, to the point that Eva was afraid his schoolwork would suffer.

Eva was also worried about her boss. Henry was noticeably slower getting in and out of chairs. Though his cardiologist had changed his medicine, his blood pressure remained erratic. While she continued to stall about answering the wedding trip question, they talked more about the struggles of parenthood.

Henry came to learn that Eva's husband, a physician, had contracted hepatitis from an accidental needle stick. He spent five years succumbing to liver failure and then was fortunate enough to receive a transplant. Two years later, he died from a multi-system infection, the result of having his immunity suppressed to stop his antibodies from attacking the new liver. As advanced as transplant medicine had become, organ rejection continued to lead to tragic results in some unfortunate patients.

Eva had spent most of his last years ministering to him, and always felt guilty that it had robbed her children of a happy childhood. Her husband had contracted the hepatitis when their youngest was still an infant, and he was sick until he died eight years later. Several years after his death, Eva became involved in a relationship. It went well for about six months until her kids started wigging out. Having lost their father, they resented the time their mother was spending with someone else, and they acted obnoxious in front of the man. It worked. They scared him off quite effectively.

Eva realized her children needed her more than they needed a father. To them, a father was someone else to take care of. Maybe her son needed some manly advice now; but she could tell him what he needed to know about condoms. Whether it happened that weekend or next year, it was going to happen sometime, and she would teach him to protect himself.

Besides, they had done fine without a father. Her husband's brother and her brother had been good uncles, and the kids were well rooted in manliness. It was time for them to function a little independently.

She had made up her mind; she would go. Then she saw Henry dragging himself down the hallway and she got cold feet again. He looked more like he needed an intensive care unit than a traveling nurse.

Chapter Forty-Nine

Sean was down to the last of his pain pills and Darcy's parents were due to arrive in three days. He didn't know how he could deal with it. He was especially uncomfortable around her dad, Rob. The guy took no interest in his daughter until the rare occasion that he was actually in her presence. Then he acted like Big Daddy, all postured to protect his little girl from evil men.

Darcy's stepmother, Noreen, had always seemed like a phony to Sean, especially when she acted like she really cared about her stepchildren or grandchildren. Even when Quinn was two, he couldn't wait to get away from Grandma Nori.

Sean sure didn't need them to show up now that everything sucked. Their timing was too perfect. It didn't look good that Darcy was working while he was limping around like a cripple. Probably still guilty for turning his daughters out when their mother died, Rob would now conclude that Darcy was living with a useless bum.

Darcy wasn't even thinking about her parents' impending visit. Two years ago, she would have been cleaning, cooking, and baking in preparation. Now she was just too busy with her job at Toblers to think about entertaining her parents. They'd have to fend for themselves.

Darcy was thinking more about how she could afford a new wardrobe. She knew the customers liked to come to the front desk just to gaze at her big violet eyes, even if it was to pay a bill. Darcy's eyes were her superpower. They were so alluring that people rarely even noticed her other facial features, which were also pretty.

The apprentice mechanic, Kenny, found far too many reasons to come to the front desk. Darcy was thrilled to feel like a desirable woman again.

A dental patient told Rosemary about a doctor that helped her with chronic pain and narcotic dependency, and that it involved acupuncture.

"Just what I most don't need," Sean complained, "more needles sticking in me."

When he finally conceded that he'd accept any treatment that would get him out of hell, Rosemary called for an appointment. She was told that Doctor Donilski had just left on an overseas vacation and the earliest appointment would be with the doctor's partner in two weeks or with Doctor Donilski in two months.

Darcy didn't even seem to care about this stuff anymore. She just let Rosemary take over. She spoke mostly to Polly in the mornings before she left for work. She avoided Sean except to lay out his pills and tell him about something that needed to be fixed. "If you feel up to it, please look at the spritzer in the kitchen sink. It's spraying sideways. And don't forget to call WhiteGuard about the out-of-network reimbursement we were supposed to have received by now."

Sean couldn't stand it when she came home from the garage and told a story about a Maserati or a Saab. She was starting to fancy herself as an import expert. For eight years she didn't give a hoot about any of the dream cars he'd worked on, and now she was going gaga for some big shot's silver Lotus.

His mother's idea was stupid. Resting was making him worse, not better, and they still hadn't found anyone who would just call in a prescription to tide him over until he got to his next appointment. He'd be totally out of medicine just when Rob and Noreen would be arriving.

Sean tried to conjure up an escape plan. He even thought about staging an accident, until the thought of returning to the hospital crossed his mind. Dealing with Darcy's parents couldn't possibly be as obnoxious as being in an emergency room.

When Corey came by at lunchtime for Sean to check out a BMW transmission, it was Sean who suggested burgers and beers. Corey was stunned. Sean never touched alcohol, but Corey realized Sean was tapering off narcotics. A beer buzz could help him get rid of the blues. It would be fun to see Sean get a buzz.

For all the years they had been co-workers and friends, Corey had never seen Sean take a drink, not even a beer. It had something to do with his mother's mother and bad genes.

Chapter Fifty

Cardiologist Nanette Tremont didn't like what she was seeing on Henry's cardiogram. He denied having chest pain but there was diminished blood flow to his heart muscles. His blood pressure records were very concerning. His pressure was rarely in the normal range and sometimes it was very high, even though Henry swore he took his medicine at the same time every day.

Nanette had sent him for more tests, and she now recommended stenting his left main coronary artery. "You're lucky" Nanette told him, "That you haven't had a major heart attack yet. If we fix it now, you can avoid the big one."

Henry only knew that he felt crappy. The blood pressure medicine made it hard to sleep and totally killed any thoughts of a sex life. Not that his back pain ever made him feel like he was in the mood for sex. It hurt all the time, despite Millany's prescription pain medicine. His gut also made sex seem like forbidden fruit. He was always backed up. Taking laxatives to offset the constipation caused by Oxycontin had turned him into an infernal gasbag.

He was just so damn tired. It was getting harder and harder for him to work long days. The more he tried to exercise, the sooner he got short of breath. It was getting hard to concentrate.

His father and his father's brother had both had cardiac artery bypass surgery, (CABG, often called 'cabbage'), in their fifties. His father never woke up from the surgery, and his uncle was now an eighty-year-old cardiac cripple with scars down his chest and up both legs. Uncle Walt had undergone two cabbages, two balloon angioplasties to open up clogged arteries, and he had stents in his carotids.

If Henry said "yes" to CABG, he'd be out of work for weeks. Stents would take less time out of his life. CLUJ wasn't going to stand for his absence. That would be the end of his job for sure.

"I can't do this right now," he told the cardiologist.

"What do you mean?" Nanette asked. "That you can't do it now, or that you're not going to do it? And when would be the right time if it were a matter of timing? I would never recommend this if I didn't think it was really needed. You talked about going to your daughter's wedding in a few weeks; that would be a good time to have a heart attack. How about at a board meeting? It's always a stunner to keel over with chest pain when your coworkers are watching.

"Think about it, Doctor Winslow. Executives do preemptive health care for a reason. Cardiac care extends life."

Henry still didn't look persuaded, but he did look scared. Nanette thought of a different approach for this die-hard professional, who seemed ready to keel over in the saddle rather than take care of himself. Working stiffs were always the hardest to convince that their hearts needed fixing. Guys with big nest eggs or nothing at all were the ones who signed up for cabbages, so long as their insurance would pay for it.

Henry sought a second opinion from an older cardiologist; one who didn't do procedures and didn't have a son who did them either. The second doctor agreed with Doctor Tremont. He urged Henry not to neglect himself.

Just when Eva thought she would never be able to make up her mind about accompanying Henry to his daughter's wedding, Henry asked her if she would please be his Power of Attorney. He begged her to not bring any of this to the attention of CLUJ.

Eva pretended she'd never have to do that.

Chapter Fifty-One

The weekend with Darcy's parents went better than expected. Rob and Noreen made extra effort to play with their grandchildren. On Saturday, Sean stayed home, while the rest of them went to a Memorial Day Parade. They barbecued in the afternoon and watched a movie for the evening.

Corey staged a Jaguar emergency on Sunday. He and Sean snuck off to a brunch and got smashed on Bloody Marys. At least Sean got smashed, which seemed to relieve his withdrawal symptoms. Corey was doing the driving and the Jag was a joy ride.

"So is Darcy a fox or what," Sean blurted out of the blue.

"What?" Corey tried to joke about it, but Sean became agitated.

"What? You tell me what, Corey!"

"Hey! Hey! Chill, Dude! You know damn well Darcy is devoted to you and the kids. She's also damn good at customer service and it doesn't hurt to have her dressing up our front desk. So just chill, and you better get sober fast. I'm not motoring around with a hostile drunk."

Corey opened the car windows and headed for the highway. He drove out to his mother's grave and spent an hour there while Sean restlessly napped. Inebriation was a better look on Sean's face than the look of pain he'd been wearing for so long.

Darcy told her folks that Sean took care of customers on the weekend like this all the time. Big executives wanted their luxury cars on Monday morning.

Stepmother Noreen wanted all the details of Sean's back pain treatment. She and her brother had both had back pain episodes and stories to go with it. Darcy's father seemed upset that his grandson didn't remember him.

They went out to dinner when Sean finally got home, Grandma and Grandpa's treat. The kids were noisy and annoying. Darcy's jaw dropped when Sean ordered a Bloody Mary. Then she thought that maybe it was okay this once because he was hurting so badly, and he had finished the last of his medicine that morning.

The kids were behaving so awfully, she felt like having a drink herself. Even though Sean had never touched alcohol, she used to indulge in a glass of wine or two at parties, before her first pregnancy. She had abstained for the past few years, but she certainly wasn't planning to have any more babies. So, what would be the harm now?

Maybe Sean wasn't cursed with "the gene." Darcy knew all about his family history and the bad episode he had when he got drunk at the age of eighteen. In one night, he had wrecked a collector's car, gotten into a fight, been arrested, gotten into a fight in jail, and broke his toe kicking a wall. When Rosemary posted his bail, he promised his mother he would never touch alcohol again. As far as Darcy knew, he had kept that promise, up until right now. It was one of the things about him that had attracted her. Her previous boyfriend drank too much.

Darcy wondered what tipsy Sean would be like. The old boyfriend needed alcohol to feel amorous. Darcy longed for Sean to feel amorous. Having men flirt with her all day at Toblers made her long for intimacy, but it was still her husband she wanted. She ordered a Bloody Mary for herself. She had never had one and if Sean was going to get horny, she wanted to be there with him. Her parents were there to tend to the kids. What if she could entice Sean into the back seat of the Pontiac in the garage? He'd be in his element and her parents would never hear them.

She put her hand on his knee and he put his hand on her hand. Such a simple gesture, but she felt a flutter. Was it sexual electricity or was she so longing just to feel that he still cared for her? Either way, she was willing to ignore his family history and have him have another Bloody Mary if it meant they could wind up in each other's embrace. She moved her hand up his thigh and he clasped it over himself.

Darcy knew the narcotic pain relievers could reduce testosterone. Sean had only been on a fractional dose for the past few weeks, so maybe his sex drive could come back. She'd been afraid the tailbone surgery had damaged nerves to his groin, so it was a relief to feel him grow hard under her hand, right there at a restaurant table. Maybe she'd get her husband back after all. They both ordered another Bloody Mary.

Chapter Fifty-Two

Eva told absolutely no one about Henry's cardiac issues when he took off from work on a Friday, but by lunchtime Monday, WhiteGuard administrative offices were all a-buzz about it. Someone working at the hospital where Henry underwent his stent procedure, leaked. Word quickly spread through the hospital and then throughout the broader medical community. Confidentiality and celebrity make for strange bedfellows.

It was CLUJ himself who informed Eva about Henry's bad heart on Monday morning. He didn't have the facts straight and thought Henry was still in the hospital. He wanted Eva to go to the hospital immediately and check up on him.

"How very clever of you to secure Power of Attorney for Doctor Winslow, Eva Rodeki. I checked his personnel folder and saw your name was added to his file after his last hospitalization, as the person to notify in case of emergency. I had no idea you two had developed such a close relationship. You are quite the charmer."

CLUJ's voice got a little softer. "You know, Doctor Rodeki, I would have no difficulty replacing our medical director with our director of provider partnerships if I had the right person to do the job. Your PhD in clinical research makes you qualified in my opinion. I don't think the board would have any problem with your being promoted. You have a long, solid track record with WhiteGuard.

CLUJ turned his back to Eva and stared out his massive window as he said, "Now please, get me a realistic analysis of what's going on with Henry Winslow."

"Doctor Winslow is in his office downstairs, Mr. Udall. He came to work a little while ago after a follow-up appointment with his cardiologist. I saw him about half an hour ago and he looked better than he has in a while. As far as I know, everything went fine with his procedure on Friday. He was doing some pre-emptive management of his potential for heart attacks. His father died from coronary artery disease."

CLUJ turned back and gave her a penetrating look. It said she needed to respond to his insinuation that he'd replace Henry with her.

"I'm flattered by your offer to be in charge of medical policy here, Mr. Udall. I'd actually love to do it, but you need a physician to manage physicians. It wouldn't matter how many PhDs I have after my name, how experienced I am, or how much knowledge I have. Managing doctors is like herding cats. Doctors don't like taking orders from nurses, and only occasionally will they take orders from other doctors. Perhaps if we sent me to medical school, I could take the helm here. I wouldn't mind getting an MD if that was in the best interests of the company."

The look on CLUJ's face made Eva sorry she'd said that. He turned from facing her back to his view of the city skyline.

"Just keep me apprised of what you know about Henry Winslow's health, Mrs. Rodeki, if you want to keep your job around here. If I have to come tell you about Doctor Winslow's next medical catastrophe, only to find out his 'power of attorney' already knows his status, you'd better have an up-to-date resume."

Eva swallowed hard. She was being used, commandeered to violate the confidentiality of a patient, and be cast as a spy. CLUJ was ordering her to do a blatantly unethical thing to a colleague or lose her job. She was being blackmailed into framing someone who trusted her with his life.

It wasn't exactly a surprise. No one was indispensable to Clarence Lowell Udall Junior. He'd get rid of her in a heartbeat if she didn't turn on Henry, and he'd have no qualms about getting rid of Henry just because the guy's health was failing.

Later that day, Eva was in the lady's room where she just happened to overhear a conversation about the medical director hitting on a new secretary "who was too thin and wore too much eye make-up," and was "way too young for him." "He's just asking for another heart attack," one of the gossips said.

Eva hung out in her stall until the women were gone. Curiosity got the better of her. She rounded the offices where the bean counters worked, and spotted a woman with luminous eye shadow, shimmering lipstick, perfect hair, and a long neck. Her spandex top was skintight. She looked to be about thirty and buff but thin, perhaps a dancer. Even the hand moving the mouse had the limp grace of a ballerina. Eva had never seen her before, but she could appreciate why she might have caught Henry's eye.

Then she wondered why this woman would want to get involved with a crippled sixty-year-old? It was a silly question. In a company like WhiteGuard, favors were the way to promotion.

Eva despised the sexism of success. She'd long ago realized that the smart girls who were also sluts, came out ahead of the pack. She prided herself on having climbed over some of those sluts on her way up the corporate ladder.

She wondered if Henry had gone looking for another wedding date or if this bombshell had fallen into his path. She couldn't blame him if he was looking for another date, after she'd procrastinated for so long. Still, she wondered if he was looking to take a proper Southern lady to his daughter's wedding, or would he be happier to have a slinky harlot hanging on his arm in the presence of his ex-wife and kids?

Was he that vain? Was she that easily replaced by a bimbo? Just this morning, she was risking her job to defend him. Bye-bye to the notion that he was looking for a skilled nurse to travel with. How foolish was she? She was glad she hadn't accepted his invitation. He was probably a dirty old man anyway.

As soon as she saw him, she'd let him know she couldn't go with him. He'd survived his cardiac procedure without a catastrophe; she didn't want to be his power of attorney anymore either. Being sandwiched between CLUJ's power and being Henry's "power" was a dilemma Eva didn't need.

Chapter Fifty-Three

Making love in the Pontiac had been the best moment Darcy and Sean had shared since the day he was hurt. Just lying in the back seat of that great old car with Darcy on top of him had been exciting. Knowing that her father was a room away added a thrill. Sean was both relieved and ecstatic that he had been able to perform, and he was amazed and delighted that having a few drinks in him had enabled him to get past the pain and enjoy his beautiful wife.

The next day was his first without any prescription pain pills. He could hardly walk. He had tapered down to the point that he wasn't experiencing frank withdrawal symptoms, but the pain was more ferocious than it had been for all those months since he was injured, and weeks since Burke had lopped off his tailbone. He considered the day as the ultimate test of his survival instincts. There had been so many days during the past few months when he had thought about killing himself.

Darcy had taken her parents to the airport before heading into the office. Arthur had closed the garage for the Monday holiday, but Darcy had promised she'd do the end of the month accounting and payroll. Sean decided to go with her just to take his mind off the pain. Polly was available to babysit the kids, and Sean knew he'd feel useless just hanging around the house with this outsider commanding his children's respect. Polly was so wonderful, she just added to Sean's feelings of failure.

While Darcy worked at the computer, Sean tinkered with a Triumph that Arthur was rebuilding. Still savoring their sex from the night before, he wanted to make love to her again. He was fantasizing about all the places they could do it in the garage. He was noticing that thinking about sex was somewhat of an antidote for his pain. So, he let his fantasies runs wild.

Darcy hadn't gotten dressed up for the day since there were no cus-tomers. She was just wearing jeans and a T-shirt, but watching her at the front desk from the perspective of a customer still seemed like a turn-on. The more intently she looked at the computer, the more attractive she seemed. He wanted her as badly as he wanted to be free of his pain.

"Let's do lunch, pretty lady," he announced, when he couldn't think of a better way to interrupt her. She read his vibes and put her work away. When they finally got a table amidst the Memorial Day crowds, he was careening between his pain and his desires. He was sure she'd give him a holy hell if he ordered a drink. She didn't.

They were in walking distance of Tobler's, so they could walk back to the garage and pick the car up later if necessary. Darcy had felt the hotness of his gaze when she was sitting at the reception desk. She also felt the longing to be physically reconnected. If a drink or two facilitated those feelings in him, so be it. She would gladly risk the family genetic potential for alcoholism in exchange for seeing and feeling the old Sean again; the romantic car-nut who made her feel that she was truly loved.

Darcy watched the look of pain on Sean's face fade away by the sec-ond margarita. By the third one, he was smiling and pawing at her under the table. She felt competent to drive after one drink. There was no point in having Sean try to walk back to Toblers, because the pain level caused by walking could cancel out the amorous effects of the drinks.

When she got them back to the garage, they were both excited. Sean led Darcy to the cot that the Toblers had moved from the van to the storeroom for Sean to lie down on when his pain was bad. Amidst shelves and baskets of auto parts, the smell of motor oil, and the phone ringing at the front desk, they made love. Then they they stayed cud-dling on the cot for a while. As they took comfort from each other's embrace, they each wrestled with the torment of their situation. Darcy wondered if Sean would ever again be able to enjoy life without pain. Sean wondered if he would even be able to get up off the cot he hurt so badly. He was craving another drink.

Chapter Fifty-Four

As many times as she saw Henry for blood pressure checks, Eva couldn't bring herself to tell him that she was declining the wedding date. He wasn't pressing her about the weekend, so she assumed he did have a back-up plan. She'd been using her son's puppy love as her stalling mechanism. She'd tell Henry about some silly thing the kid had done, and Henry would reminisce about his own adolescent experiences.

There were extraordinary differences between Henry's coming of age and her son's life, but the biggest seemed to be that Henry didn't have jealous sisters. Eva had concluded that if she did go away and leave her seventeen-year-old daughter in charge, her son would get away with nothing. Then there would be an ongoing war between the kids that they'd all have to weather for a while. There was also still the issue of telling Henry about their mutual past.

Eva and Henry had to attend another CLUJ meeting. The bean counters were reporting a significant increase in bills from chiropractors. People who had previously gone only to MDs were using chiropractors for the first time. Some stupid traction device was costing WhiteGuard a fortune. How could the insurer possibly be paying for people to have their spines stretched by two belts attached to weights, every day for four to eight weeks? Some back stretcher rep had managed to sell a dozen of these machines throughout the region in the past eighteen months, and CLUJ needed his medical team to put a stop to that nonsense.

CLUJ also gave them each a list of new medicines that the pharmaceutical director of the company had decided shouldn't be covered. Then, there was a list of older medicines that now needed special preauthorization.

"These medicines are very expensive. They must be replaced with cheaper substitutes." Henry was assigned to come up with very strict medical criteria for insurance coverage of these drugs.

Eva was assigned to find out which doctors were prescribing these drugs the most and send them all notices of how their costs graphed out higher than average.

Neither Eva nor Henry was able to pay much attention to CLUJ's rants. They were both distracted by the presence of his new personal secretary, none other than the ballerina with a skintight spandex top and too much eye make-up. Eva was watching the woman ignore Henry. Henry was trying to watch the woman without being watched.

Eva stayed late that night to analyze the data she had pulled on the drugs from CLUJ's newest hit list. When she did get home, her daughter was hysterical. She had stayed after school to attend the prom committee meeting, but it was postponed. A friend drove her home earlier than the bus would have arrived. She found her brother and his 'whore' doing 'it' in the living room.

"He has no respect for this house, Mom. You can't leave him here alone with me. I'm never sitting on that couch again."

"What makes you think I can stop it?" Eva asked.

"Take away his cell phone forever," her daughter shouted.

This was about the worst punishment that could ever befall a teenager, but it was a way to ground them. However, Eva suspected that even a cell phone-ectomy wouldn't cool her son's raging hormones. All she could hope to do was teach her son to protect himself, respect his partner and the people he lives with.

"What do you know about this girlfriend of his?"

"Mom, you've seen her, she lives in the yellow house at the end of the block. She acts and dresses like a prostitute."

"But what do you actually know about her? I'll bet she was just a cute little girl a year ago. I wonder why your sister doesn't know her. They're more the same age."

"I think she goes back and forth between her mother and father and goes to a private school. It's her father that lives in the yellow house. She dresses really slutty."

"I may have a talk with the girl's father then. Hopefully we can work as a team to make sure your brother and this young girl don't take unnecessary risks. May you someday have a boyfriend whose mother will care as much about you. In the meantime, you better learn to get along with your brother. This won't be the last time he's going to bring home someone that you don't like. He is quite the hunk."

Eva's sleep was fragmented with dreams of her kids having drunken orgies. She worried that her lack of disapproval regarding her son's sexuality would encourage her daughters to become sexually active. In her heart, she had a double standard. She hoped her daughters would wait until they were in a serious committed relationship, but she knew that they could easily be drawn into the casual sex of their generation. All she could offer them is what she had just lectured her son about. Don't be careless. Don't be cruel.

Eva fell asleep counting the number of doctors she'd have arguments with over the company's plans to stop reimbursing for medicines without pre-authorization. When she wasn't dreaming about teenage mischief, she dreamt about resuscitating Henry on the floor of the chapel at his daughter's wedding. She promised herself she'd let him know one way or another tomorrow.

Chapter Fifty-Five

Rosemary smelled alcohol on Sean's breath when she stopped by the Friday after Memorial Day. She was furious. She would have been less upset to find out he was buying narcotics on the street. A lot of her life had been a horror story because of alcohol.

Rosemary McIntyre Garmen Cauthers had grown up in a small town where her father Richard was the chief of police; her mother Sharon was the town drunk. When Rosemary was born, Sharon had not yet succumbed to full-fledged alcoholism. The problem escalated during her second pregnancy and intensified during post-partum depression after the birth of Rosemary's brother Joseph.

When her brother Kevin was born the following year, the effects of fetal alcohol syndrome were present, although Rosemary wouldn't know that until many years later. By the time Sharon gave birth to her youngest son Patrick, fetal alcohol effects were full-blown. Patrick died from a seizure at age seven months. Sharon started to drink more heavily after that.

When Rosemary was in third grade, she often came home to find her mother passed out. Kevin would be undressed and unfed. She'd make sandwiches for her brothers and herself if there was enough food. Her father rarely got home before eight pm. He'd bring home leftovers from the police station, usually stale pastries. That's what the kids mostly ate.

Kevin was not only deprived of a functional mother; he was also neurologically impaired. His teachers described him as extremely hyperactive, impulsive, and learning disabled. Older brother Joseph had milder learning disabilities.

Rosemary hated to go home after school. She knew her mother was sick, but she didn't know why or what to do about it. She could hardly stand her rotten little brothers. Still, she didn't realize that her family was abnormal until about age ten when she started to spend more time at a friend's house. Her friend's parents didn't sit around on the weekends drinking gin and tonics. Her friend's mother didn't keep a bottle of gin on the kitchen counter. The refrigerator at her friend's house was full of food. Her friend's mother often sent her home with leftovers.

Years later, Rosemary came to realize that everyone in her neighborhood seemed to understand what was going on with the McIntyres, but no one ever said or did anything about it except for those foil wrapped gifts of meatloaf from her girlfriend's mother.

The older Rosemary got, the less she hung out at home. Joseph had started sneaking hits from the gin bottle when he was twelve, and Sharon was so drunk at this point that she didn't even notice where else the booze was going. Rosemary grew tired of trying to be a parent to her mother and her brothers, while her father pretended that nothing was wrong. The worse it got at home, the more time he spent at the police station; the more time Rosemary spent with friends.

Her father died from a heart attack when Rosemary was sixteen. Her mother proceeded to drink most of his death benefits. Unless Rosemary swiped some money and went grocery shopping, there was nothing in the house for the kids to eat.

When twenty-year-old Dale Garmen married eighteen-year-old Rosemary McIntyre, she was already two months pregnant with Sean's brother Michael. Marriage was her escape route.

Sean's father Dale was also an ace mechanic. He had graduated from the agricultural college with a degree in farm machinery repair and was hired by a tractor manufacturer right out of school. The Garmens bought an old house with a big barn for Dale's machinery projects. Michael was three years old when Sean was born. They were a happy family until Dale was killed in a tractor explosion, shortly after Sean turned two.

About that time, Rosemary's brother Joseph was also looking for an escape route from his mother's home. He had stopped drinking after

Rosemary moved out and had assumed the burden of taking care of his mother and brother Kevin. He managed to graduate high school and was working as a warehouse laborer. He could help his widowed sister pay the mortgage. Rosemary took him in.

Joseph lost his job at the warehouse. Rosemary got a job in a dental office. It worked out because Joseph was able to stay home and care for Michael and Sean, while Rosemary went to dental hygiene school and worked. Then, Joseph met a single mom at a park where he took the boys to play. He later moved in with the woman and her kids, but then he started to drink again. His blood alcohol level was five times the legal limit when he was found dead in his overturned car.

Joseph's death turned out to be a sobering event for Rosemary's mother. Sharon finally went to rehab and tried to resume her relationship with Rosemary and the grandchildren with whom she had never bonded. She also tried to reconnect with Kevin, who had moved in with some other young derelicts. He worked in a factory that made bolts, and according to Sharon, drank like a fish. He wanted nothing to do with his mother, drunk or sober. Sharon blamed herself for her children's tragedies. She was seeing a therapist.

Rosemary was inspired that her mother was finally taking responsibility for the mess she had made of all their lives. She wanted nothing more than to see the woman recover and get to be a real grandmother to her fatherless sons. After her mother was sober for ten months, Rosemary took her in to replace the babysitters she had hired after Joseph moved out. She arranged her dental office schedule around her mother's AA meetings. She was amazed that her mother continued to go to meetings every day in the morning, and some nights as well.

Four months after moving in with Rosemary and the boys, a drunk driver killed Sharon when she walked out of the church where her evening AA meetings were held. The killer was another attendee of Alcoholics Anonymous, a thirty-six-year-old man who had just gotten his license back after a drunk driving conviction. It was the first time he had driven in six months. On the way to the AA meeting, he bought a bottle of tequila. He polished it off in his car instead of going to the meeting. When he realized the AA meeting attendees were leaving the church, he panicked about being seen drinking in his car, and backed out of his parking spot without looking.

Rosemary had some semblance of a real mother for a mere four months, and then she was alone with her two boys. Dale Garmen's family helped out to the extent they could, and Michael and Sean had some good grandparenting.

When they were teenagers, Rosemary did everything in her power to discourage her sons from drinking. One year, she tracked down her brother Kevin who she'd learned was a street person in Chicago. After extensive hunting, she found him in a soup kitchen. She took her boys there to meet him for their anti-alcohol education.

"Everyone in my family has been lost to alcohol. Promise me you won't ever drink." Rosemary had said this to her sons on so many occasions that Michael wrote her words into a poem. They both promised their mother they would never drink. They both broke their promises in their teens.

Rosemary still prayed nightly that Michael wouldn't become an alcoholic. His wife was a party girl, and Rosemary feared that her son was in denial about his genetic burden. Sean on the other hand had apparently learned his lesson. He was eighteen when he realized that he did stupid things when he drank, and he seemed determined to not succumb to the family curse, at least until now.

Rosemary was horrified to think that Sean had replaced narcotic pain relievers with alcohol. "Somewhere in this great country," she told him, "There has to be a doctor who can help you."

Chapter Fifty-Six

Henry Winslow was having a brutal day. So was Eva Rodeki and everyone else in WhiteGuard's offices whose job it was to take calls from patients, physicians, and pharmacists. The list of drugs that would soon need special pre-authorization had been circulated.

The phone lines were burning up with providers who didn't see the point of having to fill out forms and go through a waiting period to get authorization for a drug that the patient was already doing well on, needed, and was ultimately entitled to get.

Patients were furious or frightened about having to pay out of pocket for certain drugs or go without. Everyone manning the complaint phones read from a list of scripted responses:

"Pre-authorization assures drugs are being used appropriately."

"We'll have a very efficient staff to process authorization requests."

"All the substitute drugs are proven effective."

"This is the most responsible way for us to take care of all of our insured."

The accountants estimated that the restricted drug coverage would earn the company more than a million dollars within six weeks of implementation. WhiteGuard's cost for the program would be one measly salary to a data entry person to process the drug pre-authorization papers for those who didn't have computer access. All that lackey had to do was punch the diagnostic codes into the computer from the forms filled out by requesting physicians. The computer would decide whether that code number was an acceptable use of the drug, and then generate a response as to whether the request was approved or denied.

If denied, the provider could fill out a different form to appeal this decision. This process would repeat itself on a second appeal and if a substitute drug wasn't found by then, the computer would permit coverage of the drug on the third request. It was predicted that most providers would find a substitute before completing the drawn-out process. CLUJ considered it a win-win.

Despite all the calls she had handled that morning, Eva was unprepared for the one that her assistant passed to her. "You have to talk to this doctor. She is not to be placated."

Eva only talked to the angriest people after several others before her had failed to defuse them. She was ready to be assailed by a Doctor Louise Baily until she found herself straining to hear the weak voice of a dying patient.

Doctor Baily was a twenty-seven-year-old medical fellow with an inoperable brain tumor. Fentanyl was the only narcotic that effectively relieved her headaches. She was expected to survive another few months. Was WhiteGuard really going to make her doctor jump through six weeks of hoops to obtain her medicine? If she couldn't get an answer right then, she threatened to sign herself into a hospice immediately, which would cost WhiteGuard a whole lot more.

"All I want is to die at home in the company of my husband and my little dog. Why would WhiteGuard do this to me?"

Damn CLUJ and his policies. The only person to whom he had given the authority to make exceptions was the medical director. Eva checked out Louise Baily's file. WhiteGuard had paid for two brain surgeries, and multiple courses of radiation and chemotherapy, all in the past thirty months. There was little doubt that this patient was going to come to a tragic end. This one had to be brought before Henry.

Eva had tried hard to avoid interacting with him all day and had thought that the phone call barrage was going to save her. But she promised Doctor Bailey she'd get her an answer before the day was over. It was finally time to make up her mind and let Henry know whether she was going to accompany him to the wedding.

Chapter Fifty-Seven

Rosemary went to her personal physician and told him the story. By the time she got into see him, she was sure that Sean had been drinking every day of the previous week. She begged her doctor to please write a prescription for pain pills to sustain Sean until he could get in to see the specialist. She explained what a hard-working family man her son was, and it was inhumane for so many doctors to just let him suffer.

Her personal physician was unmoved. He advised her to check Sean into a substance abuse rehab facility immediately. He thought it would be entirely unprofessional for him to substitute narcotics for alcohol.

"They're all just addictions," he scolded. "If Sean is in that much pain, he should be under the care of a pain specialist or go back to Doctor Burke." He was sorry he didn't have the power to get Sean an appointment sooner. He thought Rosemary should use the time to get him treatment for alcoholism, especially since it was so prevalent in her family.

In despair, Rosemary did call several alcohol rehab facilities. "What if the alcoholic has terrible physical pain?" she asked the admissions counsellors. They all told her that physical pain wasn't their domain.

Rosemary finally wangled some Vicodin from one of the dentists at Riverside. She and her husband took Sean and Darcy to dinner and told them that they knew that Sean had turned to alcohol and that they hoped he would use the medicine instead.

Sean was stunned she knew. He thought he had carefully concealed it. She said he didn't smell or show anything physical; it was just how he behaved. His voice would be a little louder, his disposition a little edgier.

He would seem more impulsive. It was something a mother could tell. Sean realized that he could not deceive her. He also knew that she was devastated.

"It's only because of the pain, Mom. Believe me, I don't want to end up like Uncle Joseph or Uncle Kevin. As soon as I get hooked up with a pain doc, I promise I'll stop. I just want to be normal again. The pain won't let me do that."

'There's twenty Vicodin in here, Sean. Your appointment is in six days. Please, please don't spend another week drinking. Promise me you'll stop immediately. You're hesitating, Sean. You already like the alcohol too much. I can see it in your expression. You already don't want to stop, even with the medicine to substitute.

"Don't you see? That's the alcoholism gene, Sean. You've hardly even started and already you don't want to quit. Don't you see? You have the disease. This could be the end of everything you've worked for. This could be the end of you, Sean."

"You mean what's left of me, Mom. I already ended. I'm not even thirty years old and I'm a crippled old man. I can't work, I can't play with my kids, I can't make love to my wife, I can't even take a dump without tremendous pain, and I can't sleep. It's not much of a life, Mom, and I'm sick of it. I'm sick of everything."

"Of course, you are. We're all sick of it too. It hurts us all to see you like this. All I'm asking is that you put the bottle down and use the pills for one measly week, not even a week, just six days. Have faith that this specialist can help you. At least don't bring alcoholism to your appointment when everything else might get turned around. Just six days to have hope instead of hopelessness. Because hopelessness is all you'll ever get out of the bottle. Please, promise me that you'll stop immediately."

Sean knew she was right, but he was finding it immensely hard to look her in the eyes and say, "I promise." If it was that hard to do that, then he realized he must really want to keep drinking. Even sitting there in this moment, he desperately wanted a drink. He absentmindedly peeled at the label of the pill bottle his mother had put down in front of him. He searched for something to say short of, "I promise." He couldn't look at her. His physical pain was hammering at him.

A prickly silence arose between them.

Chapter Fifty-Eight

Doctor Millany was impressed as to how much better Henry Winslow appeared when he came in for his prescriptions. His complexion seemed less pasty. His breathing seemed easier, and his blood pressure was lower. The tired old man aura had faded a little. So, the interventional pain specialist was not surprised to learn that Henry had undergone stent reperfusion of his main coronary artery.

On the other hand, he was surprised by all the complaints that Winslow brought to the visit. Henry reported that the original pain that had started after his fall on the ice was as bad as ever. There was more pain in both legs because, he surmised, the kyphoplasty cement was impinging on his spinal cord. His bottom felt numb, and his rectum wasn't working. He also had erectile dysfunction.

Additionally, Henry complained that he hated being dependent on narcotics. Moreover, the twice a day dosing of Oxycontin that Millany was prescribing was inadequate and he could barely work, let alone travel. He needed it four times a day instead of the two doses he had been allocated. Despite the manufacturer's claims that the drug released slowly for twelve hours, Henry found its benefits wore off in about seven hours, forcing him to have severe pain for ten hours out of every day.

Leonard Millany deduced that Winslow had a lot of stress in his life in addition to his pain. He was kicking himself for taking this guy on as a medication patient. He could envision Henry becoming one of those chronic pain sufferers whose dose continuously spiraled upwards. He used to suspect all such patients of abusing or diverting their medicine. His opinion was changed by data that indicated that some people metabolized these drugs much more efficiently than others.

Around the turn of the millennium, regulators started to pressure pain doctors to obtain blood levels of the narcotics they were prescribing, so they could catch the patient who was selling instead of taking their medicine. Physicians in turn complained that there were no standards to interpret blood opioid levels. Then, when researchers started to study drug blood levels, they discovered that some people on low doses had high blood levels, while others on high doses had low blood levels. It was the opposite of what was expected.

Ultimately, it was realized that some people didn't have much of the enzyme needed to break down narcotics, so the drugs would build up in their system and show as a high blood level, even on a very low dose. These were the patients that tended to complain of so many side effects that they could never tolerate a therapeutic dose.

Other people's systems seemed to develop remarkably efficient enzyme factories that chew up and spit the drugs out so fast, that no matter how much they took, the medicine was rapidly cleared out of their bodies. These were the patients that kept complaining that the medicine only worked if they took more of it.

As much as this knowledge helped Millany and other physicians to understand the behavior of patients, it did not relieve the anxiety doctors had about prescribing high doses. High pill counts made pharmacists uncomfortable. Law officials and many doctors who were not students of pain research still believed that people on high doses had to be selling their medicine. That made many pain doctors stop prescribing narcotics. Leonard Millany was one of them.

What irony! He had taken Henry on as a medication patient to gain favor with the health insurance company, and now Henry was becoming the very kind of patient that the insurance company was trying to wheedle out, a chronic pain patient needing high doses of expensive medicine on an ongoing basis.

Just then, Doctor Millany remembered having received notice of a new pre-authorization process that WhiteGuard had instituted to put the brakes on prescriptions for Oxycontin and other expensive drugs. How he wanted to throw it in Henry's face. He slipped out of the room to go read the fine print. The document said there would be no exceptions unless approved by the WhiteGuard medical director. He almost laughed out loud. At least he'd have the fun of putting Henry on the spot about having to approve his own exception to the policy.

Henry squirmed like an eel in a fishnet when Millany told him he didn't know how they'd handle the new WhiteGuard policy requiring the insurer to pre-approve all Oxycontin prescriptions. Henry couldn't believe that he hadn't foreseen that. The strongest narcotic that WhiteGuard hadn't put on its pre-auth list was methadone, because compared to other long-acting narcotics, methadone was cheap. Trying not to seem unscrupulous, he asked Millany if he could switch to methadone.

Millany had used methadone for his uninsured patients for all the years that he prescribed narcotics. It was the only opioid that many could afford. But it was always tricky to get someone started on it or transferred to it from other opioids.

Because of methadone's particular chemistry, its beneficial effects build up slowly over several days. Patients used to quicker acting narcotics often increased their initial dose on the presumption that the drug wasn't working on days one and two, only to be found comatose on day three. Knowledgeable pain doctors carefully warned patients about this. All too often, patients ignored the warnings. Henry would be too smart to make that mistake. Millany figured his best course was to change Henry to methadone, now that he had caught the medical director at his own game.

Henry felt the difference by that night. The methadone felt like it wasn't working. He knew he needed to be patient and give it a few days, but he wasn't a patient man. By eight in the evening his pain level had him doing mental and physical contortions. He was also really pissed that Eva had turned down his wedding invitation after procrastinating for so long. Damn her and her kids. Now he had less than a month to find another date. He had no intention of going to this family affair as a loner.

Damn his ex-wife and kids. Damn if his craving for a drink wasn't getting the better of him. He decided to go to that nearby restaurant and just have one. He deserved to have a good steak and one shot of fine bourbon.

Chapter Fifty-Nine

Sean kept his promise to his mother and carefully rationed out his Vicodin. It barely helped, but it was better than nothing. He took his last pill just before leaving for his appointment with the new pain specialist. If someone was going to stick acupuncture needles in him, he wanted to be prepared.

Had Rosemary not insisted on accompanying him, he would have broken his promise and had a few drinks on the way to see the voodoo doctor. She probably knew that, but Sean had to admit to himself that she was accompanying him not to monitor him, but because she really cared. Unlike Darcy who'd lost her mother, he had one who truly loved him.

The office seemed stark for someone who was so busy that it took weeks to get an appointment. The woman at the front desk went through his pile of papers very carefully, making sure they were all completed. He had received the fat packet in the mail, and it had been another pain in his butt to fill out all those nosey forms.

He hadn't read the information they had sent along with the forms, but Rosemary had read it all. She had also done an Internet search and seemed to think that acupuncture was worth trying for pain and narcotic dependency. She was also babbling about a bunch of other therapies that she'd read about in the literature sent from the doctor's office. None of it was anything Sean had ever heard of.

Rosemary said one of the dental patients had been to this doctor and thought he was quite exceptional. She went on and on about how one of the dentists was using stem cells and Sean couldn't listen anymore. He was afraid to let himself have hope.

Sean tried to read one of the pamphlets while waiting, but he found himself distracted by the appearance of another patient sitting across from him. She was an attractive young woman dressed in a business suit. She wore huge sunglasses and dabbed at tears pouring down her right cheek with her right hand. Her left hand gripped her right wrist. She was noticeably pale. The woman at the desk kept assuring her that Doctor Krauss would be right with her.

Ten minutes after going in to see the doctor, the woman sauntered back into the waiting room without the sunglasses and with little needles sticking around her eye and in her hand and wrist. Her facial color had gone from ashen to pink and Sean realized she must have felt really sick before she went back to see the doctor.

"Why won't they do this in the ER the woman asked the receptionist? When I get a migraine on the weekend and you guys aren't around, I have to use the stupid ER. I spend hours on an IV until I stop vomiting, and then it takes me another whole day to recover from the medicines they give me. Sometimes I wait an entire day before I go to the ER, thinking I can break out of it; and then I wind up there for ten hours the next day because I'm so dehydrated."

"I know, Grace. If we could get reimbursed like an emergency room, our doctors could afford to do emergency services after hours. As it turns out, local insurers aren't paying a dime for acupuncture. Write your congressman. Tell them a few dollars' worth of acupuncture could prevent thousands in ER treatment." Tonya the receptionist sounded passionate.

Grace sat back down in the waiting room. A few minutes later, Tonya took the needles out. Grace paid cash and left.

Another patient with needles in his ear came out of the treatment area and told Tonya he hadn't craved cigarettes since he started the acupuncture.

Finally, Sean was escorted to a treatment room where Doctor Ernest Krauss introduced himself. He looked to be in his sixties, but he was trim and fit. With an exceptionally soft voice, he interviewed Sean at length about everything in the forms and more. He also asked Rosemary some questions.

Krauss watched Sean get up from lying down, sit and arise from a chair, take off and put on his socks, and other ordinary movements. Then he felt Sean's hip bones as he sat, walked, squatted, flexed, arched, and twisted his torso. Next, he felt his back and buttocks in numerous places while Sean lied on his belly.

With Sean on his back on the exam table, Doctor Krauss announced that he had found a dislocated sacroiliac joint and he was going to maneuver it back into place. He bent Sean's right knee, pushed the thigh out to the side and whomped on Sean's hip. Rosemary could hear a clunk from across the room. Then he had Sean get up and move around.

"This is unbelievable," Sean said as he walked across the room. He sat down in a chair, got back up and scratched his head. "It's gone. It's finally gone; the pain that started right after I fell, the one that shoots from my low back around the butt into my groin, and makes that click clack, isn't there now. That's the first time I've sat down and walked without that pain."

Then he sat down and got up again and there was another clunk. The pain returned.

"Not good that it popped out again so fast, but then it's been dislocated for months. We're going to have to belt it into place, and then weld it into place with a course of prolotherapy."

Krauss went on to explain that the sacroiliac joint between the hipbone and the sacrum at the base of the spine, had been loosened by Sean's fall. "The ligaments that keep the pelvic bones attached to the spine are stretched and weak, and not holding the bones in place anymore. A joint is only as strong as its weakest ligament," he said.

"The pain is coming from the bones shifting back and forth with motion of the trunk or the hip. The wobbly joint is prompting the muscles around it to contract to try to stabilize it. Unfortunately, those muscles wind up in spasm, which causes more pain, and then the spasmed muscles press on nerves which cause even more pain. To make matters worse, the muscles around the sacroiliac joint are the big powerful muscles of the low back and buttocks, so the torso and leg are affected too. It's a vicious cycle."

Krauss's explanation terrorized Sean. It sounded way too much like the song and dance routine Maynard Burke had given him before he took out his "fishhook" tailbone. He started to perspire and whenever he could catch Rosemary's eye, he glanced at the door. It took a whole lot more explaining before Sean could be persuaded that Krauss didn't want to remove anything; he simply wanted to inject a solution to strengthen the weak joint, a kind of treatment called prolotherapy. He said it would take a few treatments, but it was the only safe and effective treatment to fix a loosened-up sacroiliac.

Sean let him manipulate the joint back into place again. Once more, he was amazed that he felt some immediate relief from the pain. This time Doctor Krauss didn't want him to move around. He wrapped a big wide belt around Sean's butt and hips and made it snug. He said there was a chance the belt would keep the bones in place. After a few minutes Sean was thrilled at how that area of pain was so much better, but the pain in the area of his removed tailbone seemed worse than ever. In fact, not having the other pain made the tailbone pain seem much worse.

"Now if you can relieve my burning butt, you've got free car service for life."

"Could be very simple," Doctor Krauss replied. "Sometimes we just put some plain old anesthetic in the surgical scar and a lot of pain goes away. It's called neural therapy and it's practiced widely in Europe. The theory goes that newly developed scar tissue blocks the flow of nerve impulses, blood and nutrition to the surrounding tissue. Needling the scar tissue seems to help it develop new neural connections, new capillaries, and better circulation. Sometimes, nothing happens and sometimes the effects are dramatic. I've had patients burst into laughter or tears within minutes of doing scar injections. Sometimes the benefits wear off quickly; sometimes they're permanent. Most patients do best after a few treatments. The risks are just about nil."

Sean was so impressed with how much better his sacroiliac felt that he consented. The injections were moderately unpleasant, but nothing as awful as what he had experienced with Millany's shots. Within minutes after the injections, the burning sensation where Burke had operated was ninety percent gone. Sean literally cried for joy. The absence of pain was overwhelming.

When he was able to convince himself that this was really happening, Sean professed readiness to do anything else Krauss suggested. He underwent an acupuncture treatment and had his first prolotherapy injection to his sacroiliac, even though he was warned that the joint might feel worse for the next few days. He was so amazed at what had been accomplished in an hour that he had complete faith in whatever Ernest Krauss said or did.

Krauss had him rest for a half-hour after the treatments. He sent him home with a prescription for Percocet because there would be pain when the injected anesthetic wore off. He also gave him a jar of CBD ointment. He wanted Sean to apply it to the painful areas the next day to combat any pain caused by the injections.

"It's important to treat the pain he said, but under no circumstances should we use ice or any medicine that has anti-inflammatory effects, such as aspirin, ibuprofen, or prednisone. Prolotherapy works by creating micro-injuries that stimulate the body's natural healing capacity. The micro-injuries will make you feel worse for a day or so, and we don't want you to suffer, but the inflammation is necessary. By stopping inflammation, anti-inflammatory medicines cause delayed, incomplete healing.

"I know this is probably very different from what you've learned in the past, but stopping swelling that develops when one is injured, flies in the face of nature. People shouldn't even apply ice to their acute injuries because ice just stops the flow of blood to the damaged tissue. Blood is supposed to rush into damaged tissue to bring oxygen, nutrition, and growth factors. Blood brings specialized cells to scavenge up the injured and dead cells, and then brings in other specialized cells that spin new collagen to rebuild the tissue. Inflammation is the first critical step in the body's processes for repairing itself. It's counterproductive to stop that inflammation, yet that is what our medical culture has long been doing."

Sean recalled having been treated with ibuprofen and ice packs when he first hurt his back. He wondered why other doctors didn't know any of what this doctor was saying. He was also perplexed as to why none of the other doctors had diagnosed his sacroiliac problem.

Krauss explained, "The sacroiliac is a very misunderstood joint. Most clinicians don't appreciate that it can dislocate, because they don't consider it a mobile joint in the first place. Also, the sacral and iliac bones are thick, and dislocation cannot be visualized on any kind of imaging. In the past, orthopedists who understood that the sacroiliac could become unstable, tried to fix it surgically with disastrous results. Not having an operation for this problem seemed to cause the orthopedic specialty to ignore the joint for the past few decades.

"Recently, there's been renewed interest in sacroiliac problems because they tend to develop after surgical fusion of the sacrum to the lumbar spine. Someone has even developed some special hardware to nail the sacrum and the iliac bones together, but as in the case of most new surgical procedures, no one knows what will happen long term to the bones and the joints of the people who are desperate enough to sign up for this procedure.

"As for why American medicine promotes the stopping of natural inflammation, I can only guess it's because we're an impatient people. We don't want a sprained ankle to keep us from playing softball tomorrow, and since ice reduces pain and swelling, we feel better faster for using it. However, the quick fix undoubtedly compromises the eventual outcome.

"Sports medicine doctors are starting to understand this, but American medical culture is very slow to change, especially when the drug manufacturers bombard the public and the medical community with the notion that anti-inflammatory medicine is a remedy for acute trauma. Anti-inflammatories do have a role in the treatment of chronic inflammation that has outlived its usefulness, but I can't recommend them for someone who's just been injured."

Satisfied with Krauss's explanation, Sean's thoughts turned to the prescription for Percocet. Only twelve pills, but at least Krauss cared enough about his pain to have offered something. If his pain stayed this good, he thought he could live without the medicine. He focused on his pain again. There was still some there. It was a heavy ache in both of his legs that had started after the epidural steroids. Now that the other two more obnoxious areas of pain weren't boring into his consciousness, he was first realizing things about this other kind of pain, and he told Doctor Krauss about it.

"Let's get a new MRI," Krauss said. "What you're describing now doesn't sound like sacroiliac pain or surgical scar pain, and I think we need to look and see if there's another structure generating this pain. The MRI from last fall looks healthy, but you've had a lot of interventions since then. Tell Tonya at the front desk to squeeze in a follow-up for you in about two weeks."

Chapter Sixty

After three days on methadone, Henry was still having a hard time. The drug was starting to work well for pain, but the side effects were awful. He felt more fatigued and foggy-brained than on Oxycontin. Methadone also made him itchy, and more constipated.

Trying to figure out how to get switched back to the other medicine, Henry did some more reading. He learned that methadone is often more effective for nerve pain than other narcotics. That made sense because the deep ache in his legs that had started after the kyphoplasty cement leakage was feeling somewhat better. However, the original pain in his back, butt, and groin remained the same.

Henry started to read about back pain from alternative sources that he would normally ignore. An article about sacroiliac joint point caught his attention. When he had done his orthopedic training, this joint had hardly been mentioned. Historically, orthopedists had scraped cartilage out of painful sacroiliac joints and fastened the bones together with hardware. The procedure produced poor outcomes which resulted in less interest in this diagnosis.

In his web search, Henry kept coming across alternative practitioners claiming they could help people with sacroiliitis. Chiropractors were manipulating the joint. Interventional pain doctors were injecting steroids into this joint, and then there were these radical guys claiming they could stabilize a wobbly sacroiliac with prolotherapy injections. Physical therapists and other rehab types were teaching people how to walk and bend differently, and most of these clinicians seemed to be prescribing a sacroiliac belt to hold the joint together.

Henry also read about a new surgical approach whereby special nails could be hammered into the sacral and iliac bones to hold them together. The procedure was reported to relieve pain, though there were some nasty complications, and the long-term outcomes were unknown.

Henry learned that WhiteGuard was reimbursing an orthopedist who had done several cases. He called the surgeon and learned that this doctor had stopped doing the procedure because half of the patients had problems from it. One of the patients fell on his butt six months after the surgery and suffered serious fractures of both bones.

Despite the opinion of some physicians that an injured sacroiliac joint was the cause of low back pain in as many as forty percent of sufferers, there was still no agreement about its diagnosis or management.

Henry was taken aback by how many practitioners were advertising prolotherapy services on the web. When WhiteGuard had made a policy decision to not cover this treatment several years previously, there were only a handful of practitioners in the region who were doing it, and very little research to support it.

Now, it appeared that there were dozens of physicians who had incorporated it into their practices. The University of Wisconsin had been offering prolotherapy training through its medical school, and even some prestigious institutions like Mayo Clinic had endorsed it.

Previously, WhiteGuard and other insurers had been able to take the position that there was insufficient research to support the effectiveness or safety of prolotherapy. Now, Henry was astounded to realize that some respectable journals had published research demonstrating that "prolo" was safe and effective.

Henry the medical director could readily see that this form of treatment would again become a hot-button issue for the insurance company. Henry the back pain sufferer wondered where he could go to try it, without his identity as WhiteGuard's medical director being known.

Henry was getting desperate enough to get devious. He could get prolotherapy or his preferred Oxycontin simply by assuming a false identity and paying out of pocket. He'd have to have someone in the tech department change the name on his imaging studies. He'd also need some phony ID. Fortunately, there were people at WhiteGuard who could manufacture such documents.

Henry fantasized about showing up in doctors' offices as Nicholas Johnson, a locksmith. His father had been a locksmith before his bad heart killed him. As he planned his false identity, Henry started to wonder how many doctors were left in the community who would accept a new pain patient. WhiteGuard reached into most of the region, and he might have to travel far to find a pain doctor who didn't know who he was, or who hadn't scaled back their practice because of insurance restrictions, or who hadn't been scared off by the arrest of Judd Fleishman. He might have to go really far. There was no way he could afford to go jaunting three states away every time he needed a prescription.

Maybe though, he could go somewhere for a trial of prolotherapy. It did seem highly likely that his sacroiliac joint was the problem, and he was flabbergasted that neither he nor Burke nor Millany had considered it.

Then he started to wonder if he could dare show up in Donilski's office as himself on the pretense that WhiteGuard was taking another look at prolotherapy, and he was there to personally evaluate it. Wouldn't Donilski bend over backwards to help him out? As Eva had pointed out, this physician was appealing WhiteGuard's upcoding charges and they hadn't yet kicked him off their panel.

It seemed like a good idea for a few seconds until Henry stopped to consider that WhiteGuard had already made so much trouble for Donilski, that he might take Henry on as a patient just to get revenge and do something horrible to him. When he carefully considered it, he would be taking a personal risk. He wasn't that brave.

He wouldn't be seeing Millany for another week, so he was stuck with methadone for the time being. He'd still consider getting the phony ID.

Henry finished up in his office and hobbled over to the WhiteGuard call center. As he waited for his dinner date to lock down her computer, he pondered how to ask this woman if she would accompany him to Jill's wedding. This was only their second date. He hoped a romantic dinner and some good wine would facilitate the invite.

Chapter Sixty-One

Sean cursed Doctor Krauss for about thirty hours after the prolotherapy shots to his sacroiliac joint, but when he woke up on the third day after treatment, there was some definite improvement in the pain that shot around to his groin. Each day afterwards, it seemed to hurt a little less.

The burning in his butt from Burke's tailbone surgery was almost completely gone, but the other pain that came after Millany's shots seemed worse. He had a heavy ache in his thighs and a tingly sensation in his feet. Occasionally a sharp pain shot down one leg or the other. He was pretty sure these symptoms had been there before Doctor Krauss treated him, but he hadn't paid all that much attention to them because the other pains were so much worse. Now, he couldn't stop paying attention to them.

His pain pills were gone. He'd used most of them when the sacroiliac pain had been obnoxious on the first two days after the procedure. The CBD ointment had helped the pain in the areas where he'd been injected, but it didn't seem to do anything for his leg pain.

Getting the MRI that Doctor Krauss had ordered turned into another WhiteGuard hassle. It took the better part of the week to go through the authorization process and then Sean couldn't get on the schedule to have the MRI for another week. In the meantime, his follow-up appointments with Millany and Burke came up.

Both Sean and Rosemary were conflicted about what to tell these doctors. They wanted to know why neither had ever checked Sean's sacroiliac joint, because if that had been discovered in the beginning, he never would have had Burke's surgery, or steroid injections, or all the other miserable stuff he had suffered through for a good part of the past year. Rosemary was researching malpractice lawyers.

Sean on the other hand was afraid to confront these physicians. He was hoping one of them would prescribe more pain medicine because he still hurt enough that he was having a hard time resisting the temptation to turn back to alcohol. If the brilliant Doctor Krauss hadn't been able to identify the source and treatment of this other pain, then Sean might still need help from someone like Millany, though he couldn't think of anything helpful that Millany had done.

Still, he couldn't see the value of starting a lawsuit if one of these doctors could just help him to get rid of the pain. He'd heard too many stories from car-nuts about how they sued some mechanic for messing up on their luxury vehicles, only to spend a fortune going to court to get back nothing but a big fat fee for their lawyers. Sean's only goal was to get his life back. Then, there were the issues concerning Quinn's arm

They needn't have worried about what to say to Burke. He reportedly got called away to an emergency before they got in to see him. A physician's assistant, who they had never met, looked at Sean's surgical site and said it was healing nicely.

Quinn's casted arm was x-rayed, and the digital image was relayed to Burke at the hospital. Word came back that the bones looked good, and the cast could be removed. Quinn was so entertained with the remote-controlled toy car that he didn't utter a peep as his cast was cut off with a noisy power saw. He did get upset when he saw his shriveled arm with scaly skin and a big scar.

The physician's assistant checked Quinn's strength and reflexes. He said that an adult would be sent to physical therapy to help redevelop the muscles, but that in a young child using the arm normally, the muscles would redevelop on their own. He proceeded to show Sean and Rosemary some exercises to help the stiffness of the wrist and elbow, and suggested they let Doctor Burke recheck it in a month.

There was no way Sean was going to get help with his pain from this source. He thought it would be pointless to tell this stranger anything, or to bother to ever come back. Rosemary wondered if there was really an emergency or whether Burke had just chosen to avoid them. She asked at the front desk whether Quinn would be seen by the doctor who operated on his arm or by a physician's assistant when they rescheduled.

The receptionist said Doctor Burke always liked to see his own work, but she could never guarantee who would be present at their next appointment. After all, the surgeon was on staff at three hospitals and had to manage serious emergencies almost daily. It was customary for physician assistants to manage follow-up in the office.

Rosemary imagined that they'd only get to see Burke face-to-face again if they returned to get the hardware out of Quinn's arm. It was time to consult with another orthopedist to find out if even that was necessary. She suspected that Burke would operate on her grandson again whether he needed it or not.

When Sean told Doctor Millany about his experiences with Doctor Krauss, Millany remained expressionless. "That's great that you got that level of relief. I'm going to make a point of learning more about these techniques myself. I'd also like to get the results of your new MRI when it gets done. So, what can I do to help you now?"

"Some pain meds would help a lot," Sean responded. "I don't need nearly as much as I needed before, maybe only one or two Percocets a day, just for workdays. I get started on a car and after a while, my legs ache so much, I have to get off my feet for a while. It really slows me down and it's hurting my employer."

Leonard Millany seemed pensive. He kept looking towards Rosemary who was taking notes every time he spoke. He could smell a malpractice suit. There was nothing in his notes about checking the sacroiliac joint. Musculo-skeletal medicine was not his strong suit. He had come to the specialty of pain management from anesthesiology, and his forte was placing catheters in body parts and instilling medications, radio waves, or acrylic cement.

He had heard about sacroiliac dysfunction when he had studied back pain, but it wasn't a condition that was easily diagnosed or treated. There was a fair amount of disagreement amongst experts as to whether it was really a common cause of "garden variety" back pain, the kind of pain that sent millions of people to doctors every year; the kind of pain that wasn't visible on imaging.

Some doctors claimed that if anesthetic injected into the sacroiliac joint took the patient's pain away, then the joint was probably the cause of the pain. The cure was another matter. All Leonard Millany knew about prolotherapy, was that the insurers wouldn't pay for it.

What Millany did know, was that the medicines he injected could sometimes cause inflammation instead of curing it. Although this occurred rarely, it was a horrible thing when it happened, and he was concerned that this could be what was going on with Sean Garmen by the way the man was describing the newer symptoms. Either the steroids, or the preservatives mixed in with the steroids, might cause inflammation of one the coverings of the spinal cord.

Of the three coverings surrounding this cable of nerves, the middle covering, the arachnoid, is the most vulnerable. Arachnoiditis is an extremely painful and debilitating condition and there are no good answers for it. Unfortunate patients who suffer from it often became totally disabled.

Millany hoped that's not what would be seen on Sean's new MRI. It wouldn't be a malpractice issue for him because every patient who underwent epidural steroid injections signed a consent form in which they were informed that arachnoiditis was a possible risk of the procedure. The fact that the patients had no idea how serious the risk was, didn't absolve their responsibility in consenting to the procedure as far as the courts were concerned.

Millany was more worried about malpractice for not having considered sacroiliac dysfunction as the cause of Sean's original pain. He would have to do some homework to ascertain if he could be sued for missing it. In the meantime, it seemed prudent to make extra nice to this patient. If all this poor guy needed to do his job was ten Percocets a week, and if prescribing it would save him from this family suing, he would write the script.

"Let's give you a dozen tablets a week," he offered. "I'll write you for a month's worth and we'll see you back in a few weeks when we have that MRI."

Chapter Sixty-Two

It took Henry two more dinner dates before he broached the subject of his daughter's wedding with Felicia. He wasn't really interested in a relationship with her, but he was determined to bring a pretty woman with him when he went back home. Felicia was certainly pretty enough with her sensuous lips and Kardashian physique. She was a thirty-four-year-old nurse who had recently joined WhiteGuard as a call center specialist. She had only been on the job for about a week when the gossip channels identified her as a divorcee on the hunt.

Henry wasn't the only one who had taken notice. One of his staff had informed him that Felicia had also been seen dining out with one of the lawyers from Sperling's department. But she continued to accept dinner invitations from Henry, and after three such dates, he popped the question.

"It's such short notice," Felicia said. "I'm going to have to really scramble to make some arrangements for my kids; but I'd love a weekend out of town, especially in a charming old Southern city that I've never been to. Let me see if I can get my ex to take the kids for the weekend, and I'll let you know."

Henry cringed. If Felicia said "no," there was no time left to find another date. He'd invested all this time and money in her and still might be left out in the cold. Then an idea popped into his head. He resolved that if she did turn him down, he'd just pay the bucks and hire a woman from an escort service. He reasoned if he used an escort service at home, he wouldn't even have to pay for airfare and hotels. He'd just have to line up a service from a town far enough away that nobody local would recognize her.

He wondered why he hadn't thought of it before. How foolish of him to have spent all this time courting Eva and now Felicia. He could rent a stunning woman just for the evening, and not have to worry about anything else.

When he got back to his office, he did a fast search for escort services and found so many it made his head spin. Some of the pictures of the women on some of the websites made him think he'd never again pursue a professional associate. Now, he was hoping that Felicia would say no. She talked too much anyway.

As he drove away from his office, Henry contemplated how he was going to solve his methadone problem. After the first week of using this medicine, the itchiness was a little better, but the fatigue was still dragging him down. Henry had always been a high-energy guy who could work, study, and play at full speed with only a little sleep. Now, he could barely focus when he did work or read, and he felt exhausted, even if he spent a quiet weekend at home. His energy had improved a lot after his cardiac stenting, but since he started the methadone, he was tired in other ways.

He hated to admit it, but he also missed the Oxycontin because it made him feel good. He would look forward to taking his next dose. Methadone didn't uplift him that way, and he would get around to taking it only when the pain got really obnoxious. However, he had figured out during his dinner dates with Felicia, that methadone along with a glass of wine, did make him feel pretty good. Not that it helped the fatigue, that problem was still there, but that sense of well-being he got from taking the methadone and wine together was very welcome.

Henry reasoned that he had been able to limit himself to just two glasses of wine on the dinner dates, and there was no reason why he couldn't do the same at the end of his workday. It would only be until he got back in to see Doctor Millany and get changed back to Oxycontin. He had an appointment next week, so the most he'd have to rely on the wine was a few days. He'd be very careful he promised himself. He'd just buy two bottles and make them last until his appointment next week. That would be it.

He pulled his car into the parking lot of a strip mall with a liquor store. He sat listening to his conscience for a few minutes. It was warning him that this was a huge mistake. He was just about to restart the engine and drive away when his cell phone rang. It was Felicia. She sounded happy. Her ex could take the kids and she was free to come with him for the weekend. She was excited about meeting his children.

When the conversation ended, Henry limped into the liquor store. Then, he couldn't help but notice that his favorite brand of bourbon was on sale.

Chapter Sixty-Three

Darcy accompanied Sean to his next visit with Doctor Krauss. She wanted to meet the miracle worker who had given her husband so much pain relief, and had given them hope. Rosemary had missed a lot of work going to all these appointments with Sean, and Darcy had become so proficient at Toblers that it wasn't a problem if she took a few hours off.

As Sean filled out his paperwork, rating his pain and results from the last treatment, Darcy read some of the pamphlets in the waiting room. A pamphlet about prolotherapy explained that twisting a joint past its normal range of motion stretched out the ligaments and capsules that hold the bones together. Once sprained, weakened ligaments allow excessive motion in the joint. Over time, the extra motion causes the bone surfaces to rub together, wearing them out prematurely and leading to arthritis.

The pamphlet stated that prolotherapy injections strengthen the ligaments and help prevent further joint deterioration. Darcy wondered why so few doctors knew about this. According to the pamphlet, doctors had been doing similar treatment for centuries. In the 1800s, doctors injected saltpeter into hernias. This strengthened weak spots in the abdominal wall and stopped the intestines from poking out.

In the twentieth century, doctors realized they didn't have to use harsh chemicals like saltpeter to do the job; injecting a few drops of sugar water got the same results. More recently, doctors learned to inject painful joints with the patient's own platelets, elements in the blood that contain tissue growth factors that promote healing. Professional athletes are often reported to be getting platelet-rich-plasma shots. The problem with "prolo" and platelet-rich plasma (PRP) injections, according to the pamphlet, was that most insurance companies won't pay for it.

Darcy sighed. The medical bills for Sean and Quinn were piling high and even with WhiteGuard paying a lot of it, the Garmens budget had been badly dented. WhiteGuard had also recently raised the cost of the group policy for Arthur's business, so Arthur's budget was also compromised. The eighteen percent rate increase would likely make some small business owners drop their health insurance plans.

After salaries, Arthur's biggest expense was health insurance. It cost him a huge chunk of his income to provide good benefits for his people. Darcy worried about what they'd do if Arthur could no longer keep up with the expensive premiums and how her family was ever going to make it if the medical bills didn't stop.

When they finally got called into Doctor Krauss's office, he seemed a little flustered. "The hospital has yet to fax me over your MRI report and I've had Tonya bugging them for it since this morning. We'll just have to do without it for the moment. How have you been doing since the last treatment?"

Sean responded that his tail-end pain seemed to be almost completely gone. The sacroiliac pain was maybe thirty to forty percent better, but it felt best if he wore the belt and wasn't too active. The leg pain and tingly feet persisted.

Krauss repeated his physical exam and then thumbed through Sean's chart. "Let me see; when was it that you had that epidural steroid injection? Here we go, it was early May, about six weeks ago. Hmm! Without that MRI we still don't have all the answers, but here's what we can do today if you're game. I'd like to do a little more scar therapy to turn that 'almost-gone' burning sensation in your butt into 'completely gone.'

"Your response to the initial prolotherapy is very good this soon, and the joint feels less wobbly, so I'd like to repeat those injections. This time, I'd like to use platelet-rich plasma. All I need is an ordinary blood draw from you to get the platelets. Then we can do some more acupuncture to see if we can help with the leg pain. More needles this time.

"I'm all yours, Doc," Sean said, as Darcy cringed at the cost. An hour later, Sean was as happy as a pincushion could be. He left the office with anesthetic in his tailbone scar and sacroiliac joint. The leg pain also seemed better. Krauss had even given him a script for a few more pills in case Doctor Millany's medicine wasn't enough to cover him on those nasty "post prolo" days. He promised he'd call as soon as he could get a hold of the MRI.

Darcy stopped back at the reception desk and wrote another check for partial payment. Seeing how much better Sean was made the money seem unimportant. Poverty had to be better than Sean in pain.

"How lucky we are to have found this doctor," Darcy remarked as they drove away. "Let's go celebrate and break your promise to Rosemary just one more time. No one at Toblers looked like they'd be working late today, and I know of a nice little cot in the storeroom."

Chapter Sixty-Four

Henry had repeatedly rehearsed what he would say about his need to switch his medication when he got back in to see Doctor Millany. The morning of his appointment, a curve ball came hurling his way.

When the new pre-authorization policy on expensive drugs first came out, Eva had asked Henry to make an exception for a young physician who was dying of a brain tumor and needed fentanyl to control her headaches. Even though Henry had taken all the prescribed steps to process this exception, the computer program had continued to send the patient, her doctor and pharmacist denial notices.

One of CLUJ's computer whizzes had spent hours trying to bypass the program, and Eva thought it had been taken care of. She called the patient, and her prescribing physician, a Doctor Hahn, to advise them that the medical director had granted an exception. But no matter what pharmacy the patient's husband brought the script to, he was told that the network computer showed that WhiteGuard wouldn't pay for the medicine. The young couple didn't have thousands to pay for a month's supply.

Doctor Hahn was livid. He had to make a huge commotion to be able to even get to talk directly to the medical director. He informed Henry that he had been taking care of cancer patients for twenty-seven years and had seen the most dreadful suffering imaginable, but this patient's battle was one of the most heartbreaking he'd ever witnessed.

He described in gory detail how many pieces of Louise Baily's head had been sliced away and how, without her pain medicine, the young doctor could do nothing but lie in bed and cry. The rapidly spreading tumor, which had left her blind and partially paralyzed, had now affected her speech center, and she could no longer talk. Maybe she'd hang on another two weeks. If Doctor Winslow couldn't get this problem solved, he'd file malpractice charges against him personally, as well as bring a suit against WhiteGuard for negligence.

Henry didn't know how he was going to solve the problem, but he assured Doctor Hahn that he'd find a solution before the day was over. He first went to WhiteGuard's top geek to see about it and was shown a list of five additional patients whose exceptional needs he had approved, who were also having the problem. The techies had been working on the computer program night and day, without success. Now they were rewriting the program, but it could take more days to fix the glitch.

Henry next contacted the director of pharmacy services. In as much as Henry was dealing with irate physicians, the head pharmacist was on the phone nonstop with outraged pharmacists who were on the front line dealing with furious patients. More than one pharmacist was forced to call the police to remove desperate patients who refused to leave the pharmacy without their medicine.

"What about your emergency charity fund that we used to use for patients in exceptional circumstances? Henry asked.

"Frozen. CLUJ specifically restricted its use for patients wading through the preauthorization process. I tried to get in to see CLUJ myself because of this Doctor Baily thing when it first came to my attention, and I still can't get on his calendar. I've called up there every day this week and that new secretary of his just keeps telling me that she's given him the message."

Henry hobbled up to CLUJ's office. New secretary wasn't at her desk and knocking on the inner door got no response. Henry attached a post-it note to her computer screen stating that he needed to see CLUJ immediately, for whatever good that would do.

He went to see Clinton Sperling. After explaining the situation, Sperling advised him that there probably was a viable lawsuit in Doctor Hahn's threats, and whether CLUJ liked it or not, he was going to take the authority to unfreeze that emergency fund and get Doctor Baily her medicine. After another hour of hassling with the accounting department to guarantee the pharmacy reimbursement, Henry was able to tell the Bailys they could fill the prescription.

This wasn't how he'd planned to spend his morning, but he was grateful that the issue came up when it did. Had it not, he would have gone to Millany that afternoon claiming that WhiteGuard had granted him an exception. Then, his name would wind up on the list of people who the techies were trying to work through the system, and everyone at WhiteGuard would know that the medical director was taking Oxycontin. He could just imagine how the headlines would read if someone leaked it to the press: *Whiteguard Medical Director Takes Drug Denied to Their Insured.*

Thank you, Doctors Hahn and Baily, he thought. I'll just stick with my cheap old methadone and evening bourbon, for the time being. Oxycontin helped his pain the best with the least side effects, but it was ridiculously expensive. And, like everyone else, Henry felt entitled to have his health insurance cover it.

Chapter Sixty-Five

Darcy had a martini and Sean had two. He was inclined to try anything that didn't have gin in it, since that was the liquor that his mother always referred to when she talked about the family curse. He was feeling better than he had been for the better part of the past year, but once they got to the cot in Toblers' storeroom, he was unable to maintain an erection. Darcy blamed it on his being numb in the nerve department and they went home to play with the kids instead.

Just as Doctor Krauss had warned, Sean was sore after treatment. Krauss had advised that injecting the platelets caused a more dramatic inflammatory response but with better results in the long term. Sean felt considerably worse than the first time, but five days later, he knew that the joint was getting better, and he felt good enough to go back to work.

Sean did well for about a week. Most of the original pain had showed steady improvement, but the newer pain in his legs was getting worse, and the Percocet did little to relieve it. Some days he had strange sensations in his feet. He and Darcy became upset when Tonya called to tell them that Doctor Krauss wanted him to come back in about the results of the new MRI. She set up an appointment for the next week.

When Rosemary came to visit on Sunday, she observed Sean to have new problems. He'd shudder occasionally and then kick a foot out as if a bug was biting it. He just shrugged when she asked him what was wrong. She insisted on going with him to his next appointment to see Krauss.

Doctor Krauss started by telling them there was nothing major on the MRI, but he wanted to know how Sean was doing before going over it. Sean told him about his new symptoms. Rosemary was distressed to hear about the leg weakness and bizarre sensations. She was even more distressed watching Krauss's reaction to this information.

Doctor Krauss reexamined Sean and commented that the sacroiliac joint seemed more stable. He then said that in light of Sean's symptoms and some vague findings on the MRI, he was worried about another problem, something called arachnoiditis.

"A rack of what? And how did he get that?" Rosemary asked.

"Arachnoiditis is inflammation of the middle covering around the spinal cord."

Doctor Krauss took out an anatomy book and showed them illustrations of the three layers of protective coverings around the cord as it runs through the backbones."

Sean was shaking his head as he asked, "Did Burke's surgery cause this?"

"Probably not," Krauss answered. "There are several different things that can cause this. The most common cause is spinal surgery. Just getting blood on the arachnoid can inflame it, but there's no arachnoid in the coccyx, so Burke's tailbone removal probably didn't cause it. Infection is another cause. Occasionally injected medicines irritate the arachnoid. In some cases, the cause is never identified."

"How would we know if that's what I have?" Sean asked. "Is that what the MRI shows?"

"Maybe. It can be hard to tell in early stages. If the arachnoid is acutely swollen, that may be visible on MRI. As the inflammation settles down, imaging may not show anything abnormal, but in some cases, the arachnoid develops scar tissue after the inflammation goes away. Scarring might only become visible sometime later. Sean's MRI might be showing very slight inflammation. If we repeat the MRI in another month or two, it will help us to know what we're seeing now."

Rosemary was looking at the pictures and noticed the arachnoid was also called a meninge. "So, if the meninges are swollen, is that meningitis?"

"Technically yes; although typically if someone is said to have meningitis, it's due to an acute infection. Unless Sean had an illness somewhere along the way that I don't know about; it's highly unlikely that Sean has infectious meningitis."

"I've been miserable Doc, but I can't remember being sick during any of this. Maybe I had a cold in December when the kids got sick, but that's it."

"So, what do we do now?" Rosemary asked

Krauss shook his head. "It's hard to know. Symptoms can keep changing as the arachnoid swells, recovers, and ultimately scars down. If one tries to surgically remove the scar tissue, more scar tissue will usually grow in its place, making symptoms worse."

"What kind of symptoms?"

"It's extremely variable; there can be pain, tingling, weakness, numbness, and other strange sensations in the legs. Sometimes the symptoms are bad with the inflammation, then they improve, then they get worse again when the scar tissue starts to develop. Occasionally, the inflammation goes away without scarring and everything improves. Other times, the scarring causes irritation to other areas of the arachnoid and more symptoms develop. It's very hard to predict. It can be different in every patient."

Rosemary felt like Doctor Krauss was beating around the bush. "So, is this the result of the prolotherapy?" she blurted out.

"No, the prolo has nothing to do with this because I did not inject anything in or near the spinal cord or the arachnoid. The prolo injections were out here by the joint." He pointed out the difference in the anatomy pictures.

"It couldn't be, Mom, because I started to have these symptoms before I came to see Doctor Krauss. I distinctly remember first noticing these symptoms after Doctor Millany did the last steroid shot.

"I thought steroids were supposed to cure inflammation. You're saying they caused it?" Rosemary asked.

"Under the circumstances, that seems most likely. Sometimes the steroid liquid crystallizes, and the crystals inflame the tissue. The timing does point to the epidural injection. Truthfully, we may never know for certain."

"So how do we fix this?" was Sean's question.

Ernest Krauss didn't have to answer in words. His expression said it all. "Arachnoiditis is an incurable condition that's very hard to manage." He went on to explain that it could get much worse. Sean could lose control of his bowel and bladder. Sexual dysfunction was another symptom. Rarely, the arachnoid could become irritated all through the spinal column and even involve the brain. Some patients developed arm symptoms in addition to leg symptoms, and some complained of headaches and neck pain as though they had meningitis. Mental changes were also possible.

"If this is what Sean has, only time will tell the outcome." Doctor Krauss wished he could offer more, but the best he could do was give Sean more pain medicine and try some more acupuncture. Neither would cure him, but one or the other might give him some relief.

Sean admitted the Percocet didn't have much impact on his leg pain, especially the sharp shooting pains. Krauss said that was a common issue with arachnoiditis, it was often resistant to pain medicine. He suggested trying another nerve-quieting drug called pregabalin, since Sean had not been very tolerant of an older one called gabapentin, when it was prescribed earlier in his course.

Krauss wrote the prescription but warned them that it could take a while to get an authorization from WhiteGuard, and then more time until the drug started to work.

Chapter Sixty-Six

Giving the bride away had been about the only moment of his trip that Henry hadn't hated. Felicia had talked his ear off the whole time they were in flight, mostly about her cheating ex-husband. At times, Henry tried to respond, but Felicia's prattle was more of a monologue than a conversation.

Somehow, it seemed fitting that someone who talked a lot better than they listened, would wind up at WhiteGuard's call center. She was probably masterful at shaking complaining patients off the phone.

During the Friday night rehearsal dinner, Henry felt like a complete outsider. Jill had taken less than a minute to introduce him to her groom and his family and then she ignored him for the rest of the evening. For the reception dinner after the ceremony, Gloria had chosen to seat him with some old friends instead of with the family. It was awkward and humiliating and Felicia's incessant babbling only made it worse.

Then like a fool, Henry had a little too much to drink and thought it would be a good idea to dance with Felicia, especially since he'd paid a fortune for the band that was playing modern songs that he didn't know or like.

Felicia also drank a little too much and insisted on dancing some more. It seemed like a better thing to do than sit at the table and listen to his former friends gossip about people he barely remembered and could care less about. For appearance's sake, he tried to look like he and his date were having a wonderful time. By the end of the evening, his back felt like it was broken again, despite the pills and the booze.

After the cab dropped them back at their hotel, Felicia invited him to her room. She was highly insulted when he declined. The only consolation was that she didn't talk to him at all when they flew home on

Sunday. He suspected she'd go blabbing all over WhiteGuard that he was an impotent old dud, which he feared he was.

Henry couldn't believe it was possible for anyone to talk as much as Felicia. He hated himself for getting involved with her. He felt so uncomfortable around her that he stopped going to the WhiteGuard cafeteria for lunch for fear of running into her.

He next decided to come to work earlier and take longer lunch breaks so he could go to a local restaurant and have a drink with his meal. It made the methadone work a lot better and allowed him to get through his afternoon with a little less pain. He was pleased that he'd been able to use alcohol again without losing control. He reasoned that it was only circumstances that had led him down the alcoholism pathway when he was a younger, less cautious man. He was certain it wouldn't happen again.

He was glad that Eva had turned him down for the wedding weekend because they worked so closely together that any awkwardness between them would have compromised his work. He was very dependent on Eva's knowledge of community medical standards and trends. In as much as he disliked a lot of what he did for a living, his job was the only thing left in his life that meant anything to him.

At the wedding, even his son Adam had made him feel like an intruder in the family circle. Although two of his three children had claimed that they had forgiven him, it seemed they would forever resent him for their family fracture. Gloria had done a great job of turning them against him. She was so hostile and spiteful that he couldn't believe he had ever loved her or been married to her for fourteen years.

Since his blood pressure had improved after cardiac stenting, Doctor Tremont had asked that Henry record his blood pressure on a weekly instead of a daily basis. When Eva took his pressure on the Wednesday after the wedding, it was quite elevated. They took it again over the next two days and the numbers stayed high. The following week, Henry returned to Doctor Tremont to see what she would advise.

Chapter Sixty-Seven

Sean didn't think he needed to go to the cardiologist appointment that had been set up at the time of his tailbone surgery. He'd checked his blood pressure a few times at the pharmacy machine and the numbers looked okay, but his mother nagged him until he made the appointment,

Rosemary took another day off from work to go with him. Sean was starting to feel like a little kid with Mommy paying his bills and taking him to doctor appointments. Though he felt resentful, he also appreciated his mother's knowledge and wisdom.

Doctor Tremont's waiting room was full. The receptionist said that she'd gotten tied up at the hospital and was running late. Rosemary picked up a magazine and Sean studied the other waiting patients. It struck him that he was half the age of everyone there. Then he noticed that the man who'd sat down in the chair next to him was reading on a laptop. Bold letters caught Sean's eye: *Chiropractic Treatment of the Sacroiliac Joint.*

Sean couldn't read the small print without leaning over the man, but he was curious. He elbowed his mother and pointed to the screen. She also glimpsed the bold print before the man scrolled down. He was dressed in a business suit.

"Excuse me," she said, "but I just happened to notice what you're reading. Are you a chiropractor?"

"No, just a patient with a bad sacroiliac." He was clearly uninclined to get into a conversation.

Just then, Sean was called back, and Rosemary got up to accompany him. A medical assistant told Rosemary she was welcome to come with Sean when he saw the doctor, but she just needed him at the moment to get a blood pressure and EKG.

Rosemary sat back down and took the opportunity to tell the man in the suit that her son also had a bad sacroiliac, but he'd finally found a doctor who knew how to treat it. The man seemed interested, and Rosemary started to talk about Doctor Krauss, just when the medical assistant said, "you can come back now, Doctor Winslow."

On the pretense of asking about reimbursement, Rosemary went to the reception desk to peak at a sign-in sheet. Just under Sean's name was the name Henry Winslow. She wrote it in her notebook but didn't see the man again. Privacy's a joke, she thought. We need to eliminate these sign-in sheets at the dental office.

Nanette Tremont remembered Sean very well from that night in the hospital when his blood pressure was in the danger zone. She listened to his story about his injury and his journey through Burke's surgery, steroid shots, and the new diagnosis of arachnoiditis. She thought his blood pressure readings were probably okay, considering he was still dealing with pain, but they weren't ideal for such a young guy.

Nanette didn't know much about arachnoiditis, but she looked it up on her desktop. She learned that irritation of the arachnoid could affect the nerves to the heart and blood vessels. She explained this to Sean and Rosemary and asked that they continue to monitor his blood pressure and return if it was higher. She also warned him to return promptly if he ever felt like his heart was racing or skipping beats. Rosemary wrote it all down. They hadn't expected this.

Sean tried to explain it to Darcy that evening. This arachnoiditis thing was getting really scary. When Corey came by later to drop off some weed for Sean's persistent insomnia, he decided that some cheering up was needed. While Darcy put the kids to bed, Corey and Sean went out for a beer.

Chapter Sixty-Eight

Henry had forgotten who Doctor Krauss was until Eva reminded him that he was the psychiatrist who had joined Donilski's pain practice. WhiteGuard had pushed Nagel, the pediatrician, off their panel by attacking her credentials, but they were still trying to knock Donilski down with upcoding charges.

They hadn't yet figured out how to get rid of Krauss. He had the right credentials, and as an employee of the clinic, he wasn't doing his own billing. They were hoping he'd fall once they toppled Donilski.

Since his conversation with the woman in Doctor Tremont's waiting room about Doctor Krauss, Henry had read more about prolotherapy. It sounded unbelievable but he was desperate enough to try it. Even if it wasn't effective, there seemed little harm in it, and he'd found no other potential solution for his bad sacroiliac joint except the scary new surgical procedure. He started to scheme about going to see Doctor Krauss as Nicholas Johnson, the locksmith. He was pretty sure they'd never seen each other or had any direct dealings.

Donilski on the other hand might know what he looked like. Henry had given a presentation at a meeting of the local Pain Physicians' Association when he first came on board as medical director. He'd also had a phone conversation with Donilski when WhiteGuard began their investigation of his billing. It wasn't friendly.

Henry concluded that it wouldn't be worth the risk of getting recognized and caught using a phony identity. Another newspaper headline popped into his head: *WhiteGuard Medical Director Sneaks Treatment Insurer Denies to Patients.* He'd have to find a prolotherapist elsewhere. He went back to the Internet.

Within a reasonable distance, he could find only two other physicians advertising prolotherapy, and both probably knew who he was. His options seemed to boil down to taking more time off and going far away or finding some other therapy. Taking more time off would infuriate CLUJ. Eva had advised him that CLUJ was upset with his health issues. She didn't reveal that she'd been put on snitch patrol.

As Eva had previously suggested, Henry made an appointment to see the new physical medicine and rehab doc, Alan Crenshaw. Having opened his office just a few months previously, Crenshaw wasn't busy. Henry was able to get in immediately and Crenshaw was even willing to see him after work.

Henry had assumed that Crenshaw was young and recently trained. He was surprised to learn that the physician had already been practicing for a decade. Crenshaw had been employed by a rehab hospital. He left over a salary dispute and ventured into private practice.

Doctor Alan Crenshaw was unsure as to whether he should be flattered that the medical director of WhiteGuard was consulting him, or worried that he was being cased as someone who WhiteGuard planned to get rid of. He'd been very careful not to bill himself as a pain doctor because of the problems that insurers and regulators were causing those specialists. He promoted exercise and nutritional approaches instead of pain medicine for patients recovering from injuries.

The biggest part of Crenshaw's income came from doing diagnostic nerve conduction tests and steroid injections. He knew about prolotherapy, but had not sought the training. He saw no point in learning it because the insurers wouldn't pay for it. Maybe someday down the road when he was well established and could attract a cash clientele, he'd learn to do it, because he'd seen patients in the rehab hospital who'd had surprisingly good results from it. But for now, he was limiting his practice to treatments that produced income.

When Henry presented his history and theory that it was his sacroiliac joint that was causing his pain, Crenshaw felt inadequate. He used to work with a physical therapist who was talented at manipulating this joint, but he'd never been very good at himself. He suggested that they should try injecting anesthetic into the joint to see if that reduced Henry's pain. If so, then it would make sense to inject some steroid into the joint. He said he could get Henry into the fluoroscopy suite at the outpatient surgery center in about a week.

Henry knew that conventional doctors had developed a protocol for doing these injections with fluoroscopic x-ray guidance. In the past, such injections were done by manually feeling the joint. From his conversation with the woman in Tremont's waiting room, he assumed that her son had been injected by Krauss the old-fashioned way, since he knew that Donilski didn't have a fluoroscope, as did Millany and other interventionists. Crenshaw's practice probably didn't have enough income to purchase the expensive equipment.

WhiteGuard had struggled with the fluoroscopy issue for several years. Theoretically, fluoroscopy made injection procedures safer and more precise because the physician could see where the needle was, so 'fluoro' had become the standard of care. However, fluoro greatly increased the cost of doing injections, because of the high cost of the equipment, the personnel to operate it and the additional time needed to get the patient through the procedure.

It also seemed that once a physician purchased a fluoroscope, he would use it extensively to compensate for its cost, so he'd start to do all procedures with x-ray guidance, even simple injections that could readily be done without it. Before that trend became apparent, WhiteGuard had been denying reimbursement to doctors who didn't use fluoro, hoping they'd knock a bunch of them out of the game. Now it seemed the doctors who had bought the machine were costing them more. WhiteGuard's policy had backfired, and they couldn't figure out how to reverse the trend.

Adding to the controversy was the emergence of high-definition ultrasound, a superior imaging tool for guiding the placement of needles. Ultrasound eliminated the radiation risks to the patient and the practitioner, and better visualized soft tissue, such as nerves, muscles, tendons, and ligaments. But since most interventionists were now invested in their fluoroscopes, they were un-inclined to switch to the newer imaging tool. Fearing even more procedural costs, WhiteGuard had taken the position that ultrasound guided injections were not the standard of care, so they wouldn't pay for it; further discouraging physicians from switching. Ultimately, ever advancing medical technology may become unaffordable for all but the most elite.

Henry didn't know how he was going to solve this issue for WhiteGuard, but for himself, it seemed he had little choice but to take the time off and let Crenshaw stick some anesthetic in his sacroiliac under fluoroscopy. At least it might answer the question of the diagnosis. He was just so tired of the pain.

Chapter Sixty–Nine

Sean didn't get any noticeable relief from the new nerve-quieting drug. Just like the old one, it made him feel dizzy and stupid. He'd take parts out of a car and lose track of them. Doctor Krauss had said it might take some time to get used to the medicine and even more time to increase the dose to a level that would be beneficial. After two weeks of feeling like a stumbling airhead, Sean concluded he wouldn't be able to tolerate a higher dose. He tapered the medicine down and discontinued it.

His symptoms were worsening. Sharp shooting pains in his legs were becoming more frequent. The bizarre sensations he'd been having were getting more bizarre. Besides making him constipated and killing his sex drive, the Percocet made no difference at all, even if he doubled the dose, so he stopped it too.

He cancelled his follow-up appointment with Doctor Millany and scheduled an appointment with Doctor Krauss to try some more acupuncture. He felt somewhat better for a few days after the treatment and Doctor Krauss suggested he come in for acupuncture on a weekly basis for a few more weeks to see if it would control the pain. WhiteGuard wouldn't reimburse for acupuncture, but Doctor Krauss would accept the insurer's reimbursement for the visit and do the acupuncture for free.

After two more treatments, Sean thought it was well worth continuing. As Doctor Krauss had said, it wasn't going to cure him, but it did reduce some of the pain and the creepy crawly sensations that he had in his feet. It also seemed to improve his energy and mood.

The day before his next appointment Sean received a phone call from Tonya informing him that Doctor Krauss was no longer accepting

WhiteGuard insurance. He would have to pay the full price out of pocket. Visits ranged from $75-$500 depending on what the doctor did. Visits for acupuncture would be about $75-$100. Treating the sacroiliac again, as had been planned, would cost $300. Sean asked why Doctor Krauss was no longer taking the insurance, but Tonya would only say that it was a complicated issue, and the physicians were trying to resolve it.

Rosemary was greatly dismayed by the news. Paying for the nanny was already beyond her means. Her husband was a general contractor and while his business had been good in the early spring when they hired Polly, a slowdown in the local housing market was starting to impact their income. Normally he'd have jobs lined up for the fall, but now in the prime of the construction season, high interest rates were keeping people from building.

Rosemary called Krauss's office to try to understand what was going on with reimbursement and see if she could do something to resolve it. Tonya explained that it really didn't have much to do with Doctor Krauss, except that he worked for Doctor Donilski who was involved in a legal dispute with WhiteGuard. The insurer was accusing Donilski of over-billing, and they were demanding that he pay them back more than he'd actually earned the previous year. He was trying to fight them in court, but his lawyer had said it could take years to resolve. In the meantime, he had to stop accepting the insurance. He could no longer afford to get cheated out of reimbursements and simultaneously pay a lawyer to fight his case.

Rosemary couldn't really blame Krauss and his partner, but she was outraged that the insurer was causing trouble for the only physician who had helped her son. She decided to take the matter up with WhiteGuard directly. She spent hours on the phone explaining to a patient advocate and then a nurse, and then another nurse, that Doctor Krauss was the only physician who'd made a proper diagnosis and provided effective treatment. She begged them to either straighten things out with Krauss or refer Sean to someone else on their panel who knew how to help him.

It didn't seem to matter who she spoke with, she got nowhere. She called repeatedly for a few more days, hoping to speak with someone with a heart and a conscience, but all she got was the same run around. Finally, she threatened to sue. She was then offered an appointment to speak with Eva Rodeki, Director of Provider Partnerships.

Chapter Seventy

Henry was in a quandary about whether to have Doctor Crenshaw do a sacroiliac injection or see if Doctor Millany could do the same thing. He called Millany and asked him what his experience was with the procedure. Millany claimed to have done some and it was something he knew how to do. Henry sensed that Crenshaw also wasn't very experienced with the procedure.

While he was debating his options, his medication appointment with Doctor Millany came up. He'd gotten used to the methadone to the extent that he was now willing to stick with it. Researching the topic, he'd come to understand that alcohol mixed with methadone increased the blood level of methadone. The combination was giving him some decent pain relief for his difficult afternoons.

As Doctor Millany was writing his methadone prescription, Henry noticed a pile of articles on his desk on the topic of sacroiliac dysfunction. Millany had deliberately left the papers there so that Henry would think he was knowledgeable about it. It worked. Henry was impressed enough that he decided to have Millany do the procedure, and Millany agreed to treat him on the following Saturday morning, saving Henry the problem of having to take off from work.

What Henry didn't know, was that Doctor Millany had been studying the subject to discern if Sean Garmen could sue him for missing the diagnosis.

Henry skipped his methadone on the morning of the procedure. He wanted to be sure his pain was full bore so he could tell if the joint injection helped. Within a few minutes of the anesthetic being instilled in his sacroiliac, he noticed a definite improvement, especially for sitting.

"That's what we hoped for," Doctor Millany remarked, "so let's put some steroid in there."

Henry balked. "You know, Leonard, I've read quite a bit about prolotherapy and it's making me wonder if we should avoid using a steroid. These prolotherapy people believe that steroids weaken the joint in the long run; they claim that their prolo solutions strengthen the joint. It's really starting to make me wonder."

Leonard Millany picked up the pile of articles on his desk. "I've been looking into this myself, Henry. All these articles from the top journals refer to using steroids. I saw something in my Internet search about treating the joint with prolotherapy, but there's not much data to support it.

"When you think about it, if you loosened up that joint when you fell, the bone surfaces have been rubbing against each other for all these months that you've been walking around with the problem. Wouldn't you think there's some inflammation in there? One dose of steroids isn't going to weaken the joint, and it just might help. Are you sure you don't want to try standard care before going alternative?

"Besides, WhiteGuard isn't going to pay for this if I inject a prolo solution into your joint. It would put us both in an awkward situation if someone in your case review department should happen to read the record."

"I suppose you're right, Leonard. Let's see if the steroid might help. I can't take this pain anymore." As he positioned himself back on the fluoroscopy table for the injection, Henry wondered if CLUJ had someone in the case review department reading the records of all his doctor visits. Unless he started seeking care under an alias, CLUJ could know every detail of his personal medical life.

"How much would you charge for this if I was uninsured?" Henry asked.

Doctor Millany said he wasn't sure how the insurer would pay for this particular injection, but for large joint injections under the fluoroscope, he usually charged about $1,200 and the insurers reimbursed about half. Medicare paid less and he wouldn't even do this for a Medicaid patient because the reimbursement was so poor.

For an uninsured patient, he'd charge about $500. Just not having to put in a claim to the insurer saved him time, money, and aggravation. On the other hand, he didn't accept uninsured patients unless they came highly recommended by other physicians. Too many of them didn't pay their bills on time or didn't pay at all. Some big insurers took months to a year to reimburse providers.

Chapter Seventy-One

Rosemary and Sean had taken the afternoon off from their jobs to meet with WhiteGuard's Director of Provider Partnerships. There appointment was at two pm and they arrived early to make sure they could find their way around. WhiteGuard's offices were in a huge white building with glaring glass that could be seen long distance along the highway. The logo on top of the building was two stories high.

They encountered the first security check in the parking lot. They were given access when they told the guard they had an appointment with Doctor Eva Rodeki.

They had to park a long way from the entrance. As Rosemary watched Sean limp past the posh fountains and gardens surrounding the building, she had two thoughts. One was that the insurer's facility reeked of wealth. The second was that her son needed a handicapped-parking permit.

Once inside, they had to go through more security, walking through a magnetometer, identifying themselves with their driver licenses, and being given name tags containing chips that they were instructed to wear at all times they were in the building. "You'd think we were visiting the Pentagon," Sean commented.

"Well, they piss so many people off, they're probably afraid someone's going to walk in here with a weapon and blow them all the way." Rosemary whispered, "It's something I've thought of doing myself." As she spoke, she looked around for a microphone. She spotted several surveillance cameras.

Their appointment time came and went. In an hour, only one of the several people in the waiting area was taken elsewhere by a staff member. It was almost three pm when a woman in a business suit came and escorted them to an office on the fourth floor. She introduced herself as Kelsey Ashton, Doctor Rodeki's assistant, and told them she was very sorry that Doctor Rodeki was dealing with an emergency and could not meet with them this afternoon.

"Why weren't we notified?" Rosemary was almost shaking. "We waited ten days for this appointment and we both took off from work to get here. And that's after spending a week trying to resolve this over the phone. I was told by two different people that Doctor Rodeki was the person I'd have to talk to."

"I don't blame you for being upset. Unfortunately, this emergency came up just about the same time Doctor Rodeki was going to meet with you. It's just the nature of healthcare that emergencies arise without notice. Please let me assure you that I can do whatever Doctor Rodeki can do. We work in the same capacity and we both take patient concerns very seriously.

"Your issue must clearly have merit for our staff to have scheduled you to see Doctor Rodeki. We understand that your time is valuable and it's my intention to make the best use of it while you're here. Now, why don't you explain things to me in detail so I can see how best I can help."

Rosemary could smell the platitudes in Kelsey Ashton's words, and she was starting to suspect that this was all part of the insurer's stalling tactics. She had dealt with enough dental insurance representatives over her career to know that stalling was their primary weapon for trying to avoid having to accommodate their customers. Kelsey Ashton was coming across as a top-notch staller.

"So how long will I have to wait to see Doctor Rodeki?"

Kelsey hadn't expected this response, but saw it as an opportunity to stall things some more. "If you can excuse me for a minute, I'll go check and see."

She left the office and used the time to go to the bathroom. Kelsey and Eva had already reviewed Sean Garmen's records and all the notes from the call center staff on his mother's complaints, and they had no solution for him, other than to tell him he would have to pay out of pocket to see Doctor Krauss, or anyone else who did acupuncture.

Kelsey would emphasize that it was Doctor Krauss and his partner who had stopped accepting WhiteGuard insurance, and not the insurer who caused this issue. Their only real purpose in bringing the Garmens to the appointment was to get a feel for how likely this family was to start a lawsuit. Their legal department advisor was sure they wouldn't get anywhere with a suit, but it would tie up another attorney.

Kelsey returned and advised them that Doctor Rodeki's schedule was pretty backed up and it might be another week until she could make them an appointment to see her. Rosemary knew the insurer could play this game for months. She decided to just use this appointment to make the request that the insurer make a policy exception on Sean's behalf.

Kelsey played along with her best looks of concern and compassion. She listened to their story and diligently took notes. In the end, she agreed that Sean's circumstances were exceptional. She offered that she understood that arachnoiditis was a devastating condition that had no standard answers, and she promised she would have the medical director personally review the case.

"And how long will that take?" Rosemary asked.

"Doctor Winslow is a very, very busy man, but I promise you, I'll bring this to his attention immediately."

Rosemary flipped through her notebook to the visit with the cardiologist. That was the name. "Did you say Doctor Winslow?" Rosemary told herself it must be a common name and it had to be a coincidence, but she inquired anyway. "That wouldn't be Henry Winslow, would it?"

"You *know* Doctor Winslow?" Kelsey asked suspiciously.

"If it's Doctor Winslow who's about sixty, great head of silver hair, walks with a limp and has shaky hands, I do."

Kelsey was flustered. Most people claiming to know executives only knew names on the Internet. "That sounds like our medical director. How do you know Doctor Winslow?"

Rosemary thought that maybe there was some hope. "Just tell Doctor Winslow that the woman from the cardiology office is the person whose son got treated by Doctor Krauss for a bad sacroiliac."

Kelsey's jaw dropped.

Sean had difficulty walking as they left the WhiteGuard offices.

Chapter Seventy-Two

Henry's visit to Nanette Tremont opened another can of worms. Despite all the high blood pressure readings that Eva had taken, his blood pressure was on the low side in the cardiologist's office. To figure things out, Tremont had Henry wear a monitor to see what his blood pressure looked like over a twenty-four-hour period. The results only added confusion. His heart rate and blood pressure jumped around erratically throughout the day.

Doctor Tremont found out that Henry was now on methadone, which could slow his heart rate or lower his blood pressure. Henry was too embarrassed to admit to drinking alcohol at lunch and in the evening, which even he could see made his heart rate speed up.

Doctor Tremont changed his medicine and Henry hoped that would solve the problem. His pain did best when he mixed his methadone with bourbon. He also rationalized that pain increased his heart rate and blood pressure, so it didn't make sense to stop the regimen that was helping his pain. Tremont recommended that he return with two weeks' more blood pressure readings.

During the week after Doctor Millany had performed his sacroiliac injection, Henry's blood pressure continued to be erratic. What pain relief he had from the procedure ended as soon as the anesthetic wore off. He knew the steroids could take a few days to work, but they didn't. He hurt as much as ever and concluded that inflammation was not the cause of the pain. Short of risky surgery, prolotherapy seemed like his best hope.

Just as he was reconsidering trying to sneak into to see Doctor Krauss, Kelsey Ashton presented him with the case of Sean Garmen. It seemed a strange coincidence that the case of the man whose mother said Doctor Krauss had helped, would land on his desk just as he was pondering how to go see Krauss himself.

While he knew about Garmen's sacroiliac problem from his conversation with the mother in Tremont's waiting room, he didn't know this guy also had arachnoiditis. He had to review the subject. It wasn't something he had encountered when he was operating on backs. He started to wonder how many of his patients who complained that the surgery had made them worse, might have had arachnoiditis and weren't diagnosed. Poor bastards, he thought. He consoled himself that even if they had this condition and he'd recognized it, there wasn't anything he could have done about it.

Henry asked Kelsey to scan the data banks for arachnoiditis in patient records. He was curious to see what doctors in the community were doing with such patients, and how much those people were costing WhiteGuard. Maybe, if the insurer was spending big dollars on such patients, he could make a case for WhiteGuard allowing an exception to policies on acupuncture for someone like Sean Garmen. Having met the Garmens, he felt a little more responsible for them than he would otherwise feel towards someone with this level of misfortune.

Henry thumbed through Kelsey's notes a little more carefully. He was struck by the fact that Doctor Burke had likely done an unnecessary surgery on Garmen. It did appear that it was Doctor Millany's steroid shots that caused the arachnoiditis. Sean Garmen was a medical disaster. There was nothing in the complaint about the heart problems. He told Kelsey to find out why Garmen was seeing Nanette Tremont.

He couldn't stop thinking about how oddly coincidental it was that Garmen's and his paths had crossed in so many places, and now they were both frustrated that they couldn't obtain care from the one physician who seemed to be able to help them.

Chapter Seventy-Three

Three weeks went by and the Garmens still hadn't heard anything from WhiteGuard. Rosemary had called back repeatedly, only to be told by Kelsey Ashton that Sean's case was being researched by Doctor Winslow. On another occasion, she was told that Doctor Winslow had to meet with Doctor Krauss to further assess the situation, and that Doctor Krauss was so busy that they were having trouble scheduling.

Rosemary found out that was a big fat lie by speaking with Tonya. There were also times she was put on hold for so long that she had to hang up. It appeared that WhiteGuard planned to stall until they just went away.

Rosemary started to hunt for an attorney. The first few she spoke with seemed reluctant to go after WhiteGuard. They warned her that suing a huge corporation could be very difficult. WhiteGuard had a monstrous legal department, and they could keep filing motions and drag a case out indefinitely.

Corporate law protected the company in that it was not obliged to offer services that were not in their client's contracts. The insurance industry was unregulated and there were no laws that protected health insurance consumers from insurers making arbitrary decisions about what a patient needed. It all seemed very discouraging.

Through one of her dental patients, Rosemary was given the name of a lawyer named Andrea Valentine. Mrs. Valentine had won a suit against WhiteGuard on behalf of the family of a patient who had sustained a serious head injury. During the critical phase of the man's care, the insurer had denied coverage for the man to be transferred to an intensive care unit that had the expertise to properly manage his condition. The rural hospital that tried to take care of him wasn't equipped to provide the level of care he needed. After the family pleaded with the insurer to authorize the transfer for two days, the man died just minutes before a WhiteGuard representative gave consent.

When Rosemary first met with Andrea Valentine, she thought the woman was too young and too nice to do battle with WhiteGuard, but a half-hour into the interview, she felt maybe she had come to the right person.

Andrea Valentine's father had died from Hodgkin's Disease when Andrea was twelve. He died just after his health insurer denied coverage for the only treatment that might have saved him. This attorney was passionate about not letting wealthy insurance companies take people's money and then deny them appropriate care, while paying their top executives huge salaries and bonuses for increasing profits to shareholders.

Andrea didn't know much about Sean's health problems, but she promised Rosemary that she'd research them carefully and let them know if they had a case. She thought if nothing else, they could go after Burke. She'd research that as well.

In the interim, Sean's symptoms worsened. On several occasions, his legs felt so weak that they buckled, and he'd lose balance. One day, he hurt his right hand catching himself on a car to keep from landing on concrete. The hand swelled up badly. A classic "boxer's fracture" showed on x-ray.

Sean was referred to a hand specialist who manipulated the bone back into alignment, splinted it and told him to return the next day so to see if the bone ends stayed together. They didn't. The metacarpals had to be surgically pinned, especially because Sean used his hands so much. He'd be in a cast for six weeks.

Arthur took it in stride. Once again, they arranged for Sean to work as diagnostician with the rest of them doing the manual labor. Arthur saw it as an opportunity to have his apprentice, Kenny, work one on one with Sean. When there were no tough problems to be solved, Arthur insisted that Sean go home.

When the pain medicine from his hand surgery was exhausted, Sean turned back to drinking beer. It didn't really help his leg or hand pain very much, but it seemed to take the edge off his depression.

Chapter Seventy-Four

One of WhiteGuard's lawyers advised Doctor Winslow that he needed some information for a meeting he was scheduled to have with Doctor Donilski about the upcoding accusations. The attorney wanted Henry to clarify the definition of a certain kind of nerve block for which WhiteGuard had accused the physician of over-billing.

The meeting would be held on a Thursday in August. Henry took the opportunity to see if he could get an appointment with Doctor Krauss on the same day that Donilski would be out of the office. He succeeded.

Henry presented himself to Krauss as Nicholas Johnson, an uninsured locksmith with pain in his low back, buttock, and left leg. He claimed that his back surgery had been done a year ago and it hadn't helped. He reported that his old MRI and x-ray reports had been lost, and he was unable to afford new studies.

Although he had been advised that Donilski and Krauss were very thorough, Henry wasn't prepared for the kind of physical exam that Krauss did. He was amazed at how much time Krauss spent feeling each backbone individually. He was intrigued when Doctor Krauss commented that the vertebra treated with kyphoplasty felt "somewhat unusual." Henry played ignorant, but after Krauss questioned him some more, Henry said they did something to cement a fracture.

Henry wasn't at all surprised when Krauss told him that his pain was coming from a damaged sacroiliac joint. The only other junction between the spine and the lower body skeleton was the sacroiliac joint on the other side, and in his fall, Henry might have roughed that one up too.

Of course, Henry agreed to a diagnostic anesthetic injection followed by prolotherapy, after Krauss manipulated the joint back into alignment. Henry was both overjoyed at the reduction of pain and astounded by his own ignorance. The five hundred he paid out of pocket seemed like a bargain for the time and care that this physician had provided. He was ecstatic to observe that some of his original pain was gone by the end of the week.

The pain from the kyphoplasty cement leakage persisted, but the pain that started after his fall was noticeably improved. He couldn't wait to see how much more of his pain could be erased if he went back for a second prolotherapy injection. His long-ingrained faith in conventional orthopedics had been shattered.

On the same day that Henry went to see Doctor Krauss, Kelsey Ashton came to Eva with a twinkle in her eye. She announced that she thought she'd found a way for WhiteGuard to get rid of Donilski and Krauss.

When going over the notes she had taken from interviewing Sean Garmen, she concluded that these physicians were doing nerve blocks primarily to get reimbursed for what they were really doing, which was prolotherapy. She had looked at the notes from Sean Garmen's second visit for his sacro-iliac injection and they clearly indicated that a prolotherapy solution had been administered to the joint after an anesthetic injection. However, the billing code that Krauss had submitted to WhiteGuard indicated that he had only done a nerve block. Kelsey had examined a few other patient records, and after interviewing those patients, she was persuaded that this was a pattern.

Eva had already considered Kelsey's hypothesis and hoped that no one else would notice. When she'd first consulted Donilski as Lisa Banks, the doctor had said that he would do a nerve block first and she'd have no pain with acupuncture. He had specifically said that her insurance would pay for the nerve block and the acupuncture was for free. Later, as a self-pay patient, she underwent acupuncture treatments without nerve blocks, and she came to understand that nerve blocks before other treatments weren't always necessary. Initially she had thought this was just Doctor Donilski's approach to reducing patient anxiety, but she had come to understand that this was his tactic for getting paid.

Eva believed it was justifiable. Had Donilski not performed a procedure that WhiteGuard reimbursed for, WhiteGuard's patients who couldn't afford to pay out of pocket, would not be able to avail themselves of his exceptional knowledge and skills. WhiteGuard on the other hand, had the power to choose which ingredients they would pay for a physician to inject, even if their preferred ingredients didn't help the patient and had harmful side effects.

Eva had always believed physician compensation should be based on having the knowledge and skills and investing the time to make proper diagnosis and provide effective treatment. Instead, it was based on which pharmaceutical or technology was utilized. There would be no argument from the insurer if Krauss had first put anesthetic in the joint and then followed it with a steroid injection. He'd get paid for doing both. It was the height of hypocrisy for the same patient to not get benefits for a nerve block performed by Krauss for another purpose, and one that was more beneficial to the patient and for a lower cost. But Kelsey was gloating to have identified contractual legalese that would enable WhiteGuard to label "free treatment" as insurance fraud.

Eva knew that CLUJ and his legal eagles would embrace Kelsey's theory. She stayed late that day, pouring over the clinical notes that WhiteGuard had obtained in their audit of Donilski. His notes were too scant and illegible to make much sense of, but Doctors Krauss and Nagel documented more thoroughly, and their notes supported Kelsey's premise.

If Eva didn't take her assistant's conclusion to CLUJ herself, there was little doubt that Kelsey would do so behind her back. Kelsey wanted Eva's job.

Chapter Seventy-Five

During the weeks that Sean's right hand was casted, his leg symptoms continued to worsen. The tendency to weakness was getting so bad that he was afraid to stand up anywhere that he couldn't reach for something to support himself. His ability to obtain an erection was totally gone and his bladder function was also troublesome. He bought some incontinence underwear.

His Mustang project remained his chief interest, but it had also become his chief escape route. He'd hang out in his garage the entire day while Darcy was at work and Polly tended to his children. Half the time he'd work on the car, trying to use just his good hand. The rest of his time was devoted either to obtaining or drinking beer. A deli within a short distance of his home sold cold beer, and he kept a small cooler in the trunk of the Mustang to keep it chilled. By mid-afternoon he'd have polished off a six-pack. He'd try to nap until evening to be sure that he wouldn't smell of beer by the time Darcy got home. Polly would leave as soon as Darcy arrived, at which point he'd return to the garage and take a few bong hits. As best as he could tell, neither Darcy nor Polly had caught onto his routine.

Corey knew what was going on though. On those days when he'd pick Sean up to bring him to the garage to figure out a car problem, he could tell that his buddy had been drinking. Sean wouldn't seem intoxicated, but Corey detected those behavioral nuances that Rosemary had observed when Sean first turned to alcohol. He worried about it, but not to the extent that he was worried about Sean's physical condition. It was obvious that his buddy was having trouble walking, even early in the morning before he went out for his six-pack. He tried to ask him about it, but all he got was denial.

Darcy was also in denial. She kept telling herself that as soon as Sean was out of his cast and he could return to work, he'd be okay. She reasoned that it was not being able to work that made him so sullen and withdrawn, and that depression was the cause of the distance that had stretched between them. She hoped that when he got the cast off his hand, things would improve.

Andrea Valentine didn't have good news for Rosemary. According to her research, sacroiliac dysfunction was not a clear-cut issue. There was little agreement amongst medical experts as to its diagnosis and treatment, so it wouldn't be easy to accuse Doctors Burke or Millany of missing it.

Andrea also couldn't find much data to support the use of acupuncture for the treatment of arachnoiditis. She had talked to a few pain specialists who validated that acupuncture could help pain regardless of its cause, but there was just too little published on the topic. Acupuncture's acceptance in most of the world and even in some of the more progressive states, hadn't influenced local health insurers.

Andrea was still looking into the possibility that WhiteGuard could be sued for discriminating against patients who chose to treat chronic pain with acupuncture rather than narcotics. She had found data that clearly indicated that medication was more harmful and ultimately more costly to the insurance industry. She promised she'd get back to Rosemary after she did a little more investigation, but she wanted her to know the reality of the situation.

Sean was making extraordinary effort to conceal his drinking from his mother. He'd completely avoid drinking on Sundays when she'd come to visit. His mother had suffered too tragic a life already and he didn't want to upset her. She was already too distressed to see Sean declining so rapidly. She begged him to return to Doctor Krauss. She had enough money to pay for his visits after cashing in some savings bonds. There seemed no hope of being able to get the insurer to cover the costs. She was terrified that he might be drinking again.

Chapter Seventy-Six

CLUJ was joyful when Eva presented Kelsey's data about questionable billing by Donilski's practice. They had also checked on the bills from the family practice doctor that Donilski had trained and saw the same pattern, so they believed they could now get rid of the whole lot of them.

WhiteGuard's lawyers agreed. This wasn't just a case of upcoding, charging for a more complicated procedure. This was coding for one kind of treatment and doing something else. Fraud charges could be justified, and even if they lost that argument in the end, it would save them a ton of money for the years of court battle that would keep these doctors dysfunctional.

Eva was astonished when Henry argued with the plan and took the side of Donilski. He opined that the charts he'd reviewed showed that these doctors were doing legitimate nerve blocks. Henry thought it would be prudent to first assess what WhiteGuard's risks might be for calling in the Feds on fraud charges, should these physicians be able to find lawyers that could successfully refute the accusation of fraudulent billing.

Clinton Sperling countered that the risks to WhiteGuard were minimal. He knew of cases where accusations like this proved wrong and nothing had happened to the accusers. Sperling mentioned the case of an elderly physician whose billing service had repeatedly typed the wrong code number on insurance claims. It appeared that the physician was billing for a major surgical procedure when he was doing a minor one. The insurer never went to the physician to ask him why his notes didn't match the code numbers on his bills. They just assumed he was being dishonest and they sicced the fraud division of the FBI on him.

Agents with firearms barged into his office, seized his records, and threw him in jail where he had a stroke and died.

Later, it was learned that a new employee in the billing office had simply been typing a 23 instead of a 32 when she transcribed the multi-digit code numbers from the doctor's notes onto the claim forms. The doctor's widow tried to sue the Feds and the insurer, but six years after she filed the suit, the court determined that the fraud investigation was justified, and it was the physician's fault for not proofreading the claims that he paid the billing service to do for him.

In one of the few instances where falsely accused persons had successfully sued the government, it took nine years for the courts to settle the matter in the prosecution's favor. Sperling thought it was highly unlikely that Donilski and his partners could find an attorney who was bold and savvy enough to do it.

CLUJ was wringing his hands with excitement. He thought getting rid of these proliferating pain doctors was essential for their profit margin. Henry's words of caution were summarily dismissed.

As soon as Henry left the meeting, he called Krauss's office to try to get an appointment for another sacroiliac injection. He figured he had to get in there before these unfortunate physicians' practices and lives hit the skids. He didn't care whether he ran into Donilski or not. With a little bit of pleading and the luck of a cancellation, he was able to get an appointment for the end of the week.

What Henry hadn't factored into his plan was the speed with which the FBI jumped on the accusation that WhiteGuard had just made. He thought the federal agency would be busy with bigger cases and it would take them a long time before they got around to this small medical practice. Very wrong assumption!

Henry was lying on Krauss's table with a needle in his butt when two badge waving agents snapped a photo of him, ordered Krauss to take the needle out and place the syringe in an evidence bag, along with the medical chart of Nicholas Johnson. Henry was left to put his pants back on as Doctor Krauss was led away in handcuffs. Henry tried to be invisible as he walked past a crying Tonya who was handing over records to another FBI agent, but he was photographed again. He didn't know that he was photographed a third time on his way out the door.

Marty Ipolis, a reporter for the *MidWestern Weekly News* just happened to be heading into the phone store next to Donilski's office when he saw the doctors being led away in handcuffs by the men in suits. There were pictures of the physicians in the back of a big black car, and pictures of Henry and another patient that exited after Henry, accompanying the front-page story that the editor published a few days later.

Chapter Seventy-Seven

Sean returned to work on the same day that his cast was cut off. Autumn was a busy time for the Toblers as people who planned to trade their vehicles in for new models sought to make repairs they'd been meaning to make all year.

It only took a few hours for Arthur to realize that Sean wasn't going to be able to work at his usual pace. His right hand was stiff and had lost strength. He still needed help with manual tasks. More concerning though, was his walking and standing. He seemed okay when he was bending over an engine, but Arthur got nervous watching him standing under a car jacked up on the hydraulic. Sean stood with his legs wide apart and he occasionally teetered. When Arthur suggested that Ryan take over on the lifted car, Sean acted like a beaten puppy.

Corey observed the interchange between his father and friend and tried to distract Sean by asking him to help with another vehicle, but his friend continued to brood. After Sean and Darcy left for the day, Arthur confronted his sons.

"I'm not sure this is going to work anymore with Sean, boys. I think I'm going to have to start looking for another mechanic. We've waited so long to get him back and I just don't think he's going to be able to keep up anymore."

Ryan agreed. Corey didn't.

"It's only his first day out of the cast, Dad. You've got to give him more time. That hand will be much better in a week or two."

"Yeah, but did you see how bad his balance is? Unless he's holding on to something, he's not steady on his feet. I'm scared for him, Corey. What's he going to break next time he goes down? He looks like he could wind up in a wheelchair. I can't see him being able to work around here if he's in a wheelchair.

"I don't think this situation is good for him and it's certainly not good for us. I have to start looking for someone else. I know he's your good buddy, Corey. I love Sean too. But we all have to make a living here. I can't keep turning customers away because I don't have enough staff."

"Dad's right, Corey. I've got a baby on the way and I'm going to have to help Chloe more at home. I can't keep working until eight o'clock every other night."

"Ryan makes a good point, but Dad, we've waited so long already; just give him a little more time. Kenny's terrific and he learns fast. He could become a great mechanic with more experience. If Sean isn't doing better in a few weeks, then I won't argue with you, but after all he's been through; you can't let him go without giving him more of a chance. I know this job means everything to him, and I really don't think you're going to find anyone anywhere as smart as Sean."

Arthur agreed to postpone his search for a replacement for Sean if Corey was willing to put in the extra time to keep up with the work. Corey amazed him by promising he would.

After work, Corey went to see the Garmens. He and Sean went out for a beer and with considerable coaxing, Corey got Sean to admit that his legs were weak, and he really was afraid of falling. He didn't know if he could work anymore.

Then, they got an idea. They went back to the garage and built Sean a standing support out of a rolling dolly, so he could lean against a backboard while underneath a lifted car. They put side rails on it and a hand lever to lock the wheels. They added weight to the frame to make sure it wouldn't tip. Corey went home with the satisfied feeling that they had solved a serious problem.

Sean stayed and designed a secret storage area under a workbench in the back storeroom. He stocked it with a couple of water bottles filled with vodka. He didn't think it smelled as obvious as beer.

Chapter Seventy-Eight

Before anyone at WhiteGuard saw Henry's picture in the Monday edition of the *MidWest Weekly News*, phones were ringing off the hook from upset patients who had shown up at Donilski's office to find it locked up. Even WhiteGuard hadn't expected the FBI to act so quickly, and they hadn't yet formulated their back-up plan for the abandoned patients.

There were now no pain physicians left on WhiteGuard's provider panel who were willing to accept new patients, especially those taking narcotic pain medicine. These patients were desperate and enraged and things were getting ugly at WhiteGuard's call center.

It was a very distressed patient who told Kelsey Ashton that she'd read about her doctor being arrested in the *MidWest Weekly News*. She had an appointment with him tomorrow and if she couldn't get in to see her doctor, she was going to commit suicide. Kelsey called 911 to have a paramedic team go evaluate the woman. Then Kelsey left the building and picked up a copy of the newspaper at a local convenience store to see what this little publication had been able to learn about the FBI raid.

At first, she couldn't believe her eyes. Then she couldn't fathom how Henry Winslow's picture accompanied the story. The caption under his and another person's picture read: *Doctor Arrests Leave Patients in Distress.*

The reporter had interviewed another patient who'd been photographed leaving the office after Henry. She was a schoolteacher who told Marty Ipolis that she'd been in a car accident and had suffered from neck pain and headaches for two decades before coming to Doctor Donilski. She'd had two neck surgeries that hadn't helped. One made her worse. She'd been seeing Donilski for just three months and he'd helped her more than any of the several dozen other clinicians that she'd seen over the years. She told the reporter that her doctor was arrested in the middle of doing an injection to her neck. She didn't know why he'd been arrested.

Kelsey took the newspaper to Eva who took it to Henry. By the look on his face, she knew he was guilty of something, she just didn't know what. She wondered if he'd gone there to warn the physicians, although she couldn't imagine why he'd do that. Thinking about his reluctance to make the fraud accusation, she wondered if he might have gone there for treatment. She kept her thoughts to herself.

Henry stammered, "How the hell did they get a picture of me in this story?"

Eva responded that she hoped he had a good explanation because she had just heard from another distressed patient trying to go to her appointment with Doctor Krauss that morning, that the press was hanging out in front of the locked-up office. "This story will be all over the news by tonight," Eva predicted.

Henry studied the picture. He was in the doorway and the doctors' names could be seen on the glass panel next to the door. He racked his brain for an alibi. The best he could come up with was that he was taking his cellular to the phone store next door. When he saw the commotion going on in the doctors' office; he went to see what was happening.

That didn't make sense. He should have known what was happening. The lawyers at WhiteGuard would think that under the circumstances, he'd have gotten as far away from what was happening there as quickly as possible.

He didn't have much chance to think about it further. Kelsey knocked on his door to say there were some reporters in the lobby, and one of them was demanding to speak with Doctor Winslow. Henry suggested that they be told that he wasn't in.

"That won't work Doctor Winslow. I went down there to try to cover for you, but that Marty Ipolis who wrote the story for *Midwest Weekly News,* apparently has a picture of you getting into your car and another picture of your car and license plate. He's figured out who you are and that you're here. There's another guy down there from the local TV station who's asking why the WhiteGuard medical director was present when the doctors got raided by the FBI. We need an explanation and fast."

Henry went to the window and saw two different TV network trucks. His heart was beating very fast. His brain felt like it was sparking trying to think of what to say to keep the media from drawing their own scandalous conclusions.

"Just tell them I'm not available this minute, but that we'll release a statement within the hour."

He was about to head for Clinton Sperling's office for help when CLUJ came storming into his office with his booming voice, demanding to know what the hell was going on.

Henry's pounding heart felt like it was going to burst out of his chest when he started to answer that he could explain everything. He said two more words, clutched his chest, and collapsed.

Chapter Seventy-Nine

The support stand that Corey and Sean constructed worked very well, but Sean didn't. He'd start out on-task at a reasonable pace in the morning, but by the middle of the day, he'd slow down, and he kept making uncharacteristic mistakes.

If any of the customers paid too much attention to Darcy at the front desk, he'd drop whatever he was doing to monitor the situation. Within the course of just a week, there'd been some occasions where he'd made customers uncomfortable and left Darcy embarrassed. Darcy's distress over Sean's deterioration, and his jealousy over the attention she was getting, festered into a smoldering hostility between them.

Arthur's level of concern went way up when the owner of a Corvette came back complaining that his vehicle was running worse than when he first brought it in. His original complaint was that the engine was vibrating when the car idled. Sean had replaced a worn engine mount but when Corey reassessed the problem, it was evident that Sean hadn't tightened it down. It was an inexcusable mistake, and the customer was furious. He'd come two hundred miles for Toblers' expertise. He promised to write about his bad experience to a Corvette specialty publication and a website that listed Toblers as one of the top Corvette mechanics in the region.

Then the owner of a turbo diesel Peugeot presented with a stalling problem. Sean changed the cold start relay and the heater plugs, but failed to tighten a wire to the new relay. The car was being driven by the owner's son when it stalled on the top of a hill and got rear-ended, causing a whiplash injury. The owner, who happened to be an attorney, wanted Toblers to buy him a brand-new Peugeot or he'd "sue their asses off." Offers to completely rebuild his ten-year-old vehicle and pay for medical expenses wouldn't satisfy him.

Arthur was most distressed by Sean's attitude. The old Sean would have been mortified and apologetic. He would have wanted to pay for the damages. The current Sean didn't appear remorseful. He just went back to sucking on his water bottle like it didn't matter.

Corey asked Darcy what she thought was going on. She confessed that the doctors had warned them that there could be mental or emotional changes with arachnoiditis. She didn't know if it was the arachnoiditis or if he was just depressed. She also felt like he had morphed into someone she didn't know and didn't want to be with.

The final straw came when apprentice Kenny mistakenly took a slug from Sean's water bottle and announced to the whole crew that it tasted like alcohol. Even Corey couldn't defend Sean anymore. His head knew that his friend was causing them more trouble than he was worth, but in his heart, he felt that Sean was still worth trying to save. He went to his father and told him to order Sean to go to another doctor and find out if his mental lapses could be remedied before they made the final decision. He went back to Darcy and told her their plan and she agreed.

Darcy was grateful. She and Rosemary had been trying to get Sean to go seek help for his depression and he had outright refused. She thought their only hope was for Arthur to give him an ultimatum. She didn't even want to be present when Arthur confronted him. Her good-natured, sweet-dispositioned husband had developed a mean temper and could fly off the handle over anything. The kids and she had been trying to avoid him for weeks, for fear of triggering his anger.

It was a Friday afternoon in late September when Arthur told Sean he either had to get help or get out. Sean left the garage without saying a word. When he hadn't come home by nine o'clock that night and wasn't answering his cell phone, Darcy called all the Toblers. They had not seen nor heard from him since he left, after Arthur had given him the final warning. Neither had Rosemary or Sean's brother or any of his friends.

By Saturday afternoon, they filed a missing person report with the police.

Chapter Eighty

Henry found out what had happened to him by watching the evening news from his hospital bed. The first segment of the story showed angry patients being interviewed outside Donilski's office. Interviewees claimed that the doctors in this practice were the only ones that had ever helped them, and they were devastated when they arrived to find the office locked up.

The reporter who had been stationed in the strip mall parking lot said he'd heard the same thing from patient after patient who'd come to their appointment, not knowing their doctors had been arrested until he intercepted them. None of them knew why their doctors should have had any trouble with the law. All of them were upset or outraged to learn their doctors could be in jail.

The second segment of the news piece came from a reporter standing outside the WhiteGuard building. She said that the station had learned that the medical director of WhiteGuard knew what had happened to the arrested doctors. A news team had come to WhiteGuard's offices to interview him. Just as they were setting up cameras, an ambulance arrived. Moments later, a security guard ordered the news people to get out of the way so a critically ill patient could be transferred into the ambulance. The cameraman was able to get a few seconds of film that showed a man on a stretcher having a seizure. When they got back to the studio, the man was identified as Doctor Henry Winslow, the medical director of WhiteGuard, the same individual they'd come to interview. He was now hospitalized.

The three seconds of film showing him having a seizure gave Henry the creeps. He hoped he was unrecognizable unless someone studied single frames of the footage. It was a gross invasion of his privacy, like the picture in the *MidWest Weekly News*. Did having an important job really mean he was a public figure, an object of curiosity?

The anchorman gave a third segment of the story. He told viewers that according to a WhiteGuard spokesperson, Doctor Winslow who was photographed at the scene of the doctor's arrest, was there by coincidence. He was actually on his way to the phone store next door. According to the spokesperson, the arrest of the doctors had to do with fraudulent billing. The network would follow the story.

Henry almost had to laugh that the alibi for his presence in Krauss's office that he thought would never fly, was the same one that someone at WhiteGuard came up with. He wondered which of his colleagues had thought of it. He'd thank them if he could. Now it seemed so perfect.

Nanette Tremont had been called in to do another consult on Henry. She arrived about an hour and a half after the six o'clock news. Once again, she told him that he was a lucky man. Had the nurse at WhiteGuard not thumped his chest and done CPR, he might never have made it out of the building alive.

Doctor Tremont hadn't known about the seizure until she saw it on the evening news. What she did know from speaking with Eva Rodeki at the time that Henry was admitted, was that when he collapsed, he had a very rapid, weak pulse. A cardiogram done on board the ambulance showed an abnormal heart rhythm which improved when they shocked him. By the time he got to the hospital, the rhythm was still rapid, but they had since been able to control it with medication. If it stayed normal until the next day, he'd be able to go home with a prescription change.

Tremont believed the seizure was just a response to momentary lack of oxygen, but she wanted him to follow-up with a neurologist to be sure his brain was okay. According to the ambulance report she'd just reviewed; the seizure wasn't much longer than what the TV news showed. She'd do more investigation of his heart function after he was out of the hospital.

Henry was discharged Tuesday afternoon with new medication and more doctor appointments. Against medical advice, he returned to work on Wednesday morning. When he pushed the door open to his office, he found CLUJ sitting in his desk chair.

Chapter Eighty-One

After five days, the police had ruled out Darcy, Rosemary and the Toblers as suspects in Sean's disappearance. They interviewed his brother and everyone who Darcy could think of that he might have sought refuge with. They'd also gone through a list of customers he'd serviced in recent months. It had become an interstate investigation because several of the customers had come from far away. No suspects materialized, even though the angry Peugeot owner had been questioned on several occasions.

Darcy was able to provide a photo of his car. About a month before the injury that started all their troubles, Sean had purchased a 1969 Pontiac GTO from a junkyard for sixty bucks. It was a dilapidated rust-bucket, but somehow it still ran. He put a new engine, transmission, and brakes into it, and used it to go back and forth to work. He planned to restore it once he finished the Mustang. Where there was no rust, it was a distinctive maroon color. It had to get noticed somewhere.

While they waited to hear from Sean or some news from the police, Ryan's wife delivered a healthy baby boy. The joy of his birth momentarily overshadowed the fear that Sean was dead. As the days dragged on though, the hope that he would turn up alive grew dimmer. Darcy's heart grew heavier as Arthur started to interview perspective candidates to take Sean's place. If it wasn't for the support she got from Rosemary and the Toblers, she would have felt like she also couldn't go on. The fact that Corey seemed to be as bereaved as she was, somehow made her grief bearable.

Hope died twelve days after Sean disappeared. Two kids looking for a lost dog came across a rusty old car concealed amidst some shrubbery near the south shore of Lake Michigan. Their parents notified local police. The only thing found inside the vehicle was a big empty vodka bottle. The out-of-state license plate linked the vehicle to Sean Patrick Garmen.

It hadn't rained in weeks, so from a work shirt that Darcy found in the Mustang, a bloodhound followed Sean's scent to the lake. Divers searched for another week, but his body wasn't found.

Darcy and Rosemary conducted a simple funeral service at which all three of the Toblers let their tears flow. Corey vowed revenge against those at WhiteGuard who refused to help his best friend when Rosemary was begging and pleading for help.

Rosemary returned to work. The local newspapers and TV stations were still babbling about the arrested doctors and the patients who were distraught to find that no other physicians would help them. Marty Ipolis and a reporter from a major newspaper were still trying to figure out why the White Guard medical director was present on the day of the arrest. Some of the people in the dental office waiting room were talking about their own lousy experiences with WhiteGuard when Rosemary, seated at the front desk, commented she'd like to get her hands on the neck of the WhiteGuard medical director herself, because his indifference was what led to the death of her son. A new patient, Barbara Smagley, just happened to hear her.

"I can give you Doctor Winslow's personal cell phone number," she said. "He used to be my boyfriend, but he turned out to be a jerk and I broke it off."

Chapter Eighty-Two

Seeing CLUJ at his desk made Henry think he was going to have another heart attack. Whatever he was there for couldn't be good.

"How are you doing Doctor Winslow?" CLUJ asked.

The tone in CLUJ's voice made Henry think his boss wasn't really concerned about his health. He didn't know whether to say he was fine or let the monster know that it had practically killed him to drag himself into work the day after leaving the hospital. The new medicine that Doctor Tremont had started him on to control his rapid heart rate made him feel nauseous and more tired than he already was. It also seemed to aggravate his hand tremors.

"Back to my old self," he lied. "Ready to tackle whatever comes my way. And how are you, Mr. Udall?"

"Perturbed, Doctor Winslow. That Marty Ipolis from the *MidWest Weekly News* thinks there's more of a story about your being at the office of those fraudulent pain doctors. I've had two staff members tell me he's called them to ask questions, and those are just the people I know about. Is there more of a story, Doctor Winslow?"

"The story is what they've already said. I was going to the phone store for a new cell battery. I didn't even know that's where Donilski's office was until I got there, and I had no idea that it was the FBI causing the commotion next door until I walked in there out of curiosity. These news people are vultures."

CLUJ rose to his feet. "Well, I hope that's the truth, and nothing but the truth, Doctor Winslow. There are an awful lot of people out there right now who think WhiteGuard is public enemy number one, the ungrateful idiots. They want us to pay for every damn quack treatment that exists for every little ache and pain they can't put up with, and if we try to protect them from the quacks, they think we're the bad guys. Let's just hope the news vultures don't find anything else to embarrass this company."

As CLUJ walked out the door, Henry felt like his brain was shaking as hard as his hands. He hadn't thought of it before, but Doctor Krauss's best defense might be that even WhiteGuard's medical director was coming to him for treatment. He wondered if Krauss was in jail or out on bail. Either way, whoever these physicians turned to for legal help, was probably going to inform them that Nicholas Johnson, the locksmith, was actually WhiteGuard's medical director.

It had to come out sooner or later and now, he had just given CLUJ a very stupid answer that he couldn't back away from. He should have said that he was there checking the place out, using Nicholas Johnson as an alias. It was too late. He wondered how he could be so stupid. He spent the next hour looking at Internet profiles of lawyers, but he couldn't fathom how even a brilliant attorney could help him.

Henry was lost in thought when his cell phone rang. Without thinking or looking, he answered it. Rosemary wasn't expecting him to do that. She thought for sure he wouldn't answer an unknown number and she'd just be leaving a message about Barbara Smagley that she hoped would get him to call back. With him on the other end of the line, all she could think to say was, "Are you okay Doctor Winslow? I saw on the news that you were hospitalized."

"Who is this?" Henry sputtered.

"I'm sorry, Doctor Winslow. This is Rosemary Cauthers. I met you in the waiting room at Doctor Tremont's office. You were reading about sacroiliac problems, and I told you about my son and Doctor Krauss. I take it you went to see Doctor Krauss."

Henry was flabbergasted. "How did you get my number?" he demanded.

"Let's just say, Doctor Winslow, we have a mutual friend. Did Doctor Krauss help you?"

Henry couldn't believe he was having this conversation. His gut instinct was to tell the woman it was none of her business and hang up, but he also realized that she could be the person who could most readily reveal his secrets to the media. It seemed safer to be polite and find out what she wanted.

"How can I help you, Ms. Cruthers?"

"It's Cauthers. I've been waiting for a long time for you to review my son's case Doctor Winslow. Kelsey Ashton told me she was bringing it to your attention months ago."

Henry couldn't remember anyone named Cauthers whose case he'd reviewed. He'd reviewed so many cases for so many different reasons that the names were just a jumble: Cauthers, Cruthers, Coruthers, Cauthorn. All he could think to say was, "How is your son doing?"

"My son killed himself, Doctor Winslow. Maybe you were in the hospital when his obituary was in the newspaper. He couldn't live with the pain anymore and he drowned himself in Lake Michigan while we waited for your decision. He was only twenty-nine years old. He left a wife and two young children. I wanted you to know that, Doctor Winslow. I'm going to call Marty Ipolis from the *MidWest Weekly News* because I think he'd be interested in our story. Do you have anything to add that I can share with the reporter?"

Henry felt his temples throbbing and his stomach whirling. For lack of a good response, he took the woman's number and promised he'd call her right back. He just wanted to check her son's case.

"I'll be waiting at this number, Doctor Winslow. If I don't hear back from you within the hour, I'll just go right ahead and call Marty Ipolis."

Chapter Eighty-Three

Henry cursed the computer as he fruitlessly searched for a file on someone named Cauthers and any variant spelling in the system. He found nothing relevant.

As fast as he was able, he barged into Kelsey Ashton's office and asked her about the Cauthers guy. Kelsey had no idea who he was referring to. Henry scared her. He seemed to be in a panic. He looked frazzled like he did before his recent hospitalization, just after she'd told him that Marty Ipolis was seeking an interview. Sweat was breaking out on his upper lip.

"A twenty-nine-year-old guy with back pain. His mother came to see you a few months ago. He died. Do you read the obituaries? It was just in the paper?"

"Sorry, Doctor Winslow. I can't remember anyone named Cauthers."

For lack of a better option, Henry called the woman back and asked her if she'd please just meet with him before going to the reporter. He asked her to come to his office.

"The last time I came to WhiteGuard, Doctor Winslow, I spent over three hours there and accomplished nothing. My son died because of your indifference. If you want to meet with me, you can come to my office at Riverside Dental Clinic. I'll be free from twelve thirty until one."

Rosemary was shocked when he said he'd be there. She didn't even know what she'd say to him. Her only purpose in calling him was to make him aware of the outcome of the insurance company's lack of care and compassion.

No matter where he searched, Henry couldn't find a file on someone named Cauthers. It was Eva who thought to check obituaries on the

Internet and recognized the name of Sean Garmen, the poor guy with arachnoiditis. Henry was stunned that it was Garmen again. Now he remembered the mother from Tremont's waiting room, He had no idea what he would say to her, but he had to think of something to keep her from going to Ipolis.

Rosemary brought him through the dental clinic to her back office. She showed him a picture of nineteen-year-old Sean standing next to his first muscle car. She showed him another picture with his bride, and another of Sean, Darcy, and the children. She had no recent photos of Sean. He'd been such a broken man for the past year that pictures hadn't been taken.

Henry tried to explain that there wasn't anything that could be done for arachnoiditis. Rosemary countered that while they knew it wouldn't cure him, the acupuncture had made his pain bearable. "All we were asking of the insurer was to allow Sean coverage for the only treatment that helped him."

"I can certainly sympathize, Mrs. Cauthers. I feel terrible about Sean. I'm afraid that being WhiteGuard's medical director forces me to implement executive decisions that I don't always agree with."

"If the medical director isn't deciding about patient care," Rosemary wanted to know, "then who actually makes such decisions?"

"I have to confess that I can only recommend which treatments the insurance company should cover. It's our CEO who has the final say."

"So, who's this CEO who's so heartless? Is he a medical person?"

Henry figured he was probably on his way to the unemployment office anyway, so why not pass the buck. "Our company is managed by a banker named Clarence Lowell Udall Junior. He firmly believes that the insurance company should only finance conventional treatments that have solid evidence to prove their merit.

"If insurers provided coverage for all kinds of alternative treatments, there wouldn't be resources to meet the needs of critically ill people. No one likes to admit it, Mrs. Cauthers, but health or dental insurance companies must ration care to provide the most proven options to the most persons with the most serious problems."

"My son had a serious problem for which there are no conventional options. He was a responsible family man who provided highly specialized service to hundreds of other people. He was asking for so little. Why was he discriminated against?

"And why weren't we told outright that coverage for the needed service would never be approved. Why were we just left waiting for a decision that was never going to be made? Had we known that WhiteGuard had no intentions of authorizing the exceptional care Sean needed, we might have been able to turn to other resources, but WhiteGuard just put us on indefinite hold, taking away our precious time and hope.

"I'm certain that had Sean been able to afford ongoing care from Doctor Krauss, and had Doctor Krauss been able to continue practicing, Sean could have been saved. Have you ever lost a child, Doctor Winslow?"

"My twenty-four-year-old son is fighting cancer right now. He's undergoing chemo as we speak."

"Is his insurer covering his expenses?"

Henry winced. "Yes, but it's a treatment with a high success rate for a lethal disease. Yes, it's unfair that persons with more lethal conditions get a bigger portion of the health care dollar, compared to those whose diseases don't typically kill them."

"How is your son doing?" Rosemary asked.

Henry was taken aback. This woman, who was grieving for her dead son, wanted to know about his son. He was embarrassed. He hadn't spoken to Adam in two weeks. He was so wrapped up in his own misery that a thought of his poor kid hadn't even crossed his mind. Adam was supposed to have finished his chemo last spring. Now he was undergoing another round because his doctor was unsure as to whether he was cured.

Unlike the woman he was sitting there talking to, Henry hadn't gone with Adam to the doctors that were taking care of him since

Adam's surgery. He wasn't even giving Adam emotional support. He was so stressed out about paying the bills that he hardly even thought of Adam, except as another expense. Unlike Rosemary, he had no pictures of Adam or his other children on his desk.

"My son's a fighter, Mrs. Cauthers. He'll pull through. Thank you for asking."

"My son was a fighter too. Even though he was in agony this past year, he tried to go to work every day. Had he only been sent to the right doctor in the first place, none of the other things he suffered would have happened. He didn't need his tailbone removed. He didn't need steroid shots. He didn't need narcotics. All he needed was for someone to have recognized that he'd sprained his sacroiliac joint and to have treated him appropriately. Did you ever get help with your sacroiliac problem?"

Again, Henry felt humiliated. Even as a well-schooled orthopedist, he didn't know a fraction of what Doctor Krauss had learned from an unconventional, foreign-trained doctor. He was wishing he'd been given that second prolotherapy injection, but the FBI agent had ordered Krauss to hand over the syringe before the procedure was completed.

"Mrs. Cauthers, you are a remarkable woman. I can't even tell you how guilty I feel that I was unable to grant your request for your son to continue treatment with Doctor Krauss. It will probably cost me my job, but I'm going to go straight to Mr. Udall, our CEO, to let him know how tragic his policies are for people like your son. If you'll allow me the time to do that before you talk to Mr. Ipolis, I promise I'll call you back to let you know that perhaps your son's unfortunate demise will lead to a change in our company's policies. Will you allow me to do that?"

Rosemary felt like Doctor Winslow's request would take a small bite out of her bitterness towards the health insurance giant. She said she'd hold off on contacting the reporter as long as Winslow got back to her by tomorrow.

Chapter Eighty-Four

Rosemary's agreement to wait before talking to Marty Ipolis proved futile for Henry. On the evening news of the same day they'd met, another reporter had located and interviewed Tonya Smith, daughter of the arrested Doctor Stefan Donilski. Tonya told the reporter that the medical director of WhiteGuard had presented as an uninsured locksmith with a phony name, and that their physicians had no idea they were being spied on by the medical director of the WhiteGuard Insurance Company.

Tonya blamed the medical director for causing the arrest of her father and his partner after they had made earnest effort to help the man. She told the TV newswoman that the physicians in this practice did everything properly and legally and gave hundreds of patients free treatment just to avoid trouble with the insurance company. In her worst nightmare, she could not envision how anyone could accuse them of fraud. Their only goals were to help desperate patients and make a living.

Henry hadn't seen the evening news, so he was totally shocked when CLUJ told him he was fired within minutes of arriving for work the following morning. He figured it was going to come sometime later. As he packed up his desk, Eva Rodeki came by to offer condolences. She told him about the story on the news the previous evening. She also told him she understood why he'd gone to Doctor Krauss, and she hoped he'd obtained some relief. She wanted to make sure he'd take her out of his records as his "power of attorney." She wished him well.

Henry's initial instinct was to go straight to the bar and knock back a few bourbons. Instead, he called Rosemary Cauthers. He wasn't sure why he wanted to contact her again, but something made him want to talk to her some more. He wanted her to know that his desire to allow patients like her son to get assistance from the insurer was why he wound up losing his job. He was pretty sure that the news vultures would get wind of the fact that he was no longer WhiteGuard's medical director.

Mrs. Cauthers agreed to go to lunch with him. Yes, she had seen the news, and she was sorry that his attempt to get treatment from one of the only doctors in the region who knew how to help him, had led to the downfall of the doctors. She didn't yet know that it also caused Henry to lose his job.

Henry felt that somehow, he could draw strength from this bereaved woman. Something in the back of his frazzled mind made him think that her cause could become his cause, and that he could somehow save face by attaching his professional demise to the tragic loss of her son. He imagined them going to Marty Ipolis together to tell the world that it was really CLUJ who had caused such misery and loss of life.

What Henry hadn't understood was how angry Rosemary Cauthers was. After telling her that CLUJ had fired him, her anger intensified. He was astonished when she told him that after talking to him, she realized that Clarence Lowell Udall Junior was a patient at Riverside Dental Clinic, and she was wishing there was some way she could get revenge on the monster.

"That man should suffer just a little of what my son went through."

Henry agreed. He could never have imagined how miserable a sprained sacroiliac joint could make a person, and he proceeded to tell Rosemary that he too was misdiagnosed and had undergone a totally unnecessary surgery at the hands of Maynard Burke that had led him to suffer more pain and more interventions with bad results.

Rosemary just drank water as the two of them commiserated, but Henry downed a few bourbons. Before their lunch ended, he wanted to hurt CLUJ as much as she did. It wasn't just about assuaging the grief that this bereaved mother was suffering. Henry also wanted CLUJ to experience some serious pain himself, so that his policies, which were hurting so many of their insured, would come back to bite him. To

Henry, it seemed that if he had any contribution to make to health care, it was to teach a brute like CLUJ that people with chronic pain deserve real assistance.

The last thing Henry expected was for Rosemary Cauthers to say that maybe there was a way to teach CLUJ that very lesson. To his amazement, she said that if he could help, she knew of a way to do it. She promised to call him back the next day.

Chapter Eighty-Five

Clarence Lowell Udall Junior suffered from periodontal disease. The periodontist at Riverside Dental Clinic advised him to get a professional cleaning every three months. The man did a lousy job of taking care of himself. His appointment came up late on a Friday afternoon. Henry, Rosemary, Darcy, and Corey had planned everything down to the tiniest detail.

Rosemary added just a tiny amount of the drug to the water that CLUJ rinsed his mouth with. Corey said it wouldn't do anything noticeable except make him a little more susceptible to suggestion. When his dental appointment was over, he was totally bewildered as to why his Mercedes wouldn't start. He took better care of his car than he did of his teeth.

When he came back into the clinic to see if they knew where there was a nearby car service, Rosemary assured him that Art Tobler Auto Tech was the best in the business, especially for luxury cars.

Corey and Ryan towed CLUJ's car to the garage and told him they'd work on the vehicle all night if that's what it took to diagnose and fix it.

Darcy asked him if he'd like a drink. "We have coffee, soda, or water. CLUJ opted for soda. Darcy said it wasn't cold, so she poured it from the can into a glass of ice she took from a mini fridge under the counter. She quickly added the precise dose of Liquid X, the renowned date rape drug that Corey had obtained. Within a half hour, CLUJ was totally zonked.

Henry had instructed them well. He held CLUJ's pelvis down to the cot while Corey and Ryan wailed on his hip bone, jamming and yanking it back and forth until Henry could actually feel some extra motion in the sacroiliac joint. They scraped the back of his head with a wrench and smeared some grease on the back of his suit. Then they put him in the van and took him to the hospital.

CLUJ was just starting to wake up after the ER triage nurse checked him in. Darcy smiled at him. "I'm so glad you're awake Mr. Udall. You took a nasty fall. Our mechanics are fastidious about not getting grease on the floor of the waiting area, but you slipped on something and went down hard. Thank heavens you're okay.

"Your car is fixed and ready to go as soon as the doctors release you. We felt so bad about your fall that the mechanic isn't going to charge you for the tow or the repair; just a loose wire that's been fixed. Hope we can serve you better in the future."

Chapter Eighty-Six

Eva Rodeki was not relishing her role as acting medical director for WhiteGuard. Most everything she was required to do to doctors and patients was unpleasant and unethical. She couldn't wait until CLUJ finished interviewing prospective candidates for the medical director's position. She wondered how long it would take him to find another doctor that he could totally dominate.

She also couldn't help but feel a sense of satisfaction to realize that CLUJ had been injured. Watching him try to act like everything was perfectly okay, when he was obviously in considerable pain, made her job seem less distasteful. CLUJ was limping more every day. Eva could barely wait for him to ask for advice. He finally did.

"You know, Doctor Rodeki, I took a nasty fall last month. I thought the pain in my back would be gone by now. Instead, it's getting worse. I'm having trouble sitting and getting up. Who on our panel would you recommend I see to get it checked out?"

"That's going to be tough, Mr. Udall, since we've gotten rid of most of the physicians who know how to handle this. Doctor Maynard Burke is still on our panel. I'm sure he'll take good care of you."

Like she was his secretary, CLUJ ordered Eva to get him an appointment with Burke. Like an abused underling, she did.

CLUJ never made it to the appointment. The day before he was supposed to go, he was arrested for tax evasion. Apparently, the big bad banker had been cheating on his personal income taxes for years and the IRS finally caught up with him.

Eva Rodecki wondered which fate was worse: being in a jail cell with severe pain or being a patient of Doctor Maynard Burke.

Chapter Eighty-Seven

Sean Garmen couldn't fathom how he came to be lying in totally unfamiliar surroundings. Had he been unconscious? He wasn't sure. It took a few minutes for him to realize he was in a hospital bed. There was a tube coming out of his stomach. Brown liquid was dripping down the tube from a bag suspended over his bed. He felt confused and weak. There was a rhythmic hissing noise coming from somewhere. The light was too bright. He closed his eyes while he tried to contemplate the situation.

He opened his eyes again and tried to say 'hey,' but no sound came out. He desperately wanted to get up and look around, but he didn't think he could move with his weakness and the tube. The bright light distorted his vision, and he closed his eyes again. After a few minutes he reopened his eyes and squinted.

Someone was standing over him. As their eyes met his, the person yelled, "Oh my God, he's awake!"

"Where am I?" escaped his throat as a hoarse whisper.

"Unbelievable, he's trying to talk," the nurse said to the aide who had appeared at her side. "It's a miracle. Get Doctor Arnold."

"Where am I?" Sean's voice was still a whisper.

"You're in Lincoln-Madison Hospice, Mr. Driscoll. You've been in a coma for three months. Do you understand what I'm telling you?"

Sean was confused. He thought he must be dreaming. All he could say was "who's Driscoll?"

"Aren't you Jeff Driscoll?"

"I'm Sean Garmen. Who's Jeff Driscoll? Where is this place?" he rasped. His eyes were getting used to the light but his whole body felt strange, stiff, and disconnected.

Another woman was now standing at his bedside. She wore a white coat. "Incredible!" she said, shaking her head. "Welcome back. Never, ever thought I'd see this. Mr. Driscoll, you are a two-time miracle. The first miracle was that you survived a drowning, but it's even more miraculous that you're now talking."

"My name's Sean Garmen. Who's Driscoll? How did I get here?"

"Well, hello, Sean Garmen! You're here because a fisherman in a rowboat pulled you out of the water in Lake Michigan and gave you CPR. He got you to shore and called for help. The fisherman also found a tacklebox on the shore not far from where he found you in the water. The name Jeff Driscoll was painted on the tacklebox. That's the only identification we've had for you. Do you understand what I'm saying?"

"Well, I'm certain I'm not Jeff Driscoll and I don't think I know him.

"So, this fisherman, he saved my life?"

"The fisherman, the ambulance crew, the ER doctor, the ICU staff, and most probably, your lucky star. Your alcohol level was so high, and your lungs were so filled with water that no one could believe you were still alive and then, that you weaned off the ventilator a few weeks later. You were transferred from University Hospital to this facility when you didn't wake up after two weeks off the vent, and you've been here almost six weeks. For you to be awake and talking now goes beyond anything modern medicine could accomplish or explain.

"You're in a chronic care facility near Detroit. Where are you from? Is there someone we can call who might be looking for you?"

Chapter Eighty-Eight

With Darcy and Rosemary's support, Sean underwent intensive rehabilitation. It took another ten weeks for him to be back on his feet, home with his family, and trying to read mechanics' journals.

Darcy was thrilled to be reunited with the recovered Sean, the romantic car nut whose life was again about family, friendship, and accomplishments, instead of about trying to escape from excruciating pain. Quinn and Frieda were ecstatic to have a daddy they could play with.

Once home, Sean consulted with Doctor Leonard Millany. Everyone was elated when a new MRI showed no signs of the arachnoiditis seen on his previous imaging, and there were no signs of scarring. Doctor Millany surmised that lying still for three months had allowed the condition to resolve without resulting in scar tissue. Just knowing the arachnoiditis was no longer an issue relieved Sean and his loved ones of a tremendous burden.

Doctor Henry Winslow finally found relief for his painful sacroiliac joint. Eva Rodeki had referred him to the practice of Doctor Jennifer Nagel. After WhiteGuard kicked her off their panel, she found herself successful as an independent practitioner. Eva kept getting requests from policy holders for Nagel's services to be covered.

Doctor Nagel buried her hostility towards the former WhiteGuard medical director when she accepted him as a patient. When she heard his story, she reluctantly agreed to tutor him in regenerative medicine. He was fascinated by the techniques she had learned from Doctor Donilski.

Henry also underwent a new treatment for his shaky hands whereby a band worn on the wrist sends messages to the brain that extinguish the tremors. He was pleasantly surprised to realize that his hands worked well enough to perform the regenerative injections. He undertook the training and studied hard.

Doctor Jennifer Nagel's practice had been growing so rapidly that she was having a hard time keeping up, especially because she was also committed to treating some patients who had no ability to pay. She employed Henry to help, and having an orthopedist in the practice boosted their credentials. Henry was astounded to find patients lining up for their services, even though the insurers wouldn't pay. Henry didn't charge Sean Garmen for the platelet-rich-plasma treatment that cured his sacroiliac joint pain. Henry was an exceptionally hard worker and eventually, Doctor Nagel offered him a partnership.

The Toblers were almost as relieved as the Garments that Sean was recovered. None of the mechanics that Arthur had hired in Sean's absence had what it took to work with the high-performance vehicles or the high-maintenance customers that were referred to Arthur's business. A few weeks after Sean resumed working at the garage, word got around quickly to the dealerships that Sean Garmen, 'the carman,' was back on the job. The Toblers' referrals doubled the following month. Arthur raised his service rates and invested the income in a superior health insurance plan for his employees. Darcy so loved the Toblers and her job at the garage, that she and Sean worked out a schedule with Arthur that allowed them both to work without sacrificing family time.

Andrea Valentine is continuing her efforts to hold WhiteGuard legally accountable for the hundreds of thousands of dollars of expenses and medical bills that accrued while Sean was disabled.

With the help of Rosemary and Doctor Henry Winslow, Andrea also joined the defense team working on behalf of Doctors Donilski and Krauss. Their attorneys will argue that corporate administrators and law enforcement officials are not more qualified than physicians to determine how patients should be treated.

The End

Acknowledgments

I am most indebted to my many patients who were my most important teachers. The publication of this story would not have been possible without the support of editor, Nancy Costo, reviewer Amy Schapiro, and publisher, Katie Mullaly.

About the Author

Dr. Beverly Hurwitz, originally from Brooklyn, New York, has spent her professional life as a physician, educator, and author.

In her youth she won awards for scholastic journalism and served as copy editor for her college newspaper. Before attending medical school, she spent a decade as a health and physical education teacher in rural public schools.

As a medical fellow, Beverly specialized in the care of children with neurologic disability. After three decades of clinical practice, she spent eight years as a medical case analyst/writer for administrative law judges in federal and state court systems. In recent years, she has been writing novels and hiking books.

www.ingramcontent.com/pod-product-compliance
Lightning Source LLC
Chambersburg PA
CBHW072027220726

48293CB00016B/476